A Certain Kind of Justice

A K Jenkins

EQUINE
PRESS

Published 2018

This novel is set in Togo, West Africa in 2005, but the characters and events are entirely fictitious and no resemblance is intended to any event or real person, either living or dead.

ISBN: 978-0-9942604-4-4

1

Thursday 24 March

Lawrence Ashley checks his watch against the world clock at reception. He waits a few seconds until it's 04.00 pm exactly, then drops his arm and looks around him.

Ngozi watches the middle-aged man in the chinos and blue striped shirt take a few steps towards the exit, then hesitate and turn towards where she's standing behind the front desk. He pulls a room key out of his trouser pocket and dangles it in front of him, holding it by the flat wooden tag. For a few seconds he examines it, as if surprised to see it there. His movements are uncertain, a cartoon of someone deciding what to do.

Making up his mind, he goes over to reception. He stops in front of Ngozi and holds the key in front of her, shaking it gently.

— Good afternoon. Could you take care of this please?

His smile takes years off his age and she decides she likes this Englishman with his formal, polite manners.

She returns his smile and puts the key into the wooden box marked 15. He thanks her as if she's doing him an enormous favour, then pulls an A4 piece of paper out of his shirt pocket and unfolds it.

— Just one more thing if you don't mind.

Ngozi can see it's a photocopy of what looks like a hand drawn map.

— Where are you off to then?

— A place called The Jazzhole. You wouldn't happen to know it would you?

Ngozi laughs and clucks in a particularly Nigerian way.

— Only the best place in Lagos. Are you driving?

— Walking. At least that's what I'm thinking of. Good idea?

He looks at her for confirmation, then puts the map down on the counter, pushing at the creases to make it flat.

Ngozi pulls the map around so she can see it the right way up. It's a bit out of proportion, but all the main streets are there.

— It shouldn't be a problem Mr Ashley. Not at this time in the afternoon. If you follow these directions you'll be there in about twenty minutes.

He thanks her again, folds the paper carefully, and puts it back in his pocket. Pushing open the heavy glass doors, he steps out into the moist heat of a Lagos afternoon.

Even before he reaches the heavy wooden entrance gates he can feel dribbles of sweat trickling under his arms and he wonders if it was a good idea to walk. Then he remembers why he's walking: Jerro's taken the car, so he doesn't have a choice. If Marius wasn't waiting for him at The Jazzhole he'd probably just stay at the hotel. Of course he could ring, but then Dave was so keen for him to go there.

He stops under the jacaranda trees behind the pool and thinks about it. The thing is, Dave really wants him to check out the place – even drew the map for him, suggested the best time to go. If he doesn't go, he's going to get back to Lomé and kick himself for not making the effort.

He keeps walking through the hotel gates.

The security guard looks half asleep. He's sitting on a crate in the half shade of the jacaranda tree, his back against the boundary wall, feet spread out in front of him. But a sixth sense tells him someone is coming through the gate and he stands up and salutes.

— Good afternoon sah.

— Good afternoon.

Is the salute ironic or sincere? Not easy to tell. It's definitely a nod to the old colonial days and he quite likes it.

He turns to the right and counts off three intersections before he turns again, this time to the left. A couple of fan-palm trees in the front yard of a house give deep shade and he stops and checks his map again. Yes. This is the right street.

He can vaguely remember coming over to drum up some business when they first opened the school – what would it be – fifteen years ago? Something like that. He'd asked Dave to do the trips to Lagos after that because of Tracey, so it must have been the last year she was in Togo. Pathetic really. He feels embarrassed for his earlier self and how he'd thought that staying in Lomé might help save their marriage, when now he knows that his trips over here had been a chance for Tracey to spend the time with 'him'. The art teacher. He could remember the name if he tried, but it still hurts and he shakes his head and thinks about this morning's presentation.

Now that had gone well. In fact better than he was expecting. There was that one cranky man who complained that International Baccalaureate was too hard to spell and why would he make his children do something he couldn't spell himself! But most of the parents seemed keen. He smiles to himself and it's more than relief that he feels. He thinks of Fred Astaire swinging around those street lamps and feels like that. All that time and money he'd spent to get this new program in place! Now he's sure it was the right decision. If only Dave could get a bit more excited about it.

The thought of his friend and business partner reminds him of the phone call about their bank account. Suddenly he gets a sick feeling and his chest goes tight. Surely someone has made a mistake and it will all be cleared up. He's told Dave about it, so it might be sorted out by the time he gets back to Lomé. If not…. He's afraid to think of the consequences but there's nothing he can do about it right now.

He can feel the sweat collecting under his collar and he stops and looks around for some more shade. There isn't any, so he pulls a handkerchief out of his trouser pocket and wipes his neck under the collar. That feels better. He puts the handkerchief away then undoes the top three buttons and pulls the shirt back, flapping it lightly to let in more air. The road is longer than it looks on the map and he's already been walking for twenty minutes.

As he starts off again he notices a small white car pulled up against a wall on the other side of the road.

The bonnet of the car is propped open and two men in jeans and T-shirts have their heads under it, looking at the engine. He wonders if he should stop and help. When he's opposite the car he can see it's a Mazda. He knows quite a lot about Mazdas. But he also knows the locals are very handy when it comes to mechanics because they have to be. The men look across at him and say something but he decides to keep walking. Then he hears an English voice from inside the car.

— Excuse me.

He doesn't want to be late, but then maybe this chap needs a hand. It would be the decent thing to do. He looks around for cars, but the street is deserted, so he crosses the road and walks over to the car.

2

Thursday 24 March

There was something about the traffic on Awolowo Road that really got to Marius: too noisy, too much of it, too many fumes. So choked was the air that the heat seemed to wrap around him and stick there. And not a bar in sight. Still, he'd heard too many good things about this Jazzhole to give up. That enigma, Lawrence Ashley, had arranged for them to meet here – had insisted in fact. Ash, he liked to be called: head of a school in Lomé, but there wasn't much else Marius knew about him. Except for the jazz connection of course. Not the liveliest company but a decent chap.

Everyone had warned Marius that the place was easy to miss. Look out for a big pharmacy, they'd said, and at last, there it was. He stopped and stared at the other shop fronts, looking for something that said 'The Jazzhole'. Then he saw a couple of young men pushing open a grey door he hadn't noticed, and followed them.

The first thing that struck Marius was how cool it was. Busy, but dark and calm, and cool in both meanings of the word. Every surface teeming with books and music – on shelves, in piles, on tables; jazz playing that made the world seem a better place, every note exactly the right one.

— Are you looking for something in particular?

Marius paused and looked around, then realised the voice was coming from behind a pile of books on the front desk. She was a large friendly woman with laughing eyes, herself a work of art ablaze with the colours of African wax cloth.

Marius walked over to the desk with its stacks of books and old vinyls.

— Good afternoon auntie. I didn't see you there. Could you steer me in the direction of some local jazz?

The woman laughed and swept her arm towards the posters and photos that took up the space that wasn't books.

— They're all local and lots of them are jazz. Recorded on our label. I'll bet you a beer that you'll find one you haven't got.

At a glance Marius didn't recognise any familiar faces and he laughed.

— I'm sure you're right. But did you say beer. Could I be lucky enough to be in an establishment that serves that splendid beverage? I was told to expect tea and coffee.

She turned and pointed behind her to where the cafe was tucked away behind stands of CDs.

— You'll find it over there in the cafe. And good luck with the search.

Marius ordered his beer then flipped through the CDs marked Lagos. Of course there were plenty he hadn't even heard of – mostly afrobeat and hip-hop, but straight jazz as well. He picked out a few then found a place to sit down.

Some books had been left on the communal table and Marius took one at random. It didn't look much from the cover but the title seemed interesting: *Music and Justice in Nigeria.* From what he knew, this shop had been at the centre of protest music in the 1970s. Fela Kuti was the one everyone knew about, but there were plenty of others. Not that those protests changed much, but at least people had an idea what the government was getting up to.

He sipped on his beer and glanced through the list of contents. There was a whole chapter on the Fela Kuti riot in Ghana. If he believed in regret, it would be something to put on the list, missing that concert. Not that Marius could have gone: he was locked up in James Fort at the time. Looking back, it seemed he was in gaol as much as he was at university during that time. And that was closed half the time anyway.

According to Acheampo, there was plenty of evidence that the concert was provoked by the military to discredit Fela. The extracts from some of the documents were new to Marius and he lost track of time. He wasn't sure how long he'd been reading, but the beer was gone and he'd finished the chapter.

He pulled out his phone and looked at the time. 04.55, almost half an hour after they were supposed to meet. Maybe Ash had changed his mind. Marius checked his phone for messages, but there was nothing there. He liked this place but he had a feeling Ash wouldn't be the sort of person to be late. Now he couldn't concentrate – had he got the time wrong? – so he tried ringing Ash's phone. It rang out, but there could be a dozen good reasons for that. He could be caught up with some business at the hotel – probably best to head back there anyway

C u back at hotel, he texted.

By the time he'd picked out a couple of books and added them to the CDs, he still hadn't heard back from Ash, so he paid at the front desk and stepped outside.

While he'd been in The Jazzhole the traffic on Awolowo Road had gridlocked in a dense mix of car horns and engine fumes. The nearest crossing seemed miles away and Marius pushed his way between the cars, putting a hand on the front of each one as if that would stop them from moving. A couple of the drivers blasted their horns at him and by the time he got to the other side, he'd added it to his 'never do this again' list.

He tried Ash's number. All he got was a loud click, as if the phone had been cut off. Why would Ash hang up? Marius rang again. This time he got a message: "the person at the other end is not available". It was probably the network. Typical. Marius locked his phone and put it back in his pocket. There were lots of reasons why Ash might not make it to The Jazzhole but Marius still felt uneasy and was relieved when he could turn off Awolowo Road away from the traffic and head directly for the hotel.

It was a more expensive sort of neighbourhood than Marius would usually stay in. Of course it was pretty quiet where he lived in Lomé too, but nothing like this. African cities all shared some of the same things, but Lagos had more of everything.

What was he doing here anyway? Last Sunday, there he'd been, hosting a party for Eva's fortieth birthday, then the next thing he knew, people seemed to be organising his life for him. First it was Ash. Would Marius drive over to Lagos with him? Marius wished he hadn't said anything about the interview he'd lined up in Lagos. Yes he was planning to go there, but in his own time. He still wasn't entirely sure why he'd agreed to come along with Ash. Perhaps it was the man's diffident manner, so innocent and trusting, that made Marius feel he should look after him. Then Takashi had decided that they should both stay at his friend Kazuo's hotel. At least that made sense. There wasn't much that his old friend Takashi said that Marius didn't agree with. And although nothing was said, Marius guessed that Takashi would take pleasure in having some third-hand contact with one of his few Japanese friends in West Africa.

Nothing much was happening in the street. Occasionally a car drove past and in the distance he could see a few people. A large green SUV was pulled over on the side of the road. As he got closer Marius could see the group was standing around something. Everyone had a story about muggings in Lagos and he hoped this wasn't going to be one of them. Where the people were standing a high wall obscured whatever was behind it, but a hundred metres or so up from that was an imposing entrance to a new looking apartment block. The building itself was set well back from the road and wrought iron gates were shaded by some large date palms.

Still, it was curious. He walked more slowly and wondered what they could possibly be looking at so intently. Amongst the small group a couple seemed to be arguing about something, but they both looked smartly dressed, maybe on their way home from work, and Marius relaxed. The woman's voice was low-pitched but very loud and she was leaning forward, hands on hips, the man gesturing as if to say 'what can I do?'

Suddenly the woman stepped back angrily.

Through the gap Marius saw a grey head. He walked on a few steps. It couldn't be, but it was. It had to be Kazuo. He was kneeling on the ground, his head bent over something.

Or someone.

Marius broke into a run.

3

Thursday 24 March

Ash was stretched out on his back. His eyes were closed and blood had soaked the front of his striped shirt. It was running down his side, pooling on the ground and soaking into the dirt, despite the towel that Kazuo was holding over the wound.

Kazuo looked up at Marius.

— I'm so sorry.

Marius knelt beside Ash and felt around before he found signs of a pulse in the neck. It was very faint but at least Ash was still alive.

— Ash, can you hear me? Marius bent down so his mouth was close to Ash's ear. It's Marius. Come on Ash. Hold on, my good man. This is no place to die.

Marius noticed a tiny flutter of the eyelashes, then he felt rather than heard a sound. Ash's lips were closed but Marius could feel the effort he was making to say something. It was more a sigh than a word, but Ash seemed to recognise Marius and he tried again. All that Marius could make out was something that sounded like 'al'.

He would have liked to say "You'll be alright" as people did. But he could feel Ash's life literally draining away.

— Try to hold on, he murmured into Ash's ear.

Marius felt for the pulse again, then he leant right down and checked with his cheek for a breath. Nothing. A faint shudder passed over Ash's face. That's it, Marius thought. He looked across at Kazuo, who shook his head. The couple who'd been arguing fell silent, as if the grim reaper himself had arrived.

And now there was something about Ash's body that said death. Although the eyes were already closed, Marius ran the palms of his hands over them as a final gesture, then pushed himself to his feet, brushing bits of dirt and loose gravel off his hand. Blood had stained parts of the front of his loose shirt and he brushed absently at that too as he turned towards the woman. The straightened hair, styled in a bob, spoke of hours with the hairdresser, and the neat green jacket and blue patterned skirt were businesslike and expensive looking.

Marius offered his hand and introduced himself.

— Marius Ato Agyekum.

The woman impulsively held his hand with both of hers and kept hold of it while she talked.

— Efi Abeni Akunke, she said. You know him?

Marius nodded. There didn't seem to be much to add to that. He couldn't call Ash a friend, but suddenly this ghastly business had made them close in a different kind of way.

Efi released Marius' hand and her husband took it with a firm grasp.

— Oluwajimi Babajide Temilola. So sorry. I rang the police and the ambulance but where are they?

He let go of Marius' hand and made a sweeping gesture at the empty street.

Efi put her hands on her hips and turned towards her husband.

— Didn't I tell you? She pointed to the SUV. We have a driver. We have a car. The man might be alive.

— Or dead in the car on the way to hospital and how's that going to look? Come on Efi, you know how things are around here.

It looked to Marius as if Oluwajimi was used to calming down his wife.

A trapped wailing sound came from Awolowo Road, then the noise of the siren changed pitch and a white Toyota pick-up truck raced towards them, blue and red lights flashing.

It stopped just short of where Marius was standing and two officers got out. They were heavily built men whose blue uniforms showed off Buddha-like beer bellies, and Marius wondered how things were going to go. But the way they handled things was reassuring, and it was clear they were here to get the job done.

The casual onlookers had slipped away when they heard the police siren and there were only five of them left. The taller of the two officers did most of the talking.

— Does anyone know this man?

Marius and Kazuo gave them all the information they had and the shorter officer wrote it down in a tattered looking notebook.

— Did you see anything? Who was here rioter? He pointed at Kazuo who was trying to wipe the blood off his hands with a grey handkerchief.

Kazuo shook his head.

— I came out of the entrance to the Palms. I'm pretty sure the street was empty, because I checked before crossing. That's how I came to notice….The thing is I recognised Mr Ashley from the clothes he was wearing and my first thought was he'd had a fall. Maybe from the heat.

— And how was he?

— Still alive, but losing blood. I had my gym towel and all I could think of was to try to stop the bleeding.

— The time?

— Not long after four. The staff back at the hotel should know when he left there.

The officer looked up and down the long street and addressed the next question to all of them.

— How about a car? Whoever did this must have had wheels. Are you sure you didn't see a vehicle? Even in the distance.

Efi shook her head.

— We found him like this. Can you imagine? This place! area boys. It must have been them. Efi spoke in a way that left no room for a different opinion. I heard they'd been robbing foreigners on Awolowo Road. But right here outside our house?

— Which is yours?

Oluwajimi pointed to up the road.

— Up there. The complex with the palm trees out the front.

It wasn't more than a hundred metres further along and Marius was surprised that the security guards hadn't come to see what was happening.

— What of the security guards? Maybe they saw something.

— We'll ask. Oluwajimi inclined his head towards the SUV. We're still on our way home. He pulled out a gold trimmed, pearl embossed box from his jacket pocket, opened it and took out professional looking business cards that he handed to the police then to Marius and Kazuo.

— If there's anything I can help with just let me know.

Kazuo handed them his card as well. Marius made a show of searching in his pockets.

— Sorry. Must have left the cards at home, but Kazuo can pass on any news to me.

area boys. Marius knew who Efi had been talking about; they were gangs of young thugs who hung around the streets in Lagos. Mostly they extorted money by intimidating: setting up barriers in car parks and charging for parking, that kind of thing. Or they worked as groups to rob people. They didn't usually kill people but it could happen.

Efi and Oluwajimi drove off and seconds later Kazuo's driver arrived. Marius declined a lift and stayed chatting with the officers.

Like Efi, they assumed it must have been area boys. According to them, knifings weren't a surprise. The older man knew a lot about knives and when he finished talking, so did Marius. Then the officer bent down as far as he could and peered at the wound again.

— But my guess is that they used a screwdriver, he said, and his colleague nodded in agreement. That would be the trademark area boy attack. Could have been sharpened. Anyway, the autopsy will tell us more.

Marius nodded.

— What are your chances of catching them?

The officer shrugged.

— We'll do what we can. There'll be a coroner's report of course.

— And the body?

— Off to the morgue – leave it with us. Handy things, these pick-up trucks.

They'd brought along an orange body bag and for Marius it was almost the worst part of the afternoon, seeing Ash being zipped in and lifted onto the back of the truck.

He watched the pick-up drive away, bouncing over potholes in the road. It seemed bizarre; something he'd laugh about on a TV drama. But in real life there was nothing funny about it at all.

4

Thursday 24 March

When Marius opened the glass entrance doors of the hotel he had only a vague recollection of walking there. The same thoughts had kept chasing each other around in his head: Could he have done more to help Ash? Was it a random knifing as everyone was saying? A robbery gone wrong?

He was aware in a detached sort of way that he needed to get his thoughts together. And 'thoughts' was really a euphemism. He needed to get himself together, more like it. What he wanted more than anything was to wash and get out of his clothes. He was conscious of the blood on his shirt but there was nothing he could do about it. There would be things he had to do, people to ring, that kind of thing, but he wasn't ready for that yet.

The foyer was packed with a group of Japanese men in business suits. The smart suitcases marked them as overseas arrivals. Lucky for him, really. Even greeting Ngozi at reception was too much and he could talk to Kazuo later.

Thankfully he'd taken his key with him and he skirted around the group. They were handing in their passports and picking up keys and no one took any notice of him as he made for the stairs.

Once in his room he closed the door behind him and locked it with the key. Then he went back and pulled the chain across as well. He wasn't in the mood to be disturbed by someone wanting to check the minibar or count the number of towels in the bathroom.

He stood for a minute taking in the tidy, peaceful room with its little courtyard garden and the paper screens, and let out a long sigh of relief. His body started to relax and he realised he'd been holding tight to each bit of it, as if he was in danger of falling apart.

The water pressure in the shower was strong and Marius gave in to the urge to soap up over and over again. He couldn't get the image of Ash out of his mind – blood just kept pouring out of him – and the desperate way Ash tried to talk to him. Was it a name that he was trying to say? Should he try to find out? Who would know?

By the time he'd dried off and put on a fresh set of clothes the sun had set and the room was dark except for two little lights in the courtyard. He found the light switch by the door and more soft lights came on around the room.

Wrong place, wrong time. That's what Efi had said. That's what the police had said. Would it have been different if he and Ash had stayed in a different hotel? Probably. He and Ash would have been swapping stories over a beer.

That was exactly what he needed. A drink. Had he put that brandy in at the last minute? He went over to the bed where he'd dumped the faded old Adidas bag that he used as luggage. The clothes he'd been wearing earlier were in a sad looking heap on the bed. Keep them or toss them? It would look odd leaving a whole set of clothes in that tiny bin, so he found a laundry bag in the cupboard near the safe.

It was when he was stuffing his trousers into the bag that a folded piece of paper fell out. He must have picked it up without thinking, because he had no memory of doing it. Considering the amount of blood on everything else, it was reasonably clean. That must have been why he'd bothered to pick it up – to keep it from getting soaked.

Marius put the paper on the pillow and crammed the rest of his dirty clothes into the laundry bag, then he felt around in the Adidas bag and sure enough, carefully wrapped in a T-shirt was a full bottle of cashew brandy. I'm a genius, he thought. Throwing the T-shirt back into the bag he picked up the paper and the bottle and took them over to a table that was next to a couple of comfortable looking chairs near the door to the courtyard.

A beer chaser would be good as well, and he inspected the minibar. Four large bottles of Star beer, and two cold glasses. He added one of each to the table, then he sat back in a chair, put his feet up on the other one, poured a brandy and a beer, picked up the paper and unfolded it.

The paper was limp and looked more like it had been soaked in water than carried in his pocket. It had started to tear along the centrefold, and the photocopied map was faint but still legible. The distance between the hotel and The Jazzhole looked a lot shorter than it actually was, but otherwise it was accurate enough. Probably done by someone at the school, judging by the A4 paper and the way it had been photocopied. Could be The Jazzhole was a stop-off place for teachers up for the trip to Lagos.

Marius wished the paper could tell him more. Like what? A name? As if it could tell the story of those last few minutes. He held it up to the light, but still nothing.

What did he know about Lawrence Ashley? Not much really. Until last Sunday he hadn't spoken more than a few words to him. Then on Sunday he'd put on that barbeque for Eva's fortieth and somehow Ash had ended up there.

Lawrence Ashley was the head of the international school where Marius' friend Mibou did some music teaching and thinking about it, it was probably Mibou who had brought Ash along. The two of them weren't exactly friends but they were both crazy about jazz. Marius knew Ash in a casual way, from sitting together sometimes at Le Jazz Spot when Mibou's band was playing, but that was as far as it went.

After most of the others had left the party, Ash had stayed on. Mibou and the band had packed up and they were all standing around the barbeque eating the last of the kebabs. I really must have had a bit to drink by then, Marius thought. He couldn't remember very clearly how it happened, but he'd agreed to go to Lagos with Ash in the school car. Then Takashi had decided that Marius and Ash must both stay at his friend Kazuo's hotel in Lagos. When he'd woken up sober on Monday morning Marius had regretted allowing himself to be talked into any of it. He would much rather have just caught a plane and gone to Lagos by himself and now look how things had turned out.

Marius had to admit there was something that was really getting to him about this knifing. There was nothing in that particular street; not even a roadside stand, or a little store. Nowhere at all to hang out, so why would anyone, let alone the sort of person who killed Ash, be loitering there? It was almost as if they'd been waiting for him, knew he'd be going that way. Maybe they'd followed him from the hotel. That would be easy enough to check and Marius made a note to get Kazuo to help him.

Pretty much everything he knew about Ash was stuff he'd talked about on the trip over here. Hard to believe that was only yesterday. The two of them had shared the back seat of the old Mercedes – Ash had insisted – and Marius got off to a bad start, feeling awkward about being chauffeured around.

He only half-listened to Ash, if that. Then Ash suddenly stopped what he'd been saying.

— AC too cold for you Marius?

— Well, now you mention it…Marius realised that maybe it was, after all, the air-conditioning that was putting him in such a bad mood. The AC was like some cold, bone-eating monster.

— I'm sure Jerro – Ash pointed to the driver, who acknowledged him with a half smile – I'm sure he agrees with you. Nobody seems to like a car as cold as I do.

Yes, because we wear clothes that fit with the climate, Marius thought, but all he said was:

— Perhaps I'm under-dressed. He gestured in a vague way towards his loose, short-sleeved cotton top. Maybe I should have worn a suit.

As Ash was. A dark, finely striped light woollen suit with a long-sleeved shirt, cufflinks and a tie. Marius tried but failed to imagine himself in a suit.

— I could turn it down a bit, Jerro said, glancing at them in the rear vision mirror.

Ash pulled his cufflinks below the line of his coat sleeves.

— Do that Jerro. I suppose I could always take my jacket off. Now, where was I?

Ash turned back to Marius.

— Oh yes. We were talking about the new 6th form programme. The International Baccalaureate.

The words 'we were talking' didn't describe the monologue that had been going on pretty much since they started, but Marius hadn't done much to keep up his side of it.

— Problems? he asked.

— Not as such. The IB organisation has given us the go ahead for the last stage in the authorisation process. They're sending out inspectors next month and we should be ready for it.

— But, Marius prompted.

Ash looked relieved to have been given a cue.

— But there would seem to be some sort of problem with money and we need the money to get things properly in shape. Some extra things for the science labs and the art studio. Oh, and the library of course.

"Hmmmm", was all Marius could think of to say. What did he know – or care – about these things.

Ash gazed out of the window for a second, rubbing his hand down his cheeks and chin, like a caricature of a thinker. Then he seemed to make up his mind.

— I wouldn't normally talk about money but Mibou told me you're a good man in a crisis. The truth is, I'm worried. I had a call from my bank the other day – the UK one that's attached to our offshore account. It was about something trivial, but when the chap was talking to me I realised he seemed to think I'd asked for my name to be taken off the joint account. The one we keep for capital investments and things. Must be some mistake. Then some of the orders have been cancelled. I can't imagine what's going on. Never happened before.

Marius couldn't see how it could possibly concern him, but it seemed polite to find out more.

— I imagine you have people you can trust to check it out?

Ash ran both his hands through his hair, threw his head back and blew air out of his mouth as if exhaling cigarette smoke. Then he dropped his hands and swivelled around so he was half-facing Marius.

— That's just it you see! I really believed I had people I could trust. I've been over and over it and I don't know what to think. A friend told me you might be able to help.

— If I can. You'll need to fill me in a bit though. How do the finances work in the school?

As Marius listened he didn't know whether to admire or to laugh at the trust that Ash put in just two men. He'd started with "I'm not very good at paper work" but Marius quickly realised that was an understatement. It appeared there were two men who did all that. One was Ash's business partner, Dave Gordon. They'd set up the partnership to start the school, and the picture Marius got from Ash's description was of a hardworking reliable man who managed all the day-to-day running of the school. The business side of things. It surprised Marius to learn that Dave did most of the recruiting as well, students and teachers. What did Ash do, he wondered.

Then there was the registrar, George Barnes, who took care of the money – paid wages, chased up debtors, placed orders, balanced the books. Solid as a rock, Ash claimed. Ex-army – been at the school for the past ten years. Not a talkative chap – and a bit absent minded of late – but one of those folk you can just trust.

Marius wondered what he could possibly say. Ash sounded so earnest and sincere, but idealistic and naïve. Maybe lazy as well.

— Could it just be some sort of mix up by the bank then? Some bit of paperwork you didn't do?

Ash looked relieved.

— That's probably it. The bank is going to get back to me. But the other thing is that there just doesn't seem to be as much money as there should be.

— That should be easy to track, surely.

Marius had spoken quickly and Ash picked up the slight edge of impatience.

— I know what you're probably thinking. Why didn't I keep a better check on it?

Marius started to interrupt and explain, but Ash waved a hand as if to say 'I know what you're going to say – apology accepted' and continued.

— No need to apologise. You're right. I've been so caught up with this new IB diploma that I haven't had time for anything else. When I asked Dave about it he said he'd passed the orders to George. George tells me that Dave hasn't told him. Dave tells me George is forgetting things.

— But what about systems. There must be some paper trail?

Marius could feel his eyes getting heavy. Now that the car wasn't so cold all he wanted to do was sleep. They'd got off to an early start.

Ash seemed to notice and regretted the sudden urge to share his problems.

— Sorry. I shouldn't have bothered you with it. Too complicated. All be sorted out I'm sure.

He finished with an attempt at a laugh that fell flat and Marius felt awkward. He realised he was being insincere but didn't want to seem unhelpful.

— Don't worry my friend, he said, if I can think of something…

Now Ash was dead and that was all that Marius knew about him. He wished that he'd listened a bit more, asked more questions. Marius knew things could happen out of the blue, especially to someone as vague and trusting as Ash seemed to be. Lagos was not Lomé. It wasn't that he felt guilty. Not exactly. Yet he couldn't shake a feeling that he had a role to play, some responsibility that went beyond the obvious, something he couldn't yet see.

Ash had as good as asked Marius to help him. It probably took quite a bit for him to overcome the British reticence to talk about money, and when he did, the way Marius reacted had made Ash retreat back into himself. Well he couldn't do anything about it now and what was the point of going over and over the same things?

Marius screwed the lid back on the cashew brandy and put the empty bottle of Star in the bin. It would be a good time to get a bite to eat and ask Kazuo about the security guards. And there was Jerro – he should find him and make plans for getting back to Lomé.

And for that matter, why did Jerro have the car yesterday? Where was he when Ash was killed? Who were these friends of his in Lagos?

5

Friday 25 March

Marius sat in the passenger seat next to Jerro. God knows what the roads would have been like in the morning rush hour. Getting through Lagos had been fine until they hit the Badagary road. Now the bitumen surface was broken into giant potholes and traffic was all over the place, trying to find the best way through. Next time I go to Lagos, I'm flying, Marius vowed to himself.

On Kazuo's advice, they'd taken their time leaving the hotel. Much better to wait until the traffic settles a bit, he'd said. Jerro had been pushing to get away early but Marius wanted to have a chat to Kazuo and insisted. Jerro sulked.

Kazuo had been his usual calm, hospitable self when they'd met up over breakfast. Neither he nor Marius were inclined to go over the nightmarish time yesterday, when they'd been kneeling across from each other, Ash bleeding to death in the middle. There was something faintly ridiculous about it, if it wasn't so tragic. It gave them a sort of bond, nonetheless.

Last night Kazuo had gone to Ash's room. He wasn't quite sure what he was looking for and didn't think it was his place to move anything, but there was a little pile of business cards sitting on the coffee table and he'd taken one of those. There was a number for the school in Lomé and he rang and was put through to a man called Dave Gordon. After that it had been easy. Dave himself was coming over to Lagos to sort things out with the police and the coroner, and he was hoping to take the body back to Lomé.

That was a relief. Marius had been in two minds as to whether he should stay in Lagos or not, but if the partner was coming over then it made the decision easy. He could head back to Lomé with a clear conscience.

Jerro was doing a pretty good job at getting the Merc through the chaotic jumble of traffic and Marius left him to it. He found a lever between the seat and the door, reclined his seat a couple of notches and let his mind wander back over the last twenty-four hours.

Kazuo had already checked and double-checked the staff at the hotel. The security guard on duty at the time Ash had left to go to The Jazzhole was certain that no one had followed him, because he'd watched him all the way down the road until he'd made the left turn. It wasn't every day that a European went wandering around Lagos alone and in the afternoon heat, so the guard wanted to keep an eye on him. Ngozi was the only one who knew where he'd been going and she said he'd left the hotel at about 04.00 pm.

At least that tied up those loose ends. So if the murder was planned, it was done without the help of anyone at the hotel. Kazuo was inclined to agree with Efi and the police. The Area Boys had been getting tougher and more organised in the years he'd been at the hotel and it didn't seem too much of a stretch for them to hit on a random target, especially someone as noticeable as Ash.

— But what would they have been doing in that street? Marius had said. There's no crowd to disappear into, and they'd stand out like a sore thumb.

Kazuo smiled in a way that reminded Marius very much of Takashi.

— But with a car...

And Marius had to agree. Not much more than a few seconds and they could blend into all that traffic on Awolowo Road.

Abruptly the road changed into a paved expressway and the traffic thinned out. Apart from an occasional hut amongst palm trees there was mile after mile of green bush on either side. Pleasant enough. Marius pulled the back of his seat forward again and turned to Jerro.

— I guess you'll be glad to get back to your family.

— Yes sir.

Marius had another try.

— Your wife must miss you when you're away like this.

Jerro glanced sideways at Marius, a bit surprised that he knew about his wife.

— Yes, sir.

— Jerro, my young friend, this might seem odd to you, but I don't feel right about the 'sir'. How about calling me something a bit more friendly. Uncle, perhaps? You'd be doing me a favour.

— Yes, sir. Marius took no notice and kept going.

— As for me, I don't have a wife. But my son and his aunty, I think they secretly like it when I travel. Marius was pretty sure Eva would disagree. When he wasn't there, she looked after his son Dzigi, as well as her own daughter.

That got a reaction. Jerro shook his head.

— My wife, she's not happy when I'm gone-o. His mouth closed around the words in a sanctimonious sort of way. She's with child.

Marius smiled to himself at the strangely formal, almost biblical use of 'with child'. He managed to come up with some baby chat and Jerro loosened up a bit. He'd prefer the baby to be a boy but girls are good too. Good for looking after men. He found that really funny and repeated it a couple of times, laughing and slapping the steering wheel. Marius felt faintly disgusted and decided to change the subject.

— So, Mr Ashley's death. Will that make a difference to your work?

— No, not at all. It's Mr Gordon I work for. Not just driving, you know. He trust me. It's very bad about Mr Ashley, he added.

There was a surge in Jerro's voice, the chin and lower lip thrust out in self-importance, when he talked about Dave Gordon. Marius noted the absence of feeling in his last comment. It was more as if Jerro knew what he was expected to say, and he'd said it. If there was any tension between the two partners, then it was clear whose side Jerro was on.

— Yes, Marius agreed. Terrible. He had a sudden image of the blood soaked body and shook his head. Really awful. I imagine the school is going to find it hard without him.

— Mr Ashley, he love the school too much. Jerro paused and considered his words. He's a gentleman, you see, polite-o, but always – he took his hands off the steering wheel and circled them in a spiral up over his head – like that.

— So Mr Ashley was what you might call a dreamer?

Jerro seemed happy that Marius had found the right word.

— Yes sir. A dreamer. Mr Gordon, he's always working. When we go to Lagos it's very nice. Not some small-small hotel. We stay in the big one on the Island.

Marius had seen the over-sized Intercontinental Hotel just the other side of the bridge and was happy not to be staying there.

— Plenty to do in Lagos?

It seemed that Jerro finally had something that really interested him. He was like a different person. Marius listened to stories of the bars, the *joloff* rice, the important friends he'd made in Lagos. Clearly he'd been there a lot with Dave Gordon.

— Did you get a chance to catch up with your friends on this trip?

— My friends and Mr Gordon's too. I had stuff to do for him. And his girlfriend.

Marius hid his surprise. Well, not exactly surprise, just that he hadn't given any thought to that side of things. He said nothing, but gave Jerro an encouraging look.

— You know, Jerro went on, Mr Gordon's girlfriend, she has a brother in Lagos.

— Remind me. What's her name?

— Adelola. Lola. You haven't met her?

Marius shook his head.

— She's something. Jerro waved a closed fist in front of his mouth and blew on it.

Marius got the message. Hot stuff.

— And the brother's name?

— Ibi.

— Short for Ibrahim?

Jerro shrugged.

— No idea. Maybe not. Just Ibi.

— Mr Gordon must put a lot of trust in you. All that work you do for him. Marius felt sure Jerro wouldn't pick up on the inverted commas he mentally put around the word 'work'.

— Oh yes. He trusts me to look after Mr Ashley. Jerro didn't seem not to notice that he had failed to do that. Me, I helped him set up. Chairs, water. You know.

— Mmmm. What about security?

— We never have problems. Mr Lawrence, he just unlucky-o.

— What do you think? Should he have walked around by himself? He didn't seem to know Lagos very well.

Jerro lifted his shoulders in a shrug and glanced at Marius with a look that seemed to say 'how would I know? Why are you asking me?' Marius decided to push a bit more.

— I guess you had work to do.

Jerro smiled and nodded.

— Listen! You hear how the car is.

He paused so they could both hear the steady noise of the engine.

Marius pretended to listen and Jerro continued.

— Good na! Every time we're in Lagos I get proper proper service-o. Yesterday it was 4 o'clock. Mr Lawrence said to go.

— Must take a while. Any friends around there?

Jerro gave a knowing chuckle.

— You've got it. Chicken Republic – just across the road from there. You know it? Best fried chicken and *jollof* rice in Africa. That's where we hang out.

It sounded harmless enough and it made sense. The big Mercedes dealerships in Lagos would be the best place to keep the car in top condition. Marius didn't feel like pushing it any further; even Jerro might catch on that he was being pumped for information.

— Chicken Republic? he said. I'll definitely try it next time I'm in Lagos.

Which might be never. The meeting with the Ace Security Company hadn't gone so well. Marius got the impression their only interest was making money and the contract they had in mind didn't make it worth his while to do all the travelling. And much as the city was alive – vibrant, just like everyone said – it seemed like a place where you needed to hustle to get the most out of it. When he was younger, now that would have been a different matter, and it was a bit unsettling having to recognise what a boring routine he'd fallen into.

Ahead of them the traffic had slowed to a gridlock.

Jerro turned the AC back on.

— The Seme, border, he explained.

— How long do you think we'll take to get through?

— Forty minutes. Maybe longer.

They both lapsed back into silence and Jerro pulled out a cassette of Femi Kuti and slipped it into the player. *Beng beng beng* Femi was singing. Marius wondered if Jerro might have been doing a bit of that yesterday and whether that was why his pregnant wife didn't like him being away.

— Good speakers, he said.

6

Sunday 27 March

By the time they got back to Lomé it was 5 o'clock and Marius asked Jerro to drop him off at the gate. Well, where the gate would have been if they had one. The front door was open and Eva's wheelie bag was propping up a stuffed tote with a pair of shoes sticking out of it. Then he remembered and kicked himself! This was the weekend when Eva was going over to Accra for a wedding, the one she'd been planning for weeks.

Not again, he thought. Why did he always forget? It's not as if he didn't care. He silently thanked whatever fate had intervened to deliver him back home in time.

Eva was packed and ready to go, impatient and not even bothering to pretend otherwise. Of course she'd want to get across the border before dark; he'd want to do the same himself. She gave him a quick rundown of how she'd left things for him and the kids and in less than ten minutes she was gone.

Marius knew some people found it a bit strange that he lived in this old colonial house with his son, his dead wife's sister and her daughter. But it suited them. He and Eva shared some of the day-to-day stuff, Dzigi and Seri got on well together and it meant that each of them could get away for days – sometimes even weeks – at a time. Provided, of course, they didn't want to go away at the same time. When that happened, they just had to think of something else.

Dzigi was ten, Seri twelve, so it wasn't as if they were difficult to look after. Nothing like the months after Selina had died when Marius had to take a crash course in child rearing. He and Dzigi had become extra close as the six-year-old showed him how to do things. "Mummy did it this way. But mummy…" Looking back Marius was amazed at the things Selina had managed to do, given that she was running her own conveyancing business as well. Or what she'd always said was a pinch of conveyancing and a fistful of land dispute resolutions.

After the drama in Lagos some home time was just what Marius felt like. People on their deathbeds were said to regret not having spent more time with their families and Ash's sudden death made Marius think there might be something in it.

He resolutely turned down the usual drinking invitations and rather enjoyed feeling virtuous as the weekend settled into a comfortable routine: cook, eat, play chess, then the same again. At The Jazzhole, Marius had bought a book on chess moves for Dzigi and in an addictive sort of way the two of them went through all the openings and played out the games. It didn't interest Seri, but she had a friend staying and they spent most of the time in her bedroom.

There were long pauses in the games while Dzigi thought about his moves and Marius found himself going over Ash's murder. It was by no means the first death he had witnessed but that made it no less disturbing, not least because his conscience told him that he should have listened to Lawrence Ashley more carefully during that trip over to Lagos. Ash had trusted him enough to ask for help, and he hadn't paid enough attention. Tucked away in the back of Marius' mind, but not so far that he wasn't aware of it, was the feeling that if Ash had been a fellow African he would probably have listened more closely, offered to help.

But by the time Eva arrived back from Accra on Sunday evening, he was ready to get out of the house, and he had the beginnings of a plan. It wasn't really much of a plan, but a starting point would be to get some background on Dave Gordon and George Barnes. What he liked about the plan was that it meant taking a run out to Chez Miki. Mimi would be able to give him background about the school and he had to start somewhere, so why not there? Mimi had been teaching at the Lomé International Community School for a few years now, and should have some idea what was going on. And the very least he could do was to look into the money problems Ash was talking about. If he'd thought that Marius could help him out, he must have had some reason. What he probably wanted was someone who was not connected at all with the school and Marius had that qualification at least.

Chez Miki was half an hour or so west of Lomé on the coast road. When it was daylight there was an occasional glimpse of the cloudy green sea, but at this hour – Marius glanced at the clock in the old Toyota, 7.30pm – the road was dark and the constant stream of headlights coming towards him made it difficult to see the road.

It was a relief when the string of red and black lanterns came into view and he could turn into the gravel parking area in front of Chez Miki. Marius felt his usual sense of calm as he walked over the granite stepping stones between the neat stands of bamboo. He ducked as he walked though the blue and white *noren* that hung over the entrance and almost ran into Takashi who was standing just the other side, talking to some guests who looked as if they were just about to leave. Takashi raised his hand in greeting and waved it vaguely in the air towards the other side of the large open space.

Marius took that to mean 'make yourself at home' and he made his way between the carefully placed shoji screens and the square paper lanterns to a lounge area that was open to the inner garden.

There was a 'reserved' sign on the low glass-topped table, but that was to keep the space for family and friends. The rattan chairs and couches were grouped around the table to form a square and Marius chose the lounge that looked directly over the garden. He sank back into the soft cushions and caught the ineffable hint of salt and jasmine in the air, a smell he always associated with Chez Miki.

Yao arrived with a mug of Asahi special draft, courtesy of Takashi, and Marius thanked him and asked after his family. Since the early days of the drumming centre, way back when it had just been a couple of adobe huts, Yao had helped Takashi with whatever needed to be done and he was more like family than staff.

Marius sipped his beer cautiously through the frothy head and the image of a long-haired and much younger Takashi came into his mind. As always, the memory made him smile, the way Takashi had walked into his first seminar and without saying much at all, had everyone listening to him. Not even Selina had known about Marius' real reason for being at the university. He'd been working under cover, enrolled as a PhD student in the School of International Studies. What Selina thought was that they'd come to Togo to be closer to her family. Of course that was part of it. It wasn't long before Marius and Takashi discovered a mutual love of Thelonious Monk and jazz in general. There was a time when the two families did everything together – Takashi was Selina's biggest fan. After awhile, they heard about Miki, Takashi's wife who was murdered right in front of him in their Osaka jazz club. None of them imagined that Marius himself would lose Selina to illness only eight years later.

Marius was brought back to the present as Takashi put a mug of beer on the table then leaned back and brushed his hair off his face.

— Hey, Marius. Welcome. So sorry to keep you waiting. Good timing. I was talking to Kazuo just now and he asked me to pass on a message. Sounds like you had a tough time in Lagos.

— Not as bad as Lawrence Ashley!

— Poor guy. Kazuo sounded pretty upset. He told me about it, how he couldn't stop the bleeding.

— Yeah. It was awful. Kazuo did a great job, but whoever stabbed Ash knew what he was doing.

— Was there someone called Efi? I think that's the name Kazuo mentioned.

— Sure. Efi and her husband. Owu something. They called the police and the ambulance. It happened fairly close to their apartment block – one of those new places with a pool and a gym. In fact that's where Kazuo had just been, at the gym.

Takashi stood up and pulled a piece of paper out of the back pocket of his jeans then sat back down again. He held the paper up to the light for a minute, then put it on the table next to him.

— Right. Yes, Efi. Kazuo really wanted you to know what was happening, so I wrote it down. Efi said one of the security guards had been walking down the road not long before Ash was attacked. He saw a white car – a Toyota, I think.

Takashi checked the bit of paper and continued.

— No. Not a Toyota, a Mazda. The bonnet was propped open and there were two men standing there and another two in the car. Apparently the whole thing looked suspicious – the men didn't seem to be working on the car – and he thought they might be staking out the house across the road, so he took the numberplate. Memorised it, that is.

Marius put his beer down and leaned towards Takashi with his hand out.

— Interesting. Could I have a look at that paper for a minute?

Takashi passed it across and Marius held it at arm's length, squinting to bring the writing into focus. Then he handed the paper back to Takashi.

— A Lagos number. I thought for a minute that it might have been a Togo number plate.

Takashi shook his head.

— Kazuo said Efi's well known on radio over there. She has a sort of crime watch segment every morning and she broadcast a description of the car on it.

Marius was impressed.

— Good for her. Anything else? What about the police? Did you say that Kazuo had heard something?

— Sorry. I should have mentioned that before. The autopsy report said Ash was stabbed with a sharpened screwdriver.

Marius nodded.

— That's what the police said. Apparently that's what these Area Boys in Lagos sometimes use. I can't help wonder if talking about them like small kids is one reason they've got so out of control. Kazuo was telling me they almost run some parts of the city.

—Yes – Kazuo's told me a bit about that. Like the *yakuza*.

— Which is?

— Japanese mafia. Takashi hesitated. I know you'll keep this to yourself, but that's why Kazuo ended up in Lagos. He was getting away from the *yakuza*.

— Really? A gangster?

That dignified man and his friendly wife? Marius knew to expect surprises; after all, he spent half his life building stories around himself, and if he did it, why not others? Complacency was ignorance, he was fond of saying. And in a way it made sense. A background in the *yakuza* might not be a bad thing to muscle into business in Lagos. But if that's what it had taken to establish the hotel, it was deftly hidden behind the elegant façade.

Takashi smiled and nodded.

— You could put it like that. Hard to imagine, isn't it? His father was in the building industry and he sort of grew up into that world. Then he met Yukio – his wife – and she opened his eyes to the sort of world he was part of. He'd made some sort of connection with a Nigerian businessman so they managed to disappear and re-invent themselves in Lagos.

— So he might have more connections in Lagos than one might think?

— No doubt. Why? What are you getting into in Lagos? Are you taking on the work?

Marius shook his head and took a few sips of his beer before answering.

—The thing is, I find Ash's murder unsettling and I can't shake the feeling that it wasn't a random attack. Now you tell me about that car, it's got me thinking about it again. They could have been waiting for him. That would explain why the attack happened in that place. But it doesn't explain why they were waiting there.

— Maybe it was just what it looked like. Their car had broken down, Ash happened to be walking past and they saw an opportunity. Kazuo thinks that's still the most likely explanation; it might be an upmarket neighbourhood, but it's still Lagos. What they all want is for those men to be caught – it seems pretty clear that it must have been them. Do you think you're reading too much into it?

Marius looked up at the thick dark clouds back lit by a hidden moon; a perfect metaphor for the black fog inside his head. Determined to clear it, he pulled himself on to the edge of the couch, and leaned towards Takashi, his elbows on his knees.

— You're right. And one part of me agrees with you. But these are the questions that are nagging at me. He counted each point off on the fingers of his left hand. One. If it was an opportunistic robbery, why kill him? It just complicates things. Two. Why wasn't Ash's driver there? Three. What was going on with the school finances? Four. What was Ash trying to say to me as he was dying?

Takashi interrupted him.

— Lawrence Ashley tried to say something?

Marius nodded and brought the moment back into clear focus before he replied.

— It was almost literally his last breath. To be honest, it could have been a groan – you know, ahhh. But it might have been more like 'al'.

— Could it be a name? Al?

— I guess so.

— Wait. Takashi leaned across and picked up Marius' empty beer mug. Another one?

It was a rhetorical question. He stood up, caught the attention of Yao and held up the two mugs. Then he sat back down and waved at Marius to continue.

— Thanks. That's about it. Kazuo and the others are probably right.

— What did you mean about the school finances?

— He wanted me to help with a problem but he didn't say much. Just that he got a phone call from a bank in England – something about his name being taken off a joint account. Then he seemed to change his mind and clammed up. He tried to cover it up, but I could see he was worried.

— Was there a Lagos connection with the money problem?

— Not that I know of. And that's the thing. If it wasn't random there must be a motive, and what could that be? If it was the men in the white car, we could assume they were hired by someone. Who? There are plenty of connections between the school and Lagos – parents and students for a start – but it's hard to think of any that would end up in this sort of mess. You're probably right. I'll follow the money and see where that gets me. That's where Mimi might be able to help.

Takashi raised an eyebrow.

— Mimi?

— With school stuff. There's something going on, otherwise why would Ash ask me to help.

— I see. Well you won't have to wait long. I told her you were here and she's joining us any time now. Meanwhile, we have work to do. He pointed at the mugs of beer and the yam fries that Yao had just placed on the table. Help yourself.

Marius took a piece of fried yam, dipped it in the little bowl of *shito* and was just about to put it in his mouth when suddenly everything went dark. A hand was placed over each of his eyes and a familiar voice said "Guess who?"

— Mimi! Marius laughed.

She took her hands away, then sat on the couch beside him and picked up her glass of white wine.

— Nice to have you back safe in Lomé, Marius. How awful about Mr Ashley.

— Thanks. He put the whole chip into his mouth and reached over for some more. Nice to be back. How's the school taking it?

— It depends. Do you really want to know?

— Yes, I do. I was just telling Takashi about some sort of money trouble Ash asked me to look into.

Mimi put her wine on the table then curled up on the couch, her feet tucked under her. She was wearing her old floppy T-shirt that almost covered her denim shorts and reminded Marius of the eight-year-old he'd met when she'd first arrived.

— Pass me my wine can you?

Marius did that and waited.

— Well, the problem about money has been raised – though not officially. And there's other stuff going on.

— For example?

— It's hard to know where to start – school politics are pretty complicated. She thought for a minute before continuing. I guess in simple terms, the school is split into two factions. One side is anti Mr Ashley and the other is pro. Well, you know what I mean. That's how it was until a few days ago and I guess it still is.

— What side are you on?

Mimi smiled at Marius and took a sip of her wine.

—I try to keep out of it but it's getting harder.

— Well, my dear, beware that old saying. If you always give way to others, you'll end up with no principles of your own.

— Okay. Of course I have my own ideas. I just can't stand the fighting, and all those meetings.

— Meetings?

— They seem endless. Do we have to talk about this? I'm so sick of it all.

Marius could see that all she wanted to do at this time on Sunday night was relax and forget about work, but he pressed on.

— If you don't mind. It may be nothing, but there's a slight chance that Ash's murder may not have been a random attack.

Mimi sighed.

— Okay. If you put it that way. But I think I'll need some more wine. And some of these.

She uncurled her legs and leaned forward and took a handful of the yam fries.

Takashi stood up and walked over to the bar. Mimi ate the chips then brushed the oil and salt off her hands and leaned back into the couch.

— I'm ready.

— Tell me about the meetings.

— Well, there's a group of teachers who seem to think that the IB is going to ruin the school.

— IB?

— International Baccalaureate.

— Which is?

— A bit like the French Bac but with a few extra things.

— Sounds harmless enough.

—They say it's elitist. That the kids in our school won't be able to do it. Mimi paused for a minute and Marius could see she felt awkward, but she continued. They're not saying it in these words but it's like the African kids aren't smart enough for it.

— Who's 'they'? The foreign teachers?

Mimi looked relieved

— Yes. Well not all of them, but most.

— Let me guess. The local teachers think it's a good idea.

— Exactly. Hey, you're pretty smart for an African.

Marius laughed.

— It's all those bananas I eat. But seriously, it doesn't seem enough to get too worked up about. What else don't they like?

— They don't like the extra work or the money it's costing. And they didn't seem to like Ash very much.

— How so?

— They had two meetings. Sort of secret – or not official, anyway – where they talked about how they could put an ultimatum together to try to force Mr Ashley out of the school. Well, not quite, but to change things so he'd have less control. They already have another headmaster in mind.

— Sounds a bit extreme.

— These teachers said they had evidence of how he was sending the school broke. No details, but they made it sound like the school's about to collapse.

— So if Ash was forced out, who is this person they have in mind?

— They were talking about Dave Gordon. He's the other owner.

— Was he at the meetings?

— No. But I'm pretty sure he knew about them.

— What do you think? It sounds a bit of a mess. I can see why you're sick of it.

— There are two men and a woman and all they seem to do is stir up trouble. Every time I see them they're either gossiping with each other, or in little groups, and you can easily see the way they suck the other teachers in. We've asked for some proof – like accounts and stuff like that, but it's always all this talk. Anyway, I like the idea of the IB programme.

— What do you think's going to happen?

Mimi shook her head slowly.

—They'll get what they want. You know, now that Mr Ashley….

She didn't have to finish. Marius was thinking the same. How convenient.

— What about Dave Gordon? What's he like?

— Hard working, well organised. I think I can see why the others think he'd be a good headmaster. He gets things done. And I guess you could say he's quite charming. He manages the boarding houses and all the practical things but he doesn't seem to know much about the academic stuff. Nor is he interested.

— How do you mean you guess he's charming?

Mimi bit her bottom lip, thinking about it.

— He smiles a lot, makes jokes, that sort of thing.

— But?

— You're right. There's a but. Sometimes I feel as if he's putting it on.

Marius nodded. It wasn't hard to get the picture, and that particular type crossed cultural barriers: they were men who saw themselves as superior but were desperate to be liked by everyone. In their own eyes at least, they always had the right answer for everything, and they were never interested in what other people were saying or doing. And they could change like a chameleon to suit any situation.

— What about the registrar? George somebody.

— George Barnes. Mimi sipped on her wine thoughtfully and then continued. If you had asked me, let's say a few months ago, I would have said he's great. You know, a nice man, always seemed interested in Japan, not very chatty, but friendly. Now I don't know. He's changed a bit.

— How?

— Well, for one thing, he's gone crazy over a young Togolese woman.

— How old is he do you know?

— I'm not sure. Late sixties, maybe early seventies.

— And how young is the woman?

— My age. Maybe younger. No, definitely younger. Early twenties.

Takashi had come back with another round of drinks. He put the tray on the table and pulled his chair closer to Mimi and Marius then sat down.

— Unfortunately not so unusual here, he said.

They knew what he meant. In the expat scene in Lomé it was quite common to see older men with beautiful young Togolese girls. Sex for money. One of those inevitable side effects of poverty.

— Last Friday George brought her to the drinks at the club. They were holding hands and feeding each other food. It was disgusting.

Mimi's face looked as if she'd eaten something very sour.

Marius and Takashi laughed.

—What about George and Dave. Do they get on?

Mimi sighed. She realised there was a lot that she didn't notice.

— I've really no idea Marius. No more questions, hey. I guess I keep to myself a fair bit at the school. But here's an idea. A note came round today. There's going to be a memorial service for Mr Ashley on Wednesday. Come to that – it's public. You can meet them yourself.

— Good idea. Could we go together maybe.

— Sure. I'll text you when I know more.

Mimi announced that she was going up to her room and Marius took his leave soon after. Driving back on the coast road, almost empty now, Marius thought over what Mimi had said. Ash must have known something about what was going on, so why had he let it get to this point? After all, it was Ash himself who'd told him that Dave was saying things about George – something about losing his marbles – and George was complaining about Dave not telling him things.

This thing with the young woman might be out of character, as Mimi said, but Marius had heard of stranger things, and if George Barnes was preoccupied with the woman, then he could easily not have his mind on the job and forget things.

When it came to that, George Barnes might be skimming off some of the school's money to keep the woman happy and that would explain the money problems. It would be a classic situation, but finding out wasn't going to be easy. In fact right now Marius couldn't think of any obvious way to make a start, so he'd just have to wait until Wednesday. Dave and George were sure to be there and with Mimi's help, he'd meet up with them somehow. If nothing else, at least it would satisfy his curiosity. He laughed to himself. On first name terms already and they hadn't even met.

In a strange kind of way he found himself quite looking forward to this memorial service.

7

Sunday 27 March

After Marius left, Takashi sat looking out over the night garden, listening to the chorus of frogs. The noise always reminded him of the rice paddies behind the house where he'd grown up in a village overlooking Osaka. One of the things he'd found comforting when they first moved to Lomé was frogs – they were in the lagoon next to the first house they'd lived in. Other people complained about the noise but he found it soothing and so did Mimi. They would often sit out on the patio after the mosquitos had finished their dusk patrol and just listen, trying to work out from the noises the different kinds of frogs that were out there in the dark.

That was when Simone was living next door. It was years since they'd last been in touch. Odd how families can be so close and then just drift away from each other. It would be good to catch up with her again – maybe invite her for lunch one weekend.

There'd been that terrible thing with her son. Now that he thought about it, Takashi had to admit it was probably more his fault than hers that they'd lost touch. Simone was a powerful woman and put all her energy into finding the reason for Andre's death. At one point it was all she talked about, and even now Takashi wasn't sure how much was true and how much was what she wanted to believe. But to confront the suicide of a child must be horrific, and he of all people should have understood. It didn't make him feel any better to know that Marius would have helped her; he would have wanted to find the truth, whatever it took.

Suicide had been the official finding. Rumours had circulated for years afterwards but Takashi had chosen to accept the school's version of events. One of the names that kept coming up was Dave Gordon, and Simone had become convinced that he was implicated in some way. In the end, she'd lost her job over it, and soon after Takashi had moved over here and they'd lost touch.

And now Dave Gordon's name had come up again. Maybe Marius was becoming obsessed about Lawrence Ashley's death in the same way that Simone had about Andre. But Marius had been right enough times for Takashi to take notice and there could be something in what Simone had found out as well. The least he could do was to tell Marius.

8

Wednesday 30 March

Marius turned his wrist slightly so he could look at the time without making it too obvious. He'd only been here for twenty minutes but it seemed much longer than that. A lot of people had come to the service and they were jammed into the school hall so tightly that his wrist was just about all he could move. The memorial service for Lawrence Marcombe Ashley had started on the dot of 11.30 and for most of the past twenty minutes an Anglican priest had been telling them more about Ash's life than Marius felt he needed to know. The priest was dressed in purple robes that got Marius thinking about the old Roman Empire. With all the choices of belief systems around at that time, why Christianity?

Finally the priest stopped talking and handed over to some students. Clearly they'd been fond of Mr Ashley and what they had to say was moving and funny. It brought Ash the person back to mind. You didn't have to know him for long to understand his passion for education – Marius could testify to that.

Then it was the turn of Dave Gordon. Mimi had pointed him out as they came into the assembly hall — he'd been shaking hands with parents as they arrived. That was at a distance and Marius didn't get a good look at him, so as Dave walked over to the lectern, then turned to face them, Marius was surprised. Even he could see that the man was unusually good looking in a way that one didn't usually associate with schools and teachers.

Dave was quite tall and well built, dressed smartly in a dark suit and a pale blue shirt with a tie that looked as if it came from some sort of school or club. His brown hair was cut short and seemed to grow forward on his head, making a neat, flat cap. His skin was quite brown for an Englishman. In African terms he could almost be described as fair. But the really striking thing was his eyes. They were an unusual cloudy green colour with dark curly lashes that made them stand out and almost sparkle. But after watching him for a while, Marius started to wonder if there was something a bit odd about those eyes. It could just be that Dave Gordon was nervous, but Marius couldn't help thinking that they seemed expressionless, as if they were detached from the inner life of the man.

Most of what Dave had been telling them Marius already knew. He couldn't follow all of it, because of the accent. What was it? Irish? Scottish? Probably Scottish with those r's and a's. And now he came to think about it, Gordon was a Scottish name. There was that famous school there. What was it? Gordon something. Gordonstoun, that was it.

The way Dave delivered his words was carefully phrased, and each sentence had a resounding ring to it. He told them how the two of them had started the school in a house with fifteen students. Together they'd built up the school. How Mr Ashley had loved the school. They'd been business partners and friends, and it would be hard without him but he, Mr Gordon, would continue the work they'd started. He was making sure the memory of Mr Ashley would stay forever by creating the Lawrence Ashley Memorial Scholarship.

Dave paused and took out a handkerchief that he used to wipe his eyes. Carefully, first one, then the other, and the cynical side of Marius couldn't help feeling that it was a bit too much, as if it was more acting than real grief. The gesture seemed to impress everyone else, though, and the silence became deeper. Marius sensed discomfort mixed with respect.

As Dave was putting his handkerchief back in his pocket he smiled at them all and you could feel everyone relax as he made a little joke. At least Marius knew it was meant to be a joke by the relieved sort of laughter that came from some of the teachers sitting around him and Mimi.

— Big men do cry, Dave said.

Some of the students laughed as well and Dave enveloped them all with a smile that seemed to say 'I'm laughing through my tears'. Then the choir sang the last hymn and they all filed quietly and solemnly out to a grassed area that was enclosed by the two wings of the school buildings.

After the dark air-conditioned hall the glare and the heat of the noon sun was like an assault. It had the effect of breaking the mood created in the hall and it wasn't long before people were chatting in groups in whatever shade they could find, and looking as much as if they were at a party rather than a memorial lunch. But that's how it was. Marius knew well that the process of grieving was complicated and long, and overlaid with mostly normal, everyday stuff.

White marquees had been set up on the lawn, two with platters of food and the other one with drinks. People were already standing in long lines at the food tents so Mimi and Marius went over to get a drink.

Marius felt a lot better with a beer in his hand. A few other teachers had headed straight for the drinks tent as well; some of them Marius had met before, but most of them were new faces.

They stood around in the shade under the marquee and Marius found himself surrounded by language teachers. Mimi taught French and Japanese at the school and these were her colleagues. She introduced them: Claudette, French; Inga, German.

While they chatted about school stuff he looked around to see if he could pick out George Barnes. Behind him getting drinks from the ice-filled plastic boxes he could hear a couple of men talking. There was that Scottish accent again. It may have been that they didn't know how loud their voices were, or maybe they didn't care who heard them, but there was a sense of entitlement that came across. Marius resisted the urge to turn around and look at them. From the way they were talking, he wondered if they'd been at the service or whether they'd been putting away a few of the beers instead.

— Of course, one of the voices said. One wouldn't wish harm on anybody but you have to admit it's a stroke of luck.

— I'll drink to that, the other voice replied. I know I shouldn't speak ill of the dead, but you can't help but think it was his own stupid fault. Sometimes I wondered if he had any sense at all. Look at what he's done to the school! If it wasn't for Dave....

The voices started to get fainter and Marius turned discreetly and saw a couple of youngish looking teachers walking towards the food marquees. He could see what Mimi meant about a split in the school. The men looked ordinary enough but the bitterness in the way they spoke about Ash sounded really intense. Something had got them worked up. Or someone, Marius thought.

Mimi and the others didn't notice. They were speaking quietly in French, anxious not to be overheard. Thanks to Mimi's crash course Marius realised it was the IB programme they were talking about. He hadn't wanted to intrude on their conversation but now Mimi caught him by the elbow and brought him closer.

— Marius. You should hear this. Claudette is friends with Dave Gordon's secretary. Apparently there's a memo that's going to come round this afternoon.

Claudette broke in.

— *Oui*. A memo saying that Dave Gordon is now the sole owner of the school. He'll take over as head of school and it says 'implement immediate restructuring to address the financial problems'.

— We think that 'restructuring' probably means putting a stop to the IB programme. You know I was telling you about that group of teachers? Well it looks like they've persuaded Dave to do what they want.

To be honest, Marius couldn't really see what the fuss was about. A Levels, IB – same difference, surely, though he could see what Mimi meant about the IB being less Anglo centric. What he found more interesting was that Dave Gordon must surely have been behind those meetings, even if he wasn't part of them. Sole owner, headmaster? Those were big changes to have in place so soon after what was a very sudden death. But this wasn't the place to start raising those issues and he kept his thoughts to himself.

— Would it really make much difference in finances if the school went ahead with the IB? he asked.

It was Inga who answered him.

— The fees are high but that's not the big expense. It's the new courses Ash planned to introduce. She looked at Claudette for support. If you count the coordinator and other extra positions probably seven more teachers? Art, German, Physics, Advanced Mathematics, Theatre Arts. Plus more teaching spaces, extra equipment.

— And Ash always buys state-of-the-art stuff, Mimi added.

Marius started to get the idea. If these money problems really were because of the IB, no wonder it was causing such a rift in the school. What Ash had talked about was far more than a bit of extra expense, but what if someone was using that change to manipulate the staff?

— Right, I see. Big changes.

While they'd been talking Marius had been watching Dave. He looked busy, keeping an eye on everything, chatting to groups of parents then to the men serving the food. Now Dave was coming over to the drinks tent.

— Mimi, Marius whispered and inclined his head towards Dave. Introduce us.

Mimi took in the situation and nodded. She pointed to her almost empty glass of wine.

— Time for a top up. Anyone else?

Marius followed her over to the makeshift bar. The two men in white jackets behind the bar had seen Dave coming too and Marius could see them straightening up in readiness. He helped himself to a bottle of beer and the tall waiter came over to Mimi with a bottle of white wine and refilled her glass.

The trestle table that served as a bar was covered in a white cloth, crisp despite the humidity, and the waiters looked impeccable in their starched white jackets. But Dave ignored the waiters and everyone else and went straight to the ice filled tubs of drinks, dipping his fingers into each one.

Then he turned to the waiter who was up that end of the bar.

— This stuff's half melted. Get more ice.

Except for the white jacket that the waiter was wearing, he looked as if he was standing to attention in a parade ground.

— Yes sir.

Then Dave picked up one of the plastic tumblers that were neatly lined up on the white cloth.

— What's this? Can you get nothing right? Where are the wine glasses?

— Matron said…. The waiter started to explain but was cut off.

— Don't you have a brain of your own? Dave picked up a bottle of wine and pointed to it. Wine. Wine glasses.

— The glass ones sir?

The handsome face suddenly took on a mean look and Dave let out a long breath, as if he was only just keeping his patience. He stared at the waiter, leaning forward so that their two faces were close together. Then he stepped back and shook his head.

— You really are stupid, aren't you? The plastic wine glasses. The ones we always use outside.

— Yes sir. It wasn't clear if the man was agreeing to being stupid or to fetching the wine glasses, but he turned his back on them all and walked towards the main building.

Marius noticed Dave shaking his head as the waiter walked away.

Mimi didn't react and in fact Dave hadn't raised his voice and she may not even have heard. She walked over to where Dave was now helping himself to a Fanta and Marius followed her.

— Hello Dave, Mimi said. That was a very good address that you gave in there.

The transformation was unsettling. Dave turned towards Mimi and enveloped her in a smile.

— Kind of you to say so. It wasn't easy. What a terrible business.

— I still can't take it in. We're really going to miss Ash. By the way, I want you to meet a friend of mine, Marius Agyekum.

Dave turned his smile towards him and Marius held out his hand.

— Please accept my sympathies. Maybe you don't know... I was with Mr Ashley in Lagos when he was killed.

Marius saw a shadow pass over the green eyes. It wasn't something that he could physically see, more like a feeling, an understanding.

— No, I didn't know. I thought Mr Ashley was alone.

Marius was ready for questions. How bad was it for Ash? Did anyone help him? What did the police say? But nothing in Dave's voice, nothing in his body language, gave any sign of interest. Or feeling for that matter. Marius felt as if he'd said something wrong and he found himself apologising.

—

— Sorry. Not when he was stabbed, when he died. He was still breathing when I got there. If we'd been together, it might not have happened. We'd arranged to meet a place called The Jazzhole and he didn't turn up.

— Oh, aye. You must be the chap that Jerro told me about. Top place, The Jazzhole. I told Ash to be sure not to miss it.

Again the change in manner was disconcerting. Now Dave sounded happy, almost relieved, as if all that mattered was his recommendation. Marius had been on the point of sharing more about those last minutes with Ash, but now he kept away from the topic.

— That would be me Jerro was talking about. I had business in Lagos and Ash was kind enough to offer me a lift over there.

Dave was already looking around for the next thing to do, other people to talk to. But he flashed his smile again at Mimi and Marius.

— If you'll excuse me, he said, and moved over to a group of parents who had just come into the marquee.

In fact, the marquee was filling up.

— Let's get out of here, Mimi whispered. I can see George over there.

The lines for the food were quite short now and Mimi headed over to the marquee next to the stand of date palms.

— Wait a minute.

Marius thought at least Dave was right about the ice. His beer had heated up quickly and what was left in the bottle was flat and warm. He tipped it out and put the empty in one of the crates that were laid out at the end of the bar. Mimi had already joined the end of the line and Marius guessed it was George Barnes she was talking to.

He was taller and with less hair than Marius had imagined. There was a little bit of very short white hair just above his ears and round the back of his head, but otherwise he was completely bald. Marius was struck by the way he held himself, the military background unmistakable. Neatly dressed in a buttoned down short-sleeved shirt and cotton trousers, he didn't look at all like the man that Marius had pictured.

Mimi made the introductions. As they exchanged greetings Marius kept hold of George's hand for a few extra seconds. He looked more closely at the high forehead, the straight mouth, the brow and eyes close to each other but wide set. There was something familiar. He dropped George's hand and stepped back a pace, still looking at him.

— Have we met somewhere?

George put his head to one side and looked more carefully at Marius.

— Sorry. I can't place you. My memory's not what it used to be.

Mimi handed them plates and cutlery. They were at the head of the line now and there was the serious business of food to attend to. As they all put chunks of spicy chicken and salads on their plates he kept thinking about George. There was definitely something familiar about that square face and the unusual wide set of the mouth that was like a slash across his face, especially when he smiled.

The three of them found some space to sit at one of the trestle tables that was well shaded by the palms. As they were sitting down Marius suddenly realised what it was he'd been trying to remember.

— I think I have it, he said to George. Chess. I think I've played a game of chess against you.

George looked across at Marius in his collarless cream shirt. Then he remembered.

— You beat me! The tournament in Accra last year. The Indian gentleman.

Marius laughed and flapped the front of his shirt.

— Not Indian, despite the dress. But you're right about the game. I got lucky with a Morphy's Mate if I remember.

George smiled and shook his head.

— There's no luck in chess. But I say, you're telling me you're not Indian.

Marius shook his head.

— Definitely African last time I looked. Ghanaian to be more precise. But don't worry. You're not the first person to think I should be running an ashram in mother India.

George looked embarrassed as if Marius had read his mind.

— That's not what I meant.

— Sorry, just joking. But seriously, maybe we could have a game sometime.

Quite apart from a good chance to get to know George a bit better, Marius was always on the look out for a decent game of chess.

George picked up his knife and fork and carefully pushed some jollof rice on to his fork with his knife. The peas kept falling off but he persevered in an absentminded way. Marius thought he'd forgotten what he'd said but then George manoeuvred the loaded fork into his mouth and nodded while he chewed slowly until he'd swallowed the food.

— You know, that's a good idea. I'd like to do that. He started to load another forkful and stopped halfway through. Why don't you come round to mine? How would Saturday suit you?

— How about in the evening? Eight o'clock? He saw the look on George's face. Or seven?

— Seven would be better. I'll check with Gloria. If you don't hear from me, just come round. He pulled out a wallet and from that a business card and gave it to Marius. Turn it over. There's a map that should get you there.

Marius did as he suggested and tried to make sense of the map.

— Is that near here somewhere?

George nodded and reached over to show Marius on the map.

— The school's just here. He pointed to a spot on the left hand border of the card. My name's written on the letterbox.

Marius tucked the card into the back pocket of his trousers. He wasn't sure what to make of George. If Ash and Mimi hadn't put the idea of something being odd about him, he wouldn't have taken any notice, but with that in his mind he did see some rather blank moments. On the other hand, just now George had seemed brisk and businesslike. Normal. Anyway, what better than a game of chess to find out more.

The conversation moved on to other things. Mimi and Marius finished their meal while George was only halfway though his, still seeming to have a personal battle with his knife and fork.

— Time to go back to work, Mimi announced.

— I've things to do too, Marius said.

George had withdrawn into himself but he waved his fork in their direction. Don't worry about me. Slow eater. Off you go.

— See you Saturday, Marius said.

For a second George looked confused and Marius wondered if he'd forgotten about the arrangement. Then George seemed to remember. He made a show of remembering, at any rate.

— Oh, yes. See you on Saturday.

Marius walked with Mimi as far as the reception area.

— What do you think? he asked her.

— About George?

Marius nodded.

— Did you notice how much trouble he was having eating? Mimi asked. He couldn't seem to get his knife and fork working properly.

— You're right. I thought he was just slow but it was as if he was having trouble. By the way, do you know anything about his background? The military connection?

— Oh, that. Yes. Before he came here he worked for the British army. Some sort of accounting position.

—That explains it.

— Explains what?

— Well, apart from the ... oddities, he seems very fit for a seventy-year-old. And there's something about the way he squares his shoulders.

— You see what I mean about him. He was always so nice and I don't know .... with it. That's still there but there's this other side of him. He seems fine some of the time, then he seems to forget. Anyway, I have to rush. See you.

— Thanks Mimi. See you Friday.

Marius watched her hurry across the immaculate green lawn through the chattering groups of people and white marquees. It looked like a harmless celebration, but there was something toxic in the atmosphere, and he hoped that Mimi wouldn't become a victim of the fallout from Ash's murder.

When he walked out of the school gates he stood in the shade of the wall and considered. Straight home? Or call in for a drink somewhere? Then he realised the school was only a few blocks from Le Jazz Spot. There was always a chance that Mibou might be there. In fact Marius had half expected he'd run into Mibou at the service – he did some music teaching at the school. Marius was a bit vague as to what it actually was, but Mibou would definitely have some ideas about what was going on. Anyway, what he needed right now was a really cold beer to get the taste of the flat, warm stuff out of his mouth. He turned left and headed towards the *Spot*.

Ten minutes later he perched himself on a stool at the bar in Le Jazz Spot. To his left the chairs and tables in the garden courtyard looked as if they might melt in the afternoon sun, but in the bar the high thatched roof cast deep shade, and a ceiling fan plus a breeze coming through the open sides, kept the area cool.

As it turned out, Marius was the only person there, apart from Akosua, who ran the bar. Mibou was giving a lesson, she said. Akosua had presented him with a bottle of Star and a frosted glass from the very depths of the cooler and Marius sipped on the beer and chatted to her while she was cleaning up behind the bar.

— So Akosua, perhaps you can help me. Without knowing anything about him, what would you say about a chap like this: he's good at getting things done, energetic, and very organised; good looking and sociable. But when he talks to you he seems to be looking around as if there's someone more important just behind you. He can be smiling right at you but if you look at his eyes, they don't match the smile. People seem to like him, in fact some people think he's the best thing since Methuselah.

Akosua stopped what she was doing and stood with a half washed glass in her hand.

— I knew someone like that.

— Who's that? Anyone I know?

Akosua laughed.

— I don't think so. He came to start a church in our village.

— You're right. Church isn't my thing. So what happened?

— People loved him too much. But me, I didn't trust him.

Akosua finished washing the glass and put it in the rack then picked up another one.

— One of those self-proclaimed prophets?

— How did you know? That's exactly what he said he was. People gave him money. They didn't have anything much but they gave it to him. Even my family gave him money. All their money.

How often had he heard versions of that story? Trouble was, the gullibility of people was almost as depressing as the scammers who took advantage of them.

— Is he still there?

Akosua shook her head.

— He stayed for about three years, then one day he was gone with all the money he'd taken from the people. They believed it was going to be a wonderful new Heavenly Light Church – that's what he called it. But it was all for him.

— And you didn't trust him?

— No. Like you were saying, there was something about his eyes. I asked around and found out that he paid a man from another village to pretend to be a cripple in a wheelchair so he could 'cure' him! Even then no one would believe me. Take my advice Mr Marius and stay away from him. People like that can ruin your life.

— Thanks Akosua. You've given me an idea.

— And what would that be?

— False prophets are after power and money. The church is just a convenient arena to play in and I'm thinking a school could be just such another convenient arena.

Marius drank down the beer that was left in his glass and put some money on the bar, then he slid off the high stool and waved to Akosua.

— See you on Friday.

9

Thursday 31 March

Heaven save me from these idiots, Marius thought, but he brought the two men into his living room and invited them to sit down. They'd been shouting at each other when he opened the door but once inside they calmed down and chose to sit on the couch, one at each end. Marius sat opposite them on the ottoman and tried to work out what was going on. Kofi was the tall dark one, in a torn sleeveless shirt and loose fitting knee length shorts. Shorter and fairer, Ato was in a well-ironed print shirt, and creased trousers. Kofi was the one with the grievance.

The only thing that Marius had picked up so far was that it was something about what they were calling the 'light'.

— So Kofi, Marius asked. Who's paying for this electricity that you say Ato has tapped into?

— Kofi shrugged his shoulders and looked a bit uncomfortable.

Marius took a guess.

— Not you. One of your neighbours perhaps?

— The thing is he's chopping too much. Kofi pointed at Ato.

Marius looked at Ato and gave him a chance to speak but the anger had gone and Ato just sat there looking uncomfortable in his turn.

— Okay Kofi, let me guess. You're worried that the person who is paying for the electricity will notice that the cost has gone up too much and start asking questions.

Kofi looked relieved.

— You got it chief. Just that. This man here – he pointed to Ato again – does business. Me, I only take small small light.

Marius could see his point. It was a rule of thumb that usually worked. Take a little bit. A little bit of money, a little bit of electricity. It was wrong of course, but he also understood that people had to be creative to get by.

— So, Ato, what's this business?

— It's my wife sir. She does ironing.

— Does she make much money?

— Some. But if we pay for the light…. He lifted his shoulders eloquently.

Here was an impasse and Marius wasn't sure what he could do. The cost of electricity was too high for lots of people in Lomé.

It took the better part of an hour to talk through the problem. Marius ended up extending a small loan to them to get the electricity connected. Kofi's wife was going to use it to start a business of her own, then they could share the cost and pay back Marius over a year. He was fairly sure he'd get his money back; once the women had a chance to get into commerce things usually worked out. A meeting with the wives was organised and finally they left if not the best of friends, at least on speaking terms. Marius wasn't entirely sure why some of the locals used him to settle disputes, like a defacto chief; it had crept up on him and now he felt a certain responsibility to help out in that way.

After all that palaver Marius needed a beer. That and some peace and quiet. There was plenty of time before Dzigi got back from school and the local bar was just down the road. So local it didn't even have a name. If you said 'the spot', people around here knew where you meant.

It was nothing more than an annexe attached to the front of a smallish house. Built of concrete blocks, the house was painted a hectic blue colour and the usual plastic chairs and tables were set out under sheets of dark green corrugated plastic supported by posts that looked as if they were still part of a tree. It was enclosed by weathered lattice on three sides and drinks were served from the front room in the house where a bar was set up in one corner. The unit was chest high with fake leather padding and gold studs, salvaged from a derelict nightclub that some optimist had tried to start in the area years ago. The green roofing and the lattice created an eerie underwater effect that was strangely calming. In some ways, Marius felt more at home here than he did in his own place.

Plaisance was the owner of the bar and lived in the house with her daughter and son, Bibi and Jean. For Marius part of the charm of the place was that she seemed to do whatever she could to live down having a name that meant 'pleasant'. He'd come to live in the neighbourhood around about the time that Plaisance realised her husband was not coming back after years of study in the US. She'd been happy enough to support him in his engineering studies, thinking ahead to the time he'd be a big man back here. Then someone ran into him in the US and brought back the news that he had another wife and family over there. The bar she was running as a short term solution had become her life. People who claimed to know her well said she'd lost her sense of fun around about that time.

Marius waited at the table for a few minutes but nobody came to take his order so he went inside. From the room behind the bar he could hear Plaisance talking on the phone and it took a while for her to notice him. She kept talking to whoever was on the other end of the phone while she was serving him, but he smiled and thanked her anyway.

As he was sitting back down he felt his own phone vibrating in his pocket. When he pulled it out he checked the name. Takashi. He left his beer on the table and talked into the phone as he headed towards the entrance.

— Takashi. Just a minute. I'm going outside. Okay. That's better. Anything wrong? What can I do for you?

Takashi laughed.

— Don't worry about me – nothing's happened. But after last Sunday I thought of someone you might want to talk to.

— Go on.

—It's rather sad. The French teacher at the American school had a son who committed suicide. Her name's Simone. Dave Gordon's name came up in connection with the business and she did a lot of digging around about him. Nothing was ever proved and the official finding was suicide.

— Is she still around?

— Most likely. In fact I was thinking of catching up with her again. She's fierce but very nice and very smart. She used to live right next to us and I'm sure she's still there.

— You're right. I would like to talk to her. That's if she doesn't mind raking over those old coals.

— I might call around to her place tonight. You've got me interested in this school business now, and it's getting a bit close to home. Mimi thinks she could lose her job and you know how hard it's been for her to settle here.

And then, Marius thought, she might have to go back to Japan to find work and Takashi wasn't the only one who didn't like that idea. She was like a daughter to him too and it wouldn't be the same here without her.

— Let me know how you get on.

Marius ended the call and put his phone back in his pocket. As he walked inside it occurred to him how much this business with Lawrence Ashley had taken over his life. All from one car trip. Or to take it even further back, one barbeque.

He sat down and looked at his beer. The froth had dwindled to almost nothing and it had lost that first cold freshness. Then he realised he should have covered it with a coaster, and flicked a couple of half-drowned flies out of the glass.

Dave Gordon. Marius was more than a little curious to find out more about his past. There was a lot he'd picked up from that one meeting and it made him think the man was a lot more complex than people took him to be. In fact, Marius found it hard to understand how well liked the man seemed to be. And for that matter, how much trust Lawrence Ashley had put in him. Still, it was early days yet, and Marius tried to keep an open mind.

Another way of thinking about Dave Gordon was through Jerro's eyes: the big spender. Come to think of it, where would that money come from? Those hotels would cost a fortune and one could assume there would be expenses to match. If the school was losing money, that's one black hole it could be going into.

Had Ash known about it? George? He must remember to check with George on Saturday night. And it wasn't only the money. The word sleaze kept coming into Marius' head, but it was more complicated than that. Jerro had talked about a fast living sort of lifestyle that Dave opened up for him in Lagos. Not your average relationship between a boss and his driver, so why? Dave might just be a generous, friendly sort of guy, but there were other reasons why he might want to keep Jerro on side. It wasn't exactly blackmail, but if Dave Gordon included Jerro in his Lagos activities, then Jerro was not going to ask questions no matter what he was asked to do. Just what that might be wasn't clear yet.

Power and money. Reverence and fear. To test a man's character, give him power. The ancient Greeks knew that and people were still being tested and falling short. What would Dave Gordon do with his bit of power? The IB had been a convenient whipping post to build conflict on, and now it could be conveniently dropped. No doubt Dave had ideas about how he could make more money out of the school, but you'd think there were only so many possibilities: higher fees, lower expenses, bigger classes. There was something he was missing, of that Marius was sure, but what? And how to find out?

Marius looked at his empty glass and then at his watch. Should he have another one? Dzigi and Seri would be home from school now and he knew that Dzigi would like him to be there. But Jojo was with them and Dzigi would probably want to play with the kids next door anyway. He smothered the certain knowledge that he really should go back home and headed for the bar where Bibi was helping out, still in her school uniform. Maybe it's how Plaisance was once, smiling and friendly. Sometimes Marius gave Bibi a hand with her English homework, but today she said it was all done. She picked a beer from the bottom of the fridge and gave Marius a glass out of the freezer.

Back at his table, Marius savoured the cold beer. What about the way Dave had reacted when he'd mentioned about being with Ash when he died? There was a sudden attention that showed in his eyes. It almost looked like alarm and Dave was definitely aware that Marius had noticed. Whatever it was, the thing that passed between them disappeared as soon as Marius told Dave the whole story. Why would it worry him if Marius had been there when Ash was attacked? And why wasn't he more interested in talking about it, getting some firsthand details?

Then there was George Barnes. What to make of him? Maybe it was just that they'd played chess together, but Marius found it hard to think of George fiddling the books. There was no doubt he was in a position to do it, though, so best to keep an open mind. And George was undeniably absent-minded, so Dave could be right about him being forgetful. To what extent Marius aimed to find out on Saturday night. With luck it would end up being a simple mix up with the bank. Then he could accept that

Ash was a victim of a random and murderous attack and move on.

10

Saturday 2 April

Marius clasped his hands behind his head and looked up at the ceiling fan. The petal shaped bamboo blades made a soft swishing noise each time they revolved, and he let his mind go blank as he watched. It wasn't exactly meditation, but near enough.

It hadn't been the smartest thing to stay on drinking last night. How late had it been? Thank god there was plenty of time before lunch with Takashi and Simone.

Then he remembered Jojo had gone to his uncle's funeral and that meant taking Dzigi to his football game at whatever time. Marius tried lifting his head, but it felt thick and heavy, and he let it fall back on to the pillow. He closed his eyes and listened to the rhythmic swish of the fan. A few minutes more wouldn't hurt. He must have fallen asleep because when he opened his eyes again Dzigi was walking with elaborate care towards the bed, balancing a mug on a small tray.

Marius propped himself against the back of the bed and took the mug off the tray. He smiled at Dzigi and sniffed the steam coming off the mug.

— Lemon grass tea. Perfect, thank you. Come. He patted the bed next to him. Let's make some plans for today.

As Dzigi talked about his football, and how Jojo was helping him improve his swimming, it occurred to

Marius that he'd handed over a lot to Jojo. When did that start? What was so important that he couldn't make time to go and watch Dzigi play football? Or take him swimming? And what did he do instead? Talk to people. Eva had called it holding court, and perhaps she had a point.

Dzigi said he didn't need help getting his football gear and swimming stuff together, so Marius went down to put together some breakfast, intending to catch up with Eva's news, but the kitchen was empty and he realised Eva and Seri must have already left for Ghana. Again. Could Eva have a boyfriend she wasn't talking about? Of course it would be nice for her – it was a while since that disastrous relationship with the lawyer. But he had to admit he had mixed feelings. After all, the house was perfect, their arrangement was working well, and life had settled into an easy routine. Why go spoiling it?

The fridge was nearly empty, but Marius found some groundnut soup and a bowl of rice left over from a few nights back, and he dumped them in a saucepan to heat. Not ideal for breakfast, but it would have to do.

It was a few minutes before 9 o'clock when they arrived at the football field and already the air was dense and hot. Marius had forgotten how desolate the ground was: mostly dirt with a few clumps of grass, and nothing you could call shade anywhere near the field. He watched Dzigi run over to join his team then headed for a grassy hill that had a stand of shea trees growing on it. He couldn't see much that was happening on the football pitch from here but at least there were a few bars on his phone. A couple of rocks looked comfortable enough and he sat down under a tree and passed the time chatting to the friends who usually called in on Saturdays.

In the car on the way to Chez Miki Dzigi was quiet for a while. When he finally spoke, it was obvious he'd been stewing over what to say since they'd left the football field.

— You didn't see, did you?

— What didn't I see?

— Me scoring a goal!

— Just one?

Dzigi looked disgusted and he turned his back to Marius as much as he could and stared out the window.

Marius thought Dzigi should toughen up, but it had been a careless remark that reminded him more of his own father than himself. He tried to think of something to lighten the atmosphere.

— So what does Jojo do while you're playing?

Dzigi turned back towards Marius and gave him a look that could have said 'Why are you asking me that? Or then again, 'Do you really want to know?'. He shrugged and turned back to the window so that Marius had to strain towards him to hear what he mumbled.

— Runs up and down the sideline. Tells us what to do. Cheers when we score goals.

Dzigi looked back at Marius to see how he was taking it. They exchanged looks and then both of them laughed.

— Well, Marius said. It's probably best that Jojo keeps taking you to football!

Dzigi nodded and looked relieved.

Takashi's Beach Bar was built right in the sand, halfway between the sea and the dunes. An angular glass and timber affair with an open sided thatched annexe on one side, it was packed on this Saturday afternoon. Mimi was there as well as Simone, and Takashi had reserved a table for them in the annexe. From there Marius could keep half an eye on Dzigi, who finished his food in record time and went straight for the water.

The sea in front of the Beach Bar was protected from the rough surf that was more typical along this part of the coast. Twenty or thirty years ago there had been a coast road that went all the way to Benin, but the sea had eaten into the land at such a rate that the road was now under the water and it looked just like a reef if you didn't know any better. It had the same effect as a reef as well and made a big lagoon that wouldn't have been out of place on a tropical island.

Simone turned out to be just as Takashi had described. She was a tall woman, big built with a personality that matched. Years of teaching French had given her a certain French chic that showed in her accent and the stylish dress that showed just the right amount of some very attractive shoulders. Takashi had gone to even more trouble than usual with the meal, and the fish, the sauce, the salad, the dessert and the wine, were all analysed and appreciated in the French style. Marius tried to pick up the nuances of flavours the others were noticing, but 'excellent' was the limit of his food vocabulary.

When the plates were cleared and coffee served, Simone tossed back her espresso then looked across at Marius.

— Takashi tells me you want to know more about Dave Gordon.

Marius nodded.

— He told me about your son. It must have been terrible. I'm so sorry. If you'd rather not talk about it….

Simone waved a hand as if physically brushing the remark aside.

— It was years ago so yes, I can talk about it. I'll never get over it – I don't think anyone would – but I've learned to live with it.

— Do you think Dave Gordon had something to do with his death?

— I'm sure he did. Andre may have drowned himself as they said, but it was Dave Gordon who pushed him to it.

— What makes you so sure?

— It's not possible to prove, but I'll tell you how it was. Andre was just a normal fourteen-year-old boy then suddenly he started talking all the time about Mr Gordon. The swimming and the football were his whole interest because they were with Mr Gordon. We thought it was just a phase – adolescent boys and so on. The irony was that we were even pleased about how healthy it was, with all the sport he was playing. But then he got really withdrawn – he wouldn't even talk to us. Just as bad, he lost all interest in the sports. Then two days before his fifteenth birthday we got the terrible news. Of course we blamed ourselves. There was a good chance that Dave Gordon knew more than us, something that would help us understand. You know, after all the time Andre had spent with him. There was all the football practise and then round at his place with the swimming. I went to Dave's house and he didn't answer the door so I went around the back. He was sitting by the pool with Germaine, one of Andre's friends. The body language told me everything – ruffling his hair, touching his leg– and it was as if the boy was worshipping him. I just stood there looking at them, and instead of seeing this other boy I saw Andre. Then I knew why he'd changed.

— What did you do?

— I just said sorry and left. A few days later I tried to talk to Dave about Andre. Can you imagine how badly I wanted to know? But he just talked a lot of nonsense about how Andre could have been a great swimmer and what a terrible loss and all that.

There were tears in Simone's eyes and Takashi gave her a hug.

— Tell them about the students. I think that's what happened next?

Simone held her empty wine glass out to Mimi.

— I think I need another one of these please *cherie*. You're right Takashi. Some students accused me of being a bully, and biased against the Americans in the class. I knew those students and I knew who was behind it, so I decided to find out more about Dave Gordon. I won't go into it, but these things I know for sure: his sports degrees from Edinburgh and Aberdeen were fake. He was expelled from his Aberdeen high school for cheating on the 'O' levels. He tried to make it as a footballer and was good but didn't make the big time. He was arrested for dealing cocaine to the football club but the charges were dropped. Worked for an Aberdeen oil company as a procurement officer then came on a holiday to Togo and stayed here. It was Lawrence Ashley who got him the job at the school.

Marius would have loved to know how she managed to get all that information but he believed her. Takashi was right. She was intelligent in a way that few people are – reflective, logical.

— Did you tell anyone at the school what you'd found?

Simone shook her head as if she still couldn't believe it.

— I was stupid enough to think that the head would listen to me. But I should have known. If I hadn't been so distraught about Andre, I would have noticed that Lawrence Ashley, Dave Gordon and John Canning — that was the head's name — were like a triumvirate, a power to themselves. Lawrence Ashley had a meteoric rise to deputy principal and Dave Gordon was his best buddy. I told John Canning what I'd found out but he refused to follow it up. Then he accused me of being unstable and taking it out on Dave Gordon so I wouldn't have to blame myself.

Marius felt the injustice as if it had been done to him. He'd seen the pattern before and in his experience, it always had one outcome.

— Did the school fire you?

— I resigned before that could happen. Eventually I got a job at the French school and I'm still there.

— I don't know how you came through all that with your sanity.

— I have Anton, my other son, and I had to keep going because of him. It was too much for my husband though, and we split up a few years later. He never really got over it.

This was more than Marius had expected to hear and he felt humbled that she'd been prepared to share it with him. He reached across and took her hand.

— Thanks Simone.

He might have said something else but just then Dzigi came up to him, wet and sandy, and pointed out that they had to be back for Kofi's party at six. It was a fair point, so Marius sent him off to change and ordered another beer while he waited.

Listening to Simone took Mimi back to her time at the American school. It seemed impossible that the things Simone was talking about had happened while she was doing sport with Mr Gordon and learning French from Madame. But then at that age all she was worried about was making friends. What if Madame Simone was right? Without taking any notice of the others, as if thinking aloud, she put into words an idea that had been playing around in the back of her mind.

— There was a boy in my Year 10 Japanese class a few years ago. He was found hanged in his room.

For a few seconds the muffled thud of waves breaking on the manmade reef was the only sound at the table. Takashi spoke first.

— I remember that, but we have to assume it's a coincidence. Unless there's something else that you know about the suicide, that is.

— I don't know much – that's all we were told. It was devastating for everyone. His poor parents just couldn't believe it; I could hardly believe it either. He'd been such a great kid. Quiet, especially in Japanese classes, but everyone liked him. The thing I remember most about him was how thoughtful he was. When some of the others did stupid stuff, you know, mucked around, he'd always stay out of it and help get things back on track. I missed him a lot after he died. What must have been going on in his life for him to do such a thing?

86

Marius could see how easy it would be to jump to conclusions. The look on Simone's face was enough to tell him she'd already made up her mind.

— Look, it's probably a coincidence, just like Takashi said. But how about this. I'll get Jojo to do a bit of surveillance for me. He gets a kick out of it and at least we'll feel as if we're doing something, even if it's just to rid ourselves of the idea we now have in our heads.

As he walked out to the car with Dzigi, Mimi caught up with him.

— Did you know I've lost my job at the school Marius?

— Takashi told me. How long have you got left?

— Up to the end of July. They can't afford to get rid of me until after the exams. I feel like I've been going around with my eyes closed. Is there anything I can do?

They stopped at the car and Dzigi climbed into the front seat. Marius put a hand on each of her shoulders and her worried face looked up at him.

— You can be my eyes and ears at the school Mimi. But be careful.

— I'm always careful.

Marius let go of her and walked around to the driver's side. He waved over the top of the car and was happy to see her smiling again.

11

Saturday 2 April

Keeping the creases sharp, Dave Gordon carefully drapes his trousers over a wooden hanger and puts it in on a hook next to his shirt. Then he pulls on his swimming trunks, throws a towel over his shoulder and comes out on to the patio under the terracotta roof of the small changing room.

He walks across to the edge of the pool and examines the surface. It's looking good – not a leaf to be seen. He hunkers down, and cupping both hands together scoops up a handful of water and sniffs it. Good. A bit more chlorine than this morning, but not too much. The pool cleaners have done their job.

He stands up and looks over the still blue pool set in the green lawn. To his right a few date palms line the grey cement boundary wall, and to his left large sliding doors lead into the living room. Not bad for a lad from Aberdeen he thinks. It's years since he's been back there and the thought of the place conjures up a blur of cold winds and endless rain. That last time had been the worst, and all his parents could say was "when are you coming back?" and "It's time to settle down." They seemed to think their miserable council flat was some fucking castle. Stuff it. Stuff them.

Noiselessly a young boy appears beside him. He could be fourteen or sixteen, it's hard to tell. He's almost as tall as Dave and his shoulders and arms are already quite powerful. He's dressed in the school's sports uniform and is carrying an Adidas bag.

Dave touches him lightly on his arm as a form of greeting and favours him with a smile.

— I'll get changed, the boy says, and a few minutes later he's back in his swimming trunks.

Dave drops his towel next to the boy's on the white pool chair and the two of them line up on the edge of the pool.

— I'll give you a five-second start, Dave says.

The boy shallow dives and the water churns as he thrashes his way down the pool. Dave waits a couple of seconds then he's in the pool and racing after the boy. They're both strong swimmers, but Dave touches before the boy. Dave reaches over and fondles the top of the boy's head.

— Well swum. You nearly beat me.

— Next time we'll start together.

The boy uses the back of his hand to splash Dave and at the same time throws himself back under the water. Dave is ready when he surfaces and pushes him under again. The boy comes up gasping and the two of them wrestle in the water before Dave suddenly pulls himself out of the pool with his arms, twists adroitly and sits on the edge.

— Forty laps, he says. I'll time you.

12

Saturday 2 April

Marius felt as if he'd driven to Lagos and back. There was the present to buy, so that was a trip down town. Then Dzigi's friend's place had to be way out past the airport and in the opposite direction to where George lived. At least Kofi's parents were happy for Dzigi to sleep over, so Marius didn't have to do the return trip until tomorrow. Just as well. It was after 6.30 already.

Marius grabbed a quick beer and some more of the groundnut soup then headed off to find a moto-taxi. He'd had enough driving for one day.

The driver put him down near the German school and Marius asked him to wait for a minute while he used the headlight to look at the map on the back of George's business card. When the moto had disappeared around the corner the darkness was complete, and Marius had to stop and peer at the names on the gates before he found the one he was looking for. Even so, it wasn't much after the agreed time of seven when he found the metal plate that said 'George Barnes'. He hardly had time to push the buzzer before the gate was opened by an earnest young security guard in a short-sleeved brown cotton uniform.

Just inside the gate there was a small wooden chair and Marius noticed a book opened face down on it. The guard must have been reading by the light of the square lamps on top of the gateposts. *How to Succeed.* Leaning down Marius picked up the book, and using the fingers of one hand to keep the place, he used the other to turn back to the introduction.

— Looks interesting. Found anything useful?

— The guard gave Marius a half-smile.

— Work hard.

Marius laughed and held out his hand.

— My names Marius. And you're…?

— Everyone calls me Sam.

— Nice to meet you, Sam. What are you working at?

— Accountancy.

— Good choice. I hope that gets you to where you want to go. Down here?

Marius pointed to a row of paving stones set into the lawn.

— That's it. Follow the path. The door's on that side.

There were curtains pulled across the windows in front of the house. Behind them a light was on and Marius could hear women's voices over some loud afrobeat. He wondered if there was a party and what the chances were of a game of chess, and when he knocked on the door he wasn't sure what to expect.

But he didn't need to worry. It was George who answered the door and he led Marius through a narrow room with orange and black velvet couches and a giant screen. On either side of the screen the shelves were filled with videos and CDs, with large speakers at each end.

The three women on the couches all looked young and local. One was braiding the hair of another, who was sitting on the floor with her back resting against the couch. The third was holding her hands out in front of her, blowing on her fingernails. Marius could smell the acrid nail polish remover. On the screen, dancers dressed in blue and yellow African prints and two bare chested acrobats were performing to the music.

George paused in front of the woman who was inspecting her nails.

— Gloria, he said, meet…. He looked at Marius who offered his name. He wasn't sure what to do next but the woman took the matter into her own hands and held out a wrist to be touched.

— Watch out for the nail polish, she said.

George laughed as if it was all quite normal.

— Women! Come on, through here.

Marius felt better when he saw a chessboard set up on a polished wood dining table, and even more relieved when George pulled a folding partition across, closing them off from the other room. Clearly this was the formal part of the house. The L-shaped space had the table and chairs in one wing and a chintz covered lounge setting in the other.

George pointed to the screen that divided them from the television room.

— They're all going out once they get themselves done up.

— Anywhere special?

George shrugged.

— Some disco downtown I expect. You know Gloria is still young. She needs to have some fun.

It occurred to Marius that the fun Gloria was looking for might be more than a dance. There'd been something about the tight dress and her manner that suggested it, but he managed a smile that he hoped looked sincere.

— Of course.

George had turned his back to him and walked over to a carved wooden sideboard in the lounge area. He turned towards Marius and waved an arm at the table.

— Have a seat. What will you have?

Marius elected to follow George over to the sideboard and he inspected the collection of bottles neatly arranged on the top. There were more behind glass-fronted doors and Marius bent down to have a look.

— You wouldn't have a cashew brandy by any chance would you?

George looked pleased.

— You're a cashew brandy man? Excellent stuff, that.

He opened the glass doors and pulled a bottle out from the back of the cabinet, then held it up to the light and he and Marius admired the fine amber colour.

— Ice?

— No thanks.

Marius took the tumbler full of brandy and George poured one for himself, then they headed back to the chessboard and settled down for a game.

It seemed to Marius that the best strategy would be to play Morphy's Mate, the same game as he'd played at the tournament in Ghana when he'd checkmated George. As close to it as he could anyway – it would be an interesting test. On that occasion George had played an intelligent, challenging game.

It was George who picked the white pawn and he didn't hesitate with his first move at least. Pawn to King

4. Good. Now Marius had the chance to put his idea to the test and he played e5.

It didn't take long for Marius to realise that something was different about the way George was playing. Not that he'd forgotten the moves. But what he did forget, more than once, was whether he'd moved or not. It was hard to say exactly what it was, but there were times when George seemed confused, unable to concentrate, though he tried to cover it up. And he was fumbling with the pieces.

Marius kept the game going as long as he could but he ran out of alternative moves and checkmated George before he'd finished his brandy.

George tried not to show it, but it was clear he felt embarrassed.

— Well done old chap, was all he said. Best out of three?

Marius agreed and they were re-setting the chessboard when Gloria pushed open the folding partition with a flourish. She didn't so much walk across to George but pranced – hips swinging extravagantly on either side of high heeled strappy shoes that crisscrossed around her ankles. A heavy smell of perfume floated around her as she petted George, draping both her arms around his neck and leaning first to one side then to the other, giving him the sort of kisses one might plant on a baby. George seemed to enjoy it, though it was hard to tell if the flush on his face was embarrassment or pleasure.

Gloria gave George a final kiss on his forehead then pushed herself upright and flapped her hand in a kind of wave.

— Bye, bye pet. Don't wait up for me.

She didn't bother to close the partition and music was still pounding out of the speakers. George didn't seem to notice so Marius gestured with his head towards the now empty room.

— Do you mind?

George swung the board around so the white pieces were in front of Marius.

— The music? No, turn it off by all means.

Marius walked through the partition to the other room, found the 'off' button on the remote then came and sat back down again.

— Go ahead. You play white this time.

Two games later and the score was two to Marius, and one draw.

They packed the delicately carved ivory chess pieces back into the lacquered wooden box and went over to the bar for more drinks. When he handed Marius his drink, George looked a bit embarrassed.

— Sorry about the poor form. Don't seem to be myself lately. Anyway let's sit down for a bit.

Marius followed him over to the lounge area and sank back into the soft cushions on the couch. George took the chair across from him. The silence stretched to the extent that nodding and smiling was not enough and Marius decided to go straight to the point.

— I'm not sure if you know George, but I went over to Lagos with Lawrence Ashley. I was there with him when he died.

George leaned forward with his elbows on his knees and shook his head.

— Tell me about it. Was he suffering? It's been such a shock I can't really take it in.

— No, by the time I got there he wasn't suffering.

George sighed and leaned back in his chair again, shaking his head.

— The school won't be the same without him. Such a decent chap.

— Mr Ashley didn't say anything to you about a problem with the bank did he? He told me he was worried about something and it's been on my mind since he was killed. Any idea what it might be? He said he trusted you, so I thought he might have told you something.

Marius hadn't been sure what to expect, but it certainly wasn't what happened next.

Suddenly George put his brandy glass on the coffee table next to him and sat on the edge of the chair, rubbing his forehead.

— I'd completely forgotten. What with the shock of Ash being killed like that it went clean out of my mind. And I guess it seemed a bit... irrelevant. You know, now....

— What had you forgotten George?

— The bank statements. I remember now. It was just before Ash went to Lagos. I was round at his place for dinner and he asked me to check something with the bank for him. Discreet, was the word he used. He didn't want me to say anything about it to anyone, even Dave Gordon.

— Why wouldn't he check them himself?

George had difficulty finding the right words.

— It's a bit hard to explain, but Ash was... strange about any sort of official stuff especially if it involved paper work and money. I don't like to speak ill of the dead, and Ash was a good friend of mine. You might say it was like a phobia. He absolutely refused to have anything to do with money. Except spend it of course. Since I've been here it's been Dave and I who run everything. Before I came it was just Dave. And Dave manages the dollar account. The statements get posted to him — it's always been like that. When a capital purchase needs to be made he transfers the money over to the current account.

— What did Ash do at the school? Wasn't he the headmaster? Or do you call it principal?

— Headmaster. He called himself the head. What he did was decide everything to do with what the kids got taught. That was it. He used to go into the classrooms a lot — even took a class of physics. Loved giving the Thursday address at assemblies.

— So you didn't get the statements?

— No. I mean yes. I got the statements but then I put them away. They're still in an envelope in the study somewhere.

George stood up, but while he was doing it he lost his balance slightly and knocked over his glass of brandy. Marius hurried across to help wipe it up but George had already pulled out his handkerchief and was mopping at it.

— Not much left anyway, he said. And plenty more in the bottle.

He left the handkerchief on the table and went across to the sideboard to refill his glass. Marius used it to wipe up the rest of the brandy that had trickled across the coffee table and was starting to drip onto the grey tiles. He tried to contain the liquid in the soaking handkerchief and held it at arms' length to avoid the drips.

— Is there somewhere I can put this?

George looked confused so Marius dumped the handkerchief in an ice bucket he spotted on the sideboard, then rubbed his damp hands down the side of his trousers and hoped the smell would evaporate. While he was doing it, George refilled his glass with some more cashew brandy, then he took it over, put it on the coffee table and settled himself back in the chair.

— Now where were we? Something about Lagos, I think.

— You were talking about the bank statements. The ones you picked up for Mr Ashley.

— Of course. Yes. Ash asked me to pick them up for him. I had to use my connections with the bank manager to get them.

— Would you mind if we had a look at them now? I feel I owe it to Mr Ashley to get to the bottom of it.

— No, not at all. Good idea.

George got up again, this time without spilling anything, and went over to a door at the end of the lounge room. He opened it and switched on the light. Marius was relieved to see an office that was full of folders and filing cabinets, tidy and organised.

Marius pointed to the larger of the two grey filing cabinets.

— Do you think the statements might be in here?

George rubbed the back of his head with his hand and looked around.

— Or if you were about to look at them before Ash died, perhaps they're in here.

Marius leant over the desk and lifted a pile of documents out of a wooden in-box. He shuffled through them and picked out an unmarked manila envelope secured with a treasury tag. He handed it to George.

— Could this be it?

George looked relieved and took the envelope.

— Well done old chap. Of course. I put it in there ready to give to Ash and it must have got mixed up with all my other stuff. He went over to the door and switched the light off. Let's take this back to the other room.

George tore open the moldy looking envelope and pulled out a stack of bank statements.

With the statements in his left hand and licking the fingers of his right hand, George quickly flicked through them. Then he stopped, looked more carefully at the bottom sheet, turned back to the one on top and pulled two statements out of the pile.

— This must be what Ash was worried about. Come and look at this.

Marius picked up his glass of brandy and went and perched on the arm of the chair. George held up the two statements side by side so they could both read what was written at the top. At first Marius couldn't see any difference.

— Have a look on the left hand side, where it says account details.

There it was. The February statement gave Dave Gordon and Lawrence Ashley as the joint account owners. In March it was just Dave Gordon.

George took the top few statements and checked all of them.

— No doubt about it.

And not long before Ash was killed, Marius thought.

He went back over to the couch and sat down. For all he knew Lawrence Ashley may have let slip something about that call from the bank to Dave Gordon. He might not have intended to tell Dave, but that didn't mean Dave didn't know. And now here's George with the unreliable memory already knowing more than Marius was comfortable with. He needed George to check the money side of things, but would he keep it to himself? Well it was too late now – all Marius could do was hope for the best.

George put the statements on the coffee table and flipped over a couple of pages in his notebook.

— Look here Marius. There's something else going on in this account. It's not just that Lawrence Ashley's name's been removed from the account. Around about that time some very large amounts of American dollars have gone in and out of the account. Nothing connected with the school would involve those amounts. Over time, yes, but not in one go.

He looked down at the notebook.

— Here's a single deposit for two hundred thousand dollars. It's tagged as school fees, but I know we didn't take that amount of fees in February. Not only that, but apart from the big amounts, there's not nearly as much money in there as one would expect. I'd need to look at more statements, but I think Dave's been taking money out – perhaps for quite a while. What do you think we should do?

To which Marius had no real answer. Not yet, anyway.

— For the time being, we need to keep this strictly to ourselves. Is there a school board?

— No, nothing like that. It's an odd set-up – just the two partners.

— So with Ash out of the way, there's no one to say that Ash wasn't party to the change in the account names. He told me about it in the car going over to Lagos, but it would be my word against Dave Gordon, and I think I know how that would go.

— But you know, Marius, it's pretty bad that Ash is getting the blame for sending the school bankrupt with this new IB programme when all the time….

— I know. There's something fishy about those large amounts going in and out like that. I'll see what I can find out – there might be a simple explanation. But George, remember that you tell absolutely no one. Not even Gloria.

— Really?

— Yes. Really.

Especially not Gloria, but Marius kept that thought to himself.

13

Sunday 3 April

Marius stood under the shower and dropped his head forward so the water ran down his neck and onto his back. He hadn't bothered to turn on the hot tap and the water was just tepid.

He felt good after the run. Unlike Takashi, he couldn't always persuade himself that running was a good idea on a Sunday morning, and that was doubly so if he'd come home late from a jazz session at the Mandingue, which is where he'd ended up after he left George's place. Good decision though. That trumpet player from the Netherlands was fantastic and Mibou was in top form. Interesting to think it would never be repeated, but that was the thing about jazz. You had to be lucky enough to be there.

It was interesting what Takashi had said as they jogged around the Lomé streets. Could George be on some sort of drugs, he'd asked. Or taking some of the potent aphrodisiacs you could pick up, right here in the Grand Marché, not to mention the Fetish Market. With a young woman like Gloria, had Marius thought about juju? Often the juju men used a combination of both.

Marius let the water cool the heat from his body, then soaped up and rinsed himself off. He was half dry when he heard his phone ringing in the bedroom. The towel was too small to knot around his waist, so he held the two ends in one hand and hoped it would keep most of the drips off the tiled floor. He grabbed the phone on its last ring. When Jojo got back last night he'd jumped at the chance to do a bit of surveillance, and Marius hadn't even heard him leave this morning.

— Hi Jojo. What's up?

— It's the Gordon man. He's out near the airport. I'm watching him.

Marius gave up his attempt to keep hold of the towel and let it drop on the floor, then he lay back on the bed and listened.

Jojo had been drinking a Malta, sitting under the trees at a spot opposite Dave Gordon's house, when the fancy roller door of a garage set in the wall opposite opened, and a green Mercedes backed out onto the street right in front of him. When he saw the Mercedes, he knew it was Dave Gordon. The Toyota was parked quite close to where he was sitting, so he ran down straight away and got in the car. He was starting the motor when he saw the back of the Mercedes disappearing off to the right.

Luckily, the Mercedes was held up by traffic when it was turning into the Boulevard du Mono and Jojo had a chance to catch up with it. Then it hadn't been too hard to keep it in sight. Jojo followed it along the Boulevard and then up the N1. At the *Colombe de la Paix* he'd nearly lost it again with all the traffic on the roundabout, but then at the last minute he'd caught sight of the green car on the airport road and he'd been relieved when the Mercedes had pulled into a familiar drinking spot opposite the long-term car park. Dave Gordon was by himself, sitting at a table outside, and Jojo was still in the car in the car park, wondering what to do next.

— Go inside, Marius said. Get yourself some brochettes and another Malta, and wait. Ring as soon as someone else turns up.

He picked the towel up off the floor and hung it back in the bathroom, then put on a pair of jeans and a freshly ironed top. There were lots of perfectly ordinary reasons why Dave Gordon would be meeting someone at the airport bar and Marius didn't give it a lot of thought. On the other hand, if Takashi was right, then maybe he should keep a friendly eye on George. There might be something he could pick up from the gossip that circulated amongst the security men, the gardeners, the cooks, the maids, the so-called houseboys. Someone always knew what was going on. Perhaps he could start with Sam.

Marius pulled the sheet across the bed and gave the pillows a couple of shakes; it still looked messy, but it would do. Then he picked up his phone, got his wallet off the bedside table and went downstairs to the kitchen. The house felt quiet. Dzigi was still over at Kofi's place and the others weren't due back from Accra until later this afternoon.

He was hungry but not in the mood for cooking so he ate a banana and poured himself a bowl full of peanuts. That would do for now – later he could get something at the spot. He looked in the fridge for a beer, then remembered that he'd drunk the last one before he went to George's place. Now he'd have to wait until Jojo was back with the car to stock up. Instead, he poured himself a glass of water from the bottle in the fridge. It looked unappetising, so he added a half glass of cashew brandy, put them on a tin tray and took it into the living room. With the ceiling fan on, this was the coolest place in the house. Was it just him, or was it hotter than usual today?

He sat on the couch with his feet on the coffee table and nibbled on the nuts, washing them down with the brandy.

When the phone rang again Marius felt disoriented and realised he must have dozed off.

— Jojo. What's happening?

— A man just walked up to the table where Gordon is sitting. Looks like they know each other. Now he's sitting down.

— Where are you? Can they see you? Do they know you're watching them?

Jojo sounded pleased with himself.

— I'm inside. They're outside near the cars. I can't hear anything but I can see them.

Marius knew the place; you didn't need to be travelling to end up there, but the spot was an easy walk from the airport. Most people chose to sit outside at tables and chairs scattered in the dusty gravel. Löwenbräu umbrellas were fixed into the tables and there was Löwenbräu beer on tap, a legacy of the colonial past.

On the side away from the airport there was a big circular wooden building. Inside it was roughly furnished with wooden tables and benches all the way around. In the centre was a curved bar and backing on to it, and completing the circle, a charcoal grill. Here some bored looking men cooked perhaps the best brochettes in the whole of Lomé. While Jojo talked Marius thought about those brochettes and his mouth started to water.

— Who's he meeting?

— Another white man.

Marius rolled his eyes at the ceiling and sighed. Jojo had never travelled out of West Africa and to him all white skinned people looked the same. They were Europeans, no matter if they came from America or Greece. Marius told himself to exercise patience. He'd had a similar problem when he was first in Moscow, especially with the KGB agents; it sometimes seemed as if there was one man who did all the work.

— Can you tell me some more. How old is he? What's he wearing?

Jojo did his best and Marius could hear the concentration in his voice.

— Half a head of not much hair. He's just taking his jacket off – maybe he's come off a plane.

— Thanks Jojo, but so far it could be anyone. Listen, you know the camera I gave you.

— It's in the car.

Jojo, was suspicious of cameras. Not uncommon here, but Marius had shown him how to use it anyway. No, he reassured Jojo, the camera would not steal his spirit. No chance.

— Of course you can't take a photo where people can see you; not near the airport. But how about this? Where's the car? That area is huge. Could you park the car somewhere and photograph them from there?

— I'll try. They're getting drinks now. Gordon's taking a beer. And the other man, looks like he's brought his own. He's just taken a bottle out of his bag.

— Can you see what it is?

— Not from here. It looks like water.

So gin or vodka.

— What's he taking with it?

— Nothing. He's not drinking yet. Wait. Looks like they're taking some yam chips and brochettes. He's talking to the waitress, very serious. Now he's poured it into a glass. It's gone. He's pouring another one. Eating some chips now.

Vodka. For some reason, Marius felt sure of it. There'd been a few times in Moscow when he'd drunk far too much vodka. Everything Jojo said made him think of Russia. Like, who else would bring their own bottle of vodka to the bar? Interesting.

— Good work Jojo. Keep watching and take a photo if you can. But be careful.

14

Sunday 3 April

Marius put the phone down and checked the time. 2.05. No wonder he was hungry! He found a felt tip pen and used the back of an electricity bill to write a note for Dzigi, just in case he came home early.

At the spot. M

There was a magnet on the fridge in the shape of a football and Marius put the note under it. Dzigi should see it there.

Outside the sun was fierce and the branches of the mahogany trees that straggled along the side of the road hung limp and still. Marius walked under the shade as much as he could, but by the time he arrived at the spot the sweat was running down the back of his neck and under his arms. The rainy season was late this year and the heat was intensifying like a boil about to burst.

The only person at the spot was Bibi, who was sitting at a table under one of the ceiling fans, papers and books spread out in front of her. She had started to get up but when she saw it was Marius she smiled at him and sat back down again.

Marius greeted her with a *namaste*, pulled a chair from the table opposite and put it in a place where the table wasn't covered with books.

— Homework? he asked.

She nodded and pushed a piece of paper towards him. When he reached over and picked it up he saw it was a poem.

Bibi sounded frustrated.

— What can I say about this? I'm supposed to write a commentary.

Marius looked at the title. *Chanson d'Automne*. Verlaine. Shouldn't be too hard.

— I tell you what, he said. How about you get me a beer and some of your excellent fried plantain, and I help you with your commentary?

Bibi laughed.

— I asked God to help me, then you came along!

She was teasing him and Marius laughed. Bibi headed inside and Marius caught the cheeky look over her shoulder as she went into the bar. She knew exactly what he thought about religion – he'd told her about Marx's 'opium of the people'– and it made him happy that she could joke about it.

He picked up the photocopy of *Chanson d'Automne* and read through. Rather a lovely poem but sad, especially the last stanza. Thinking of past times and the idea of being blown around from here to there resonated with him. Marius put the poem on the table and leant back in his chair. He found himself thinking about Moscow, of a time in Gorky Park that was part of his set of life images.

It must have been the last September he'd been in Moscow and the year that Selina had come over to visit him. He could smell the crispness of the day: blue sky from a paintbox, bright yellow on the birch trees, the clean crunch their feet made walking through piles of dead leaves. He usually didn't think about all of that, but each line of the short poem was like a pointed stick.

Bibi came back with a cold glass and a bottle of Star on a tray. She put them on the table and opened the beer. Marius picked up the bottle and smiled at her.

— Thanks. I'll pour it.

Bibi took the tray off the table.

— I'll get the kelewele. It'll be a couple of minutes.

Marius picked up poem, his beer in the other hand, then leant back again, looking at the photocopy.

Des violons
De l'automne
Blessent mon coeur

It was making him feel…what? Loss? Nostalgia? A bit of both perhaps. Poetry! In a way it was a nice sort of hurt. Anyway, that wouldn't be any help to Bibi. Maybe if he could explain about autumn, that might get her on track.

The plate of kelewele that Bibi brought out for him was piled high with steaming plantain coloured red from the pepper and still gleaming from the hot palm oil. On top were two fried eggs: the house specialty. The plantain would take a little while before it was cool enough to eat without burning the inside of his mouth and Marius let it sit while he talked to Bibi.

He pointed at the poem.

— So how much of this do you understand?

— Well the words are easy enough but I just don't see what he wants to say. What's this thing about autumn? Why would it be crying like a violin?

Marius sipped on his beer and wondered how he could get across the idea of the sadness of late autumn with the colour and leaves gone from the trees and only the prospect of a long cold winter ahead. For Bibi, he realised, being cold was when the temperature dropped to 20 degrees at night during the rainy season.

And right here and now, the ceiling fan was barely moving the heavy, hot air.

— Okay. Tell me what you think about when I say autumn.

— I've seen pictures – bright colours, yellows and oranges, like the trees are on fire.

Marius looked at her, surprised.

— You've got it. That's the beginning of autumn.

Then he found himself telling Bibi about Gorky Park and the image that was in his head, though he left out Selina.

— It's not long before it all changes, he explained. The weather gets much colder and by November it can be really cold. By then the trees are completely bare and the leaves are brown and dead. I'm sure you can't imagine that sort of cold, but think about living in a freezer. And when the wind blows, the leaves whirl around in the air.

— *Deçà, delà*

Bibi and Marius both looked up. Marius didn't recognise the woman who'd just come into the spot, so not a regular then. Bibi had jumped up from her chair and was giving her a big hug.

Marius watched them. She'd quoted those lines from the poem so could she be Bibi's teacher? If so, she was off duty today, judging by the floppy green top that threatened to fall off one of her shoulders, and the denim shorts. Her hair was so close to the scalp it could almost have been a man's cut, but there was something about her that was stylish and Marius suddenly felt scruffy and sweaty. He stood up and held out his hand.

— Hi, I'm Marius. I was trying to help Bibi with her French homework, but maybe you'd be better at that.

The woman laughed and took Marius' hand.

— Afua. Nice to meet you. No, I doubt I'd be any better than you, I just happen to know that poem from when I was at school. Looks like they're still teaching the same things!

She gave his hand a confident shake.

Bibi was looking pleased.

— Well now you can both help me. Can I get you a drink, Aunty Afua?

— A Star would be lovely Bibi. Nice and cold if you've got it.

Marius gave her a mental tick.

Bibi went back inside. Afua sat down at the table across from Marius and cleared a space by making a neat pile of some of the notebooks and papers. He rather liked the way it showed more of the smooth dark skin of her shoulder. She noticed him looking at it and smiled, pulling the neck of her top with both hands so that it sat straight.

— This top! I should throw it out. Did I hear you talking about Moscow? Sounds as if you know the place. I've always wanted to go there – not sure why. Could be those Russian novels I read in my teens.

Marius had read his share of them too; still did sometimes, only partly to keep up his Russian.

— What's your favourite?

— Oh, *Anna Karenina* I guess. In my teens I thought it was so romantic. Now I've read it a couple more times, I think it could do with an edit. She laughed. Not everyone agrees with me! What about you?

She had the sort of laugh that invited you to join in, and Marius relaxed into it.

— I thought I was the only one with that idea. About the edit.

— Me too. Anyway, what's your favourite?

Bibi arrived back with the beer and Marius smiled at Afua and waved his hand to suggest maybe another time.

Afua picked up her beer and took a satisfied sip.

— Thanks Bibi. *Santé*, Marius. She pulled her chair a bit closer to Bibi and picked up the photocopied poem. Do you mind? she said to Marius, then she turned back to Bibi. So you want us to help with this?

Bibi looked relieved.

— Please. I just don't get it.

Marius helped where he could while he finished his beer and kelewele. He felt comfortable, just sitting and listening, while in Socratic style, Afua managed to help Bibi understand the poem. All he knew about Afua, was that she wasn't a teacher and he guessed she was a friend of Plaisance and not long back from abroad. But he really should be getting back home. Jojo would be there by now and he wanted to know more about the meeting at the airport. When he stood up to leave he put some money on the table for Bibi then spoke to Afua.

— Maybe we could continue our chat about Russian literature sometime. Do you live around here?

He ignored the pleased look on Bibi's face. Afua didn't seem to notice.

— No. I've got a place near town. I told Plaisance that I'd come round and keep Bibi company for a bit. You know Plaisance's mother is sick and she's gone to try to sort things out.

Marius didn't know, but he let it pass.

— Oh well. If you're round here again, I'm just up the road. Maybe we'll run into one another.

Afua laughed.

— Or not. Have you got your phone? She waited while Marius pulled his phone out of his back pocket and scrolled to the contact page. Okay? The number is 9496657.

Marius read the number back to check it, and left feeling pleased. As he walked back to the house he realised he was humming a tune that he'd forgotten he ever knew, and he felt happy for no particular reason.

15

Sunday 3 April

The mood was broken when he walked up the drive and found Dzigi and Kofi kicking a football around on the dried up lawn. As soon as they saw Marius they stopped and crowded around him, asking for Kofi to sleep over. That was easy. No. Tomorrow was a school day.

It was Jojo's news that Marius wanted to hear and Marius sent the boys up to Dzigi's room. Dzigi knew the rules about sleep overs, so why keep pestering him?

The first thing to do was re-stock the fridge with beer and he could talk to Jojo while they drove to the depot. They stacked the back seat with crates of empty bottles and Marius gave the keys to Jojo then sat in the passenger seat.

— So. After we talked, what happened?

Jojo put his arm across the back of the front seat and looked behind him as he reversed out of the driveway. Then he stopped, changed into first gear and set off down the road. He looked straight ahead as he spoke, intent on getting it right.

— After we talked I shifted the car like you said. From the top end I could see Gordon and the other man, no trouble. Jojo reached across and opened the glove box. He took out the camera and gave it to Marius. Maybe I got them – I couldn't see so fine.

He was speaking Ewe now and Marius felt comfortable as he changed to his mother tongue. The mood in the car lightened as well.

— We'll just have to wait and see.

Marius wasn't holding his breath. He wished the camera was like one of the old polaroids so he could just pull the fully developed photo from it. But it wasn't. He'd have to go through the process of waiting.

Jojo pulled off the road onto the gravel in front of a small, blue painted concrete brick building with a Coca-Cola umbrella out the front. The local bottle shop. When he turned the engine off, Jojo opened the car door to let in some air and continued:

— They finished their drinks and came towards where I was in the car. I thought maybe they'd seen me take the photo, but they just walked past to a car parked behind me.

Marius half listened while Jojo went into every detail. He had managed to keep the two men in sight from the car and he'd noted the writing on the bag the visitor was carrying. Antwerp duty free. Did he perhaps live in Belgium then? Porous was a word that came to mind when Marius thought of Antwerp. People and things like money could move in and out of there very easily.

— And then, Jojo was saying, the big man, the visitor, opened the boot of his car. I couldn't see what they did, but then Gordon had a suitcase that he hadn't had before. He walked right past me again and over to his car. He put the suitcase in the boot and drove off. You told me to come back here so that's what I did.

Marius wondered if he'd made the right decision, but Jojo couldn't have followed both of them.

— Thanks Jojo. You did the right thing. Any idea what might have been in the suitcase?

Jojo shook his head.

— No. But it looked like yours. The flash brown one.

That must be the old leather suitcase that he'd bought in Moscow. The Estonians were famous for them and he was rather pleased with it. In his eyes at least, it still looked as good as when he'd bought it.

— You mean something like the brown suitcase or do you mean really like?

Jojo thought carefully. It clearly took some effort and he searched the space above his head on slow replay.

— Just like yours. It had a strap through the handle with a gold lock thing.

Russia again. The vodka, now the suitcase.

Marius didn't want to jump to conclusions but this was starting to feel familiar.

He handed a bundle of CFA notes to Jojo.

— Can you organise three crates of Star for me Jojo. Make sure they add some cold ones. And buy a crate of something that you and Dzigi drink as well. I need to think about what you've just told me.

Marius looked at the quiet sandy street with the untidy string of houses. Some children were playing a clapping game on the side of the road. A moped went past slowly with a whole family on it, coming back from church judging by the Sunday best clothes.

That was normal. Russians dropping off suitcases to the head of the local school was not. A suitcase filled with money? That would fit the way a certain type of business was conducted here; it fitted with Dave Gordon removing Lawrence Ashley from the joint account; and it fitted with the recent fluctuations in that account. Drugs or arms sales. Take your pick, though Marius put his money on arms sales. There were always embargoes in place for some African countries. Togo itself had been under an arms embargo until a couple of weeks ago, during that business with the son after President Eyadéma died. Now that had been a depressing affair. Still was.

When Marius decided he owed it to Ash to follow up the money angle, digging around about embezzlement, someone fiddling the books – those were the sort of things he had in mind. But if he were right, things were on an altogether different, and much larger, scale.

In the years following his return from Moscow Marius had kept in touch with friends there, and he knew before it became common knowledge that some of his KGB opposites were making the most of the situation and becoming rich on arms sales. All those weapons in the Ukraine, Georgia, Moldova and of course Russia, were there for smart men without too many scruples to make their fortunes. And once they had the millions then it didn't matter how they got them. They were businessmen – moguls with power and influence.

Could the money going in and out of the account be from arms being sold right here? The embargo had ended, but now there was one in Côte d'Ivoire and that was only a couple of borders away.

If that were the case, Dave Gordon would be getting plenty of kickback for helping out. Did it matter? If it did, what could he do?

Marius feared that Thrasymachus might be right. He couldn't remember exactly which book it was in –*The Republic* perhaps – when he said that the just man always comes off worse than the unjust. Not a comforting thought.

16

Monday 4 April

Mimi couldn't make up her mind.

It was early Monday morning and she was sitting at her desk, not even pretending to work.

The staffroom had cubicle style desks lining three of the walls. It couldn't be described as small, but it wasn't designed for all the teachers to use at the same time. However, every Monday morning, when Ash conducted an informal, 'start the week' meeting, that was exactly what happened. There was seldom anything important that was covered in the meeting, but it had the effect of getting teachers to plan the 0730 Monday start into their weekend.

No single teacher was shouting, but the combined effect of people talking over each other was cacophonous, and Mimi was finding it hard to think.

Dave Gordon had just led the Monday meeting and he had behaved impeccably. Even his clothes were perfect. He usually wore the sort of clothes that shouted out 'sports teacher' but today he looked smart and professional. The suit was new, of that Mimi was certain. She could smell the newness. It was tailored in self-striped, grey, lightweight wool, and showed off his good looks. The shirt was the right shade of blue, and the silk tie was stylish.

He sounded genuinely sympathetic and understanding when he said how sad he was that the problems with the finances meant changes in the curriculum, and that he knew how much staff and parents had been looking forward to the International Baccalaureate. It was nothing short of tragic, he said, that he had to lose some of his best staff. Mimi couldn't help being pleased despite herself, when he'd praised her for a student performance she'd organised last week.

Then he'd come up to her after the announcements were finished and asked her how she was getting on.

— Struggling with a headache, she'd told him. Perhaps she could be excused from the assembly and take some prontaigine?

— Of course, he'd said. Look after yourself.

Mimi started to have doubts. Was this the same person Simone was talking about? Who'd fired her without so much as a thank you?

Her desk faced out over the circular drive at the front of the school and she watched students pouring in through the front doors. Now the other teachers were heading out of the staffroom to go to the assembly, and with the connecting door open, there was a noise like a herd of buffalo on the move. That was the students going up the stairs for the assembly. It was almost enough to give her a real headache.

She finished her coffee and went over to the sink to rinse her mug, trying to calm her nerves. When Claudette came up and gave her a pat on the arm she jumped.

— Sorry about the headache. If you need anything, just ask, she said.

— Thanks.

Mimi felt guilty, but she had no right to drag anyone else into what she was planning to do, even though it would be good to have back up.

Back at her desk she sat in front of the computer and stared at the *Cuisine Actuelle* recipe she'd just printed out for her first class. If she didn't make her mind up soon, she'd miss the one time of the week when she could be sure that Dave Gordon and the rest of the school would be fully occupied. Dave would be running the assembly and it would give her thirty minutes at least, by the time they got through the merit awards, the inspirational address, the hymn singing.

Mimi checked the time. 07.50. Ten minutes to go.

The letter giving her notice was in the top drawer and she took it out and read through it. Terse to the point of rudeness, and no mention of a reference. Signed Dave Gordon, Headmaster. And yet he was acting this morning as if nothing had happened.

It was Marius who had given her the idea when he mentioned surveillance. If there was something to be found might it not be right here at the school? And who better to do a search than her? But Mimi knew neither her father nor Marius would like the idea, so she had told no one at all. If she found anything useful, then she would share it, and it would be too late for them to say anything.

The time on her computer screen turned over to 0800. It was a good plan, she told herself. Act on it!

Mimi picked up an unsealed envelope off her desk, opened the door that connected the staff room with the reception area and walked past the staff toilets to the foyer. It still looked much more like the hotel it once was, than a school. Four round wooden pillars were the height of the first two floors and supported a white plaster ceiling that was criss-crossed with dark timber squares. To her left a curved staircase led up to the mezzanine floor, where the old conference rooms had been converted into an auditorium. The floor of the foyer was of polished black granite specked with brown, and the walls in front of the offices were covered in a kind of crazy paving that had been popular in the 1970s.

To her right heavy glass doors with brass handles opened on to wide stairs that ran the length of the foyer and she could see the gravel circular drive with the fountain in the middle. The dark wood and stone gave the space a somewhat heavy feel, and there was still a moldy smell left over from when the hotel had been boarded up for two or three years after the bottom fell out of the tourist business because of the political problems of the 1990s.

Adele, the school gatekeeper and secretary, was just around to her right behind the long wooden counter that had been the hotel reception desk. She was at the back of the office, working on her computer, and Mimi had to call out to her a couple of times to get her attention.

When she finally noticed Mimi, she rolled her chair back on its castors, then swivelled around, stood up and came over to the counter.

— Sorry Mimi. I thought everyone was up at the assembly. I've got all these letters to parents to get ready for this afternoon.

— You're always so busy, Mimi said. I've got an awful headache that I'm trying to get rid of before classes start.

— Can I help at all? Adele was sympathetic in a businesslike way.

— Thanks. I'll be fine once the prontaigine starts working. But I've got this letter for Mr Gordon – Mimi held up the envelope – and I wondered if it would be okay to put it on his desk? I didn't want to go in without checking.

Adele waved one hand in the air in a way that suggested it was hardly worth asking.

— That's fine. I'm sure he won't mind. He's still in his old office. You know the way. It was a statement, not a question.

— Thanks Adele. Good luck with those letters.

But Adele was already heading back to her computer.

The art teacher had set up a display of students' work on moveable screens in the centre of the foyer and Mimi skirted around them and went over to the short hallway that led to some classrooms. The door to Dave Gordon's office was on the left.

As she opened the door, she looked back towards the reception. It was mostly obscured by the artwork and what with that and Adele's letters, she felt sure Adele wouldn't notice how long was in the office. Even so…

It had taken her a while to work out what to put in the letter, which had to be genuine because she was planning to leave it on the desk. In the end it was a mixture of a request for a reference and polite disappointment at the way things had turned out. The envelope wasn't sealed. The letter wasn't signed. Mimi took it out, unfolded it and put it on the green leather top of the very neat desk.

There was a light on in the hallway and with the door open Mimi could see quite well in the half darkness. Glancing at the doorway every few seconds, she started opening the drawers of the solid wood desk. First the top drawer on the right. Nothing of interest there, just a couple of books of blank order forms. She picked them up anyway and leafed through them. As she was pushing them back into the drawer she noticed what looked like a blank piece of paper that had been underneath the order forms. Holding the books in one hand she flipped the paper over. It looked like a rough sort of map. Not that it made any sense to her but she recognised the name Jazzhole, so in Lagos then. No time to look more carefully and she turned it back over and arranged the order books just as they'd been before.

Mimi wished she had someone to keep watch, to distract Dave if he was coming back early, and she couldn't stop herself from looking up at the door every few seconds. Not exactly looking, but listening. Yes, she could say she was just putting the letter on the desk like she'd told Adele, but it would sound feeble, no matter how she said it. Best not to think about it.

She tried the bottom drawer on the right, a bigger drawer. Locked. She hadn't thought about that! It just made her more determined and she moved across to the three drawers on the left. It was in the bottom one that she found the wallet.

Mimi looked at the time. Ten minutes before the half hour was up. She stood very still and listened. From upstairs there was applause, then silence.

She took the wallet out of the drawer. Should she close the door? Probably not, that would look very odd.

Mimi sat down on the office chair and put her letter on the desk. She noticed what she hadn't seen before, a wooden pen holder, and she picked a pen from it and put it next to the letter, then she pulled the wallet out, leaving the drawer open just wide enough so she'd be able to slip the wallet back in.

Keeping her hands below the desk she searched through the wallet. A bit of herself that seemed to be outside looking on was amazed that she would do such a thing, but she kept going.

Credit cards, AMEX, Visa. Bupa card, driver's licences – UK and Togo. Then she noticed a section of the wallet that was like a secret pocket. From there she pulled out a business card and a photo.

The business card was in a language she couldn't read. She turned it over. There was a name in English letters – Sergei Krushnekov – and two handwritten telephone numbers.

She looked at the photo: about the size of a passport photo, probably taken in a photo booth. It was a young man's face, mid-twenties Mimi guessed. He was looking straight at the camera, eyebrows raised slightly, his mouth in a knowing sort of smirk. His hair was close shaven and there was dark hair over his upper lip, though not a moustache. Could be Ghanaian. She brought the photo up closer. Or come to think of it, he looked more Nigerian. There was something about the challenging look on his face; that and what she could see of his shirt, a close fitting black T-shirt with the front buttons undone, and showing a necklace that looked as if it could be made of wood or perhaps seeds.

Mimi turned the photo over. On the back was written one word: Alabi.

From upstairs there was the sound of more applause, louder this time, then shuffling. She glanced again at the open door. Still quiet out there.

Quickly she pushed the photo and card into the wallet, put it back exactly where it had been, and closed the drawer.

Trying not to panic, she grabbed the pen and signed her name. Her mouth was feeling dry again and she had trouble moistening the gum on the envelope. Finally she half sealed it and put it in the centre of the green leather inset. Her hand was shaking as she put the pen back in the holder but she took time to have a careful look at the desk, and felt better. Apart from her letter, it all looked the same as when she'd come in.

She closed the door behind her. As she walked around the art display screens and along the hallway to the staffroom she started to breathe more easily.

Then she glanced up and looked straight into the eyes of Dave Gordon coming through the auditorium door.

17

Monday 4 April

In the afternoon of the same day Marius was halfway through his third beer.

Opposite him was Dave Gordon's house. Where Marius was sitting, the leafy canopies of mahogany trees had joined together, and in the deep shade small traders had set up businesses in the dirt on either side of the road. One of them was a woman with an icebox filled with beer. She had set out a few empty drink crates, and Marius had taken two: one to sit on, one for a table.

He put a yellowed copy of *The Last Days of Socrates* face down on the crate next to him and thought about what he'd just read in the *Apology*. The bit where Socrates explained why he couldn't just mind his own business resonated. Marius smiled to himself at the double irony; he was himself being Socratic in twisting words to support his own actions. And yet reading it made him feel better about spending – wasting? – his time trying to work out what had happened to Ash. Searching for the truth – same sort of thing. Not that he wanted to die in the process, like Socrates had, but at least knowing it had been an impulse for millennia made him feel better.

A group of teenage boys in navy and green LICS uniform walked past Dave Gordon's place. One of them pointed at the wall in front of the house and said something, and the three of them laughed and jostled each other.

It reminded Marius of what Mimi had told him about the meeting on Saturday night. For a few years some of the parents had been worried about Dave Gordon, but they couldn't get Lawrence Ashley to do anything about him. It sounded very much like what Simone had told them. His behaviour with the boys was damaging. Not sexual abuse – if it was, they could lay charges against him. No, it was erratic and weird. He'd be best pals with small groups of boys. They'd become infatuated with him and fall under his influence. Then he'd start telling stories about some of the boys to the others, and that would set the boys against each other. After that, he'd treat them like dirt and pick another group. It sounded creepy.

That had been bad enough, but then they realised that he was trying to sabotage the International Baccalaureate they were so keen to have at the school. Apparently talking it down had started last September when newly recruited teachers arrived from the UK and told anyone who would listen how Lawrence Ashley was bankrupting the school, and how the IB was an elite program that was only for top students, and not suited to LICS.

At first the parents believed the stories. Why not? Much as they liked Lawrence Ashley, everyone knew he was hopeless with paperwork. But one of the parents had a friend who worked in the BTCI bank where the school had its foreign currency account, and they found out that there was plenty of money in the school account. They still couldn't persuade Ash to do anything, but now the situation had changed, so they met to discuss what to do. It was tricky because the parent who worked at the bank couldn't be seen to break confidentiality, but according to Mimi they'd decided to ask Dave Gordon to present them with a full financial statement and take it from there.

It sounded as if this was a smart bunch of parents. In a way they were one step ahead of him, but it might help their cause if Marius shared what he knew with them. And he didn't have his hands tied like the parent who worked in the bank. It could be just the thing. Pressure from parents could work alongside whatever he could do himself.

A woman wearing a loose white T-shirt over a faded cotton wrap came and stood next to Marius. She was balancing a glass-sided wooden box on her head and asked Marius to hold the box while she slipped out from under it, and then took the box from him and put it on the ground. It was filled with little puffy donuts and Marius didn't even try to resist. He bought a bag of them, and was just finishing off the last one and licking the sugar off his fingers when the gate to Dave Gordon's house opened and a woman came out and slammed it behind her.

Her hair was completely covered by a deep blue headscarf, the ends twisted and tied in a high knot in the front, and another scarf was thrown around her shoulders. The pink and blue dress she was wearing was simple, but followed the body contours in a subtle way so that the overall effect was almost demure. Almost, but not quite. It had to be Lola.

Here goes. Marius stuffed his Socrates – the smallest book he'd been able to find – into the back pocket of his jeans, left his half drunk beer on the crate, and followed her at a distance. He fell easily into the old surveillance habits, and he could see from the way she was walking that the last thing on her mind was the idea that she was being followed.

It helped that Marius realised where she was heading. She'd turned left out of the first street then left again on to the Rue Gragbade, where there were more cars but fewer people. Now she was taking another left into a familiar street, the Rue des Bars.

Familiar, but it had been a while since Marius was last here. That would have been with Takashi and Gabriel after Louis was killed. The noise in the sandy street was still the same: too loud, Hiplife competing with Afro beat as he walked past one stack of giant speakers and on to the next.

Lola clearly knew where she was going. She wasn't stopping to look at any of the bars, but Marius did, as if he was looking for a place to eat. Marius hoped she wouldn't stop at the tilapia place. The waitress there might recognise him despite the clothes.

Or not. Marius had barely recognised himself when he looked in the mirror. It had required a trip to the market and one to the barber, but the effect was worth it. He was wearing black – it seemed sufficiently different from his usual cream tops and blue jeans, and he'd gone for slim fit black Diesel pants and a black Calvin Klein T-shirt. With the close shaved hair and the sunglasses on, what he saw was a younger Marius with attitude.

Lola was almost at the other end of the street when she finally disappeared into a place on the left. It was more like a regular restaurant then the other spots around it. A terracotta roof shaded the outside paved area, and wooden folding doors divided the inside from the outside. Right now they were folded back and the space inside looked dark and cool. The ceiling fans were turning briskly and the menu on a board at the front had fish, goat soup, chicken and jollof rice on offer.

The question was, what to do now? When he'd decided in a vague sort of way to get chatting with Lola, he had imagined something a bit different. Now he wondered just what. He felt as if he stood out in these clothes and that made him uncertain, but he couldn't just stand here. That surely was going to attract attention.

Then he took off the sunglasses and immediately felt better. They'd given the people and the surrounds an orange tint that seemed to separate him from them. Without the glasses he felt normal again. What would he usually do? Go in, have a drink, a bite to eat perhaps, watch people, maybe strike up a conversation. Nothing hard about that.

The cane tables and chairs on the paved terraces looked inviting, but there was no sign of Lola so he walked straight across the patio and into the dark interior.

There was a bar on the far side of the room and Marius made for that, looking around him for Lola. Odd, he was sure she'd come in here. In the toilet perhaps. A few people were eating at the tables and there were a couple of women sitting on the high cane stools at the bar.

Marius started to feel more at home. He went up to the bar, pulled a stool out to make room for his legs, then perched himself on it.

The barman had been chatting to the two women, and still talking to them, he walked along to where Marius was sitting. The woman closest to him had her back turned facing her friend, but as Marius sat down she swiveled around and looked at him.

It was more a curious look than anything else, but Marius didn't want to cause offence. He pointed at the stool he'd just climbed on to and the empty one next to him.

— Not taken, are they?

The woman turned a bit more so she could get a good look at him.

— Doesn't look like it, she said in English, but her voice sounded friendly enough.

Marius smiled to himself. This could be easier than he thought. Lola, minus the scarves, was sitting almost next to him. She must have taken them off when she came into the restaurant. Her hair was streaked with orange on one side and the fine braids pulled up in a bunch, so he hadn't recognised her from behind.

The barman, young and bored looking, was still waiting.

— What do you have that's really cold my good man? Marius asked.

The barman pointed to the glass-fronted refrigerated shelves behind him.

— Take your pick.

Marius leant across the counter on his elbows, so he could get a better look. They all seemed to be European beers.

— Nothing local?

The barman looked condescending and shook his head.

— Okay. Give me a Corona.

Marius declined the offer of a glass but accepted the slice of lemon. It didn't taste as bad as he'd expected.

The barman had turned his back and started stacking glasses on the racks opposite the bar but Marius talked to him anyway.

— I'm just over here for a few days. Any good music spots you could recommend?

The barman looked less disinterested and stopped stacking the glasses. He looked at Marius.

— From Accra, right? He asked in English.

— Correct.

— Thought so. The man looked pleased with himself and more friendly. I've got family there. At Coco Beach.

His English was good. Maybe that's what Lola liked about this place.

— Nice place, Coco Beach. I know it well. I've got a recording studio in the

Cantonments – came over here to check out the talent.

Marius could sense the women getting interested. The barman did too and he turned towards them.

— Hey, Dora, Lola, this guy's here to check out the music scene. Any ideas?

The woman he'd called Dora leant forward so she could see Marius along the counter.

— It's a bit pathetic here. You should keep going on to Lagos.

Then Lola said half to Dora, half to Marius.

— But there's a new place that opened last month. Beat Plus – or something like that anyway. It's pretty good if you like Afro stuff.

Marius hoped he didn't sound as fake to them as he did to himself.

———
134

— Sure. We do a lot of Afro stuff. Hip, beat, jazz.

Lola gave Marius a closer look and seemed to make up her mind.

— Let's have a few drinks and I'll take you there. The music starts pretty early.

Then she turned to Dora.

— It's not really your scene.

Dora took the hint.

— Yeah. Not my scene, like you say. She pushed her empty glass towards the barman. But I'll have another one of these thanks.

Lola and Dora were drinking vodka and coke but Marius stuck to Corona. At first they sat at the bar and talked, then they moved over to a table so they didn't have to keep leaning back and forward to talk to each other. After her third vodka and coke, Dora wished him luck in finding 'proper proper' music in Lomé and left.

Now it was just the two of them, and Marius had a good idea what was in Lola's mind. He'd given her the name Sam Quist and the little he knew about music production was enough for his cover. Trouble was, in a careless moment of invention, he said he was staying at the Ibis Hotel and he was pretty sure that Lola would expect him to take her there.

She was looking relaxed after all the vodka, but pretending not to notice, Marius took her empty glass and got them both another drink. He put the glass of vodka and the bottle of coke in front of Lola, and another Corona on the table, but didn't sit down.

— Back in a minute, he said.

As he walked around the terrace to the toilet that was out the back, he pulled out his phone and found Mimi's number. He'd had two calls from her, and he'd blocked them, but now he had an idea. She picked up straight away.

— Marius. I've been trying to call you.

— Sorry Mimi. I can't explain right now. Can you call me – Marius looked at his watch – around 8.30? Are you home? Should I come out to Chez Miki later?

— Yes. Come out.

— Look Mimi, when you call I'll probably say some odd sort of things but just play along can you?

Marius could hear the exasperation in Mimi's voice but he knew she's be too curious to refuse.

— Okay. So long as you promise to tell me about it when you get here.

— It's a promise.

— Okay, I'll ring at 8.30.

When he got back to the table Lola was talking to someone on her phone. As he pulled out his chair and sat down she said "Got to go now" into the phone and put it on the table in front of her. Then she looked up at Marius and smiled.

— Okay Sam, let's get to know each other.

****

When Mimi's call came, Marius only just heard it over the music at Beat Plus. He was sitting with Lola at a table right at the back of a packed courtyard, but the band had plenty of brass, three guitars and a male singer with a big voice and plenty of amplification.

Marius picked up his phone, looked at it, then at Lola.

— Sorry Lola. This could be important. I'd better take it.

And into the phone.

— Hi Freddie. Is this important? I'm rather busy.

He held the phone tight against his ear and hoped that the music would drown out Mimi's voice saying:

— Yes, it's important.

— So is this the only time? What about tomorrow night? I'm here for a few days.

— No, it has to be tonight.

— Okay. If that's the case – Marius looked at his watch – I can be there at nine. See you then.

He waited until Mimi's phone was switched off then he closed the call and put the phone in his back pocket.

Lola had got the message. She didn't seem too put out and Marius realised he was a bit disappointed.

— Business? she asked.

Marius nodded.

— I guess you heard. A guy I need to see is leaving for a gig in Benin tomorrow morning.

Lola shrugged. She was looking at the table next to them, where three European men were just sitting down. One of them had a large jug of beer that he put in the middle of the table.

— You'd better go.

— Can I drop you somewhere?

— No. I don't need a chaperone. See you round Sam.

— Sure.

Marius turned and looked back when he got to the exit. Lola was talking to one of the Europeans. They all laughed, then Lola pulled out an empty chair, picked up her glass off the table where she'd been sitting with Marius, and sat down with them.

Marius laughed to himself. Lola was good at what she did.

A taxi was dropping off some new arrivals and he opened the passenger door as they were getting out.

— Do you know Chez Miki?

The driver nodded and Marius climbed in to the front seat and closed the door. He was still in his tight black clothes but there was no time to go home and change. And as for the hair, it would take its own time to grow again. Takashi and Mimi would get a laugh out of it at least.

18

Monday April 4

As Marius pushed aside the blue and white *noren* and stepped up to the polished wooden floor at Chez Miki, on impulse he took the cheap sunglasses out of his back pocket and put them on. In the soft lighting, he couldn't see much through the orange tinted lenses, but he managed to navigate a path across the room between the shoji screens and the customers.

As usual, Mimi and Takashi were in the reserved area over by the garden where the guest cabins were. Mimi looked up at him when he got close. What she saw was a man she didn't know, dressed in black and wearing dark sunglasses, and she leant over to Takashi, who was sitting at the other end of the couch and caught his attention by tapping on his arm. He'd been absorbed in the music and hadn't noticed anything, so first he looked at Mimi to see what she was doing. Then Marius was right opposite them and Takashi looked up, saw the strange man and started to get up from the couch when Marius took off his sunglasses and sat down on a chair opposite them.

Takashi sat down again and laughed.

— Marius!

It took a while for Mimi to stop laughing but finally she got herself back in control with a couple of sips from the glass of white wine that was on the table next to her.

Marius ran his hands over his close shaved head and looked down at the black jeans.

— What do you think? Would I pass as a music producer?

Mimi started laughing again then took a breath and stifled it.

— A pretty scary one.

Takashi looked at Marius from top to bottom, head on one side.

— I don't know. The jeans are a bit tight and I don't know about the glasses, but that haircut takes ten years off, and the black suits you. So what was the occasion?

— That was a weird phone call, Mimi said. Where were you? It sounded like a party.

— Getting to know Dave Gordon's girlfriend. Adelola. Lola.

Takashi raised an eyebrow.

— How well did you get to know her?

Marius laughed. He leant across and picked up a handful of spiced nuts from the bowl on the table and nibbled on them.

— Well, without Mimi's phone call ....

— I hope she didn't hear my voice on the phone, Mimi said. Did you notice I'd been trying to ring you?

— Yes. I'm really sorry Mimi. I haven't even asked you what it was you were calling about.

— And I haven't asked you what you want to drink, Takashi said.

Eating the nuts reminded Marius that he hadn't eaten much over the day.

— Beer thanks. And something to eat would hit the spot thanks Takashi.

— How about yakitori?

— Couldn't be better.

Mimi went to get up but Takashi was quicker and she sat down again.

— I have to go and check on the kitchen anyway, Takashi said. Yakitori all round?

— Thanks.

— Just one stick for me, Mimi said.

She pulled the bottle of Chenet out of the ice bucket and poured some more into her glass, then she leaned back into the corner of the couch and curled her legs under her.

— I've been bursting to tell you something all day. Can you guess what?

Marius tried to think. Was there something he should remember? Nothing came to him and he shook his head and smiled.

— You got your job back?

Mimi pulled a folded piece of paper from out of the back pocket of her shorts, unfolded it, then passed it to Marius.

— I had a look in Dave Gordon's office.

Marius ignored the paper.

— You what?

Mimi was too pleased with herself to worry if Marius approved or not.

— I went through his desk.

— Did anybody see you?

Mimi shook her head.

— Not in the office. They were all at assembly. I was scared though. Like, really scared. Anyway, that's what I found in his wallet.

Marius looked at her sharply and took the paper.

— This?

Did Marius really think she was that stupid?

— No. Not the paper. The names. I wrote them down when I got back to the office so I wouldn't forget. And it's probably nothing, but there was a sort of map in the bottom of one of the drawers. Face down, but I turned it over and saw The Jazzhole that you keep talking about. And the hotel.

— Hand drawn? Photocopied on A4 paper?

— Hand drawn for sure, with a fine black felt tip. But not photocopied. There was a pen like that on his desk, so I guess he drew it himself. Why?

— Ash had a copy of that map when he was killed. I still have no memory of picking it up, but somehow it ended up in my pocket. I wonder who else our Mr Gordon gave a copy to? Anyway, tell me about this.

Marius put the scrap of paper on the table and Mimi uncurled her legs and slid forward on the couch so she could point to the names she'd written.

— That one was on the back of a photo of a man. Youngish. Maybe Nigerian, maybe Ghanaian. Good looking, but a bit showy. The other one was on a business card. I don't know about the surname, but the first name is definitely Sergei and I think the second name started with Krus and ended with a v. Not sure about the bit in between. Sounds Russian.

As it happened Marius could easily find a name to fill in the blanks: Sergei Krushnekov. But Sergei was a common name and anyway, what would the Sergei he knew be doing in Lomé?

Sergei Krushnekov. The image that came to his mind was of a man in his mid twenties. His fair hair was already receding which made the pale blue-grey eyes and the forward jut of his chin more striking. He and Marius had been much the same age, and during an intense year of language training at the military institute in Moscow they'd struck up a friendship. Marius had been working on his Russian and learning Polish, Sergei Polish and French, and he'd been keen to pick up some Ewe as well. The energy Sergei had was manic and he always had some sort of business on the side. Cheap cigarettes had been one that Marius made use of.

After Marius had come back to Africa, the friends he'd kept in touch with sometimes mentioned their mutual acquaintance Sergei, but now he moved in a different world. Most of those old KGB friends had done well out of real estate, import export businesses, that sort of thing, after the collapse of the union. Sergei too had gone into business. Before joining intelligence, Sergei had served in Afghanistan with the Soviet air force, and he used that expertise to buy up cheap Soviet planes, weapons, spare parts, anything that could be traded for lots of money. At first he flew the planes himself, then he mostly did high level diplomacy, setting up deals, and had a team of mercenary pilots who would fly anywhere for a buck. Certain governments wanted to get arms to countries under embargo, countries at war, and Sergei would organise it at a price. France was one of those countries. The US another. African countries like Angola and Liberia were a major destination.

According to Marius' friends, Sergei Krushnekov now owned an old palace in Moscow and apartments in places like Paris and Hong Kong.

Mimi looked at Marius, an eyebrow raised, waiting for some sort of response.

Marius pointed to where she'd written 'Sergei Krus...v'.

— I'm pretty sure it was a Russian that Dave Gordon was meeting at the airport bar. Probably a coincidence, but as it turns out, I know someone with a name like that. An arms dealer. We've lost touch now but he was a good friend in Moscow.

The unmistakable smell of charcoaled soy sauce and chicken made him look up as Takashi arrived back holding a long plate with yakitori sticks neatly arranged on it. Yao was behind him and he laid out plates, chopsticks, hot towels rolled up in little cane baskets and a big container of rice.

As Mimi took the lid off, a rush of steam carried the smell of hot rice and Marius breathed it in as she scooped it into ceramic bowls. She put one on the table in front of Marius and pointed to the yakitori.

— *Douzo*. Help yourself.

Takashi wiped his hands on a towel then picked up a yakitori stick and pulled the meat off with his chopsticks. Marius followed suit, but Mimi said she'd eaten earlier and wasn't really hungry.

As they ate and drank, Marius told Takashi and Mimi about Jojo's surveillance at the airport bar, and the suitcase exchange.

Takashi put down his chopsticks on the *hashioki* and leaned back, pushing his hair back off his face as if it might help him to think.

— So not a suitcase full of clothes?

Marius shook his head.

— In which case he probably hadn't arrived by plane. Not a commercial one, anyway, unless he has very good contacts at the airport.

Marius picked up another yakitori stick and bit off a couple of pieces of chicken before he answered.

— Even then.... From something that Lola said, I'm pretty sure it was money. He caught Mimi's look and added. Don't worry, I'll tell you about it. But let's get back to you. What's this other name?

Marius pointed to the scrap of paper on the table.

— Alabi. Where did that come from?

— The back of a photo. It was tucked away in a sort of hidden pouch under all the other stuff.

— Tell me more about the photo. What was the impression you got? Why do you think Dave Gordon was carrying it around in his wallet.

Mimi told them about the slightly raised eyebrows, the challenging look. It could have been taken in a photo booth, but maybe it was a more intimate photo. Could have been taken close up by someone who knew him well.

— Like a boyfriend?

— Boyfriend? Really?

Marius nodded.

— Exactly. It would fit with what Adelola told me this afternoon. And with what Simone told us, of course.

— Well if you put it like that…yes. It was just like the sort of picture you might carry around of your boyfriend. I just didn't think…

— Nor me. But according to Lola, Dave Gordon is paying her to act the part of his girlfriend. The person he's really interested in is her brother. What Lola told me is that she and her brother were hustling out of the bar at the Mariott hotel in Ikoyi in Lagos. They spotted Dave as a target and got lucky. Dave still thinks that he initiated the whole thing, but apparently not.

Takashi raised an eyebrow in the direction of Marius.

— And Lola told you all this over a few drinks?

Marius laughed and ran a hand over his shaved head.

— Look at me! I don't think she believed for a minute I was a music producer. She knew I was on the make somehow and seemed happy to be able to chat about the whole thing. She probably doesn't get to be herself with many people around here. And you know I'm a good listener.

Mimi gave Marius a friendly push on the shoulder.

—Good at getting people to tell you things they don't mean too! Anyway, tell us some more. What's this hustling they do?

— They hang out in the hotel bar, as if they're guests and pick out a businessman or a tourist – usually white, but not always. Then they work out ways to get money from him. Or it could be a her. Lola said Dave seems to have fallen for her brother but the brother is stringing him along, just like he does all of the targets. Apparently he can turn it on for men and women. She called him Ibby but I'm thinking it could be a nickname. Alabi – Ibby.

— What does Lola get out of it? She must get sick of having to put on an act all the time.

— It doesn't seem to phase her at all. She just wants to have plenty of money without doing much for it. From the sound of it, she and her brother have been scamming together for years. If I can believe her story, their parents died in a car crash when they were in their teens and they've been on the make pretty much since then.

Mimi suddenly leant back into the soft cushions and looked out into the garden. Marius guessed she was thinking about her mother and when she spoke it seemed almost as if she was talking to herself.

— That's sad. She looked back at Marius. Maybe the parents were more… I don't know, middle class? She's very convincing as Dave's girlfriend. The accent and the clothes and everything don't look anything like the person you're describing.

— She's good at it.

— So what do you think they're aiming to get out of Dave? Takashi asked.

Marius shrugged.

— Whatever they can get. Money definitely. Lifestyle. Maybe more than that. Dave won't want anyone knowing he's gay. Not here. So Lola and her brother are in a pretty powerful position. And another thing, Lola knows that Dave is getting that extra money. Apparently he's keeping it secret from her and her brother – or thinks he is – but she went back to get something the other day and saw him taking money out of a suitcase and putting it in the safe in his room. He didn't know she'd seen him.

Mimi picked the scrap of paper off the table and read the name 'Alabi' a few times, trying to get a feel for the way you might say it.

Marius leant back with his eyes closed and only half listened to her. He wanted nothing more than to be back home and back in his own clothes. Then something in the way Mimi was pronouncing Alabi with an emphasis on 'Al' triggered an idea and he felt awake again.

— Wait a minute. You've just given me an idea. Do you remember the last time I was out here? It wasn't long after I'd got back from Lagos. I was talking about how Lawrence Ashley was trying to say something just before he died. It sounded like Al.

— Al. Ālabi, Mimi said. Is that what you're thinking? I guess it could be.

Takashi had been fixing up a problem with one of the guests but now he came back over and sat back opposite Mimi and Marius.

— Could be what?

— Dave Gordon's boyfriend could be the name that Ash was trying to say, said Mimi.

Marius nodded.

— Yes. It's possible.

— What are you thinking? That opens up all sorts of connections.

— I don't know what to think yet, but you're right about the connections. I'm pretty sure the driver, Jerro, was delivering something to Lola's brother while we were over there. If Ibby and Alabi are one and the same, then it's possible Ash could have seen him, maybe talked to him.

Takashi went to take a sip of his beer and realised the glass was empty. He stood up and caught Yao's attention then turned to Marius.

— Another one?

— Why not?

Takashi held up two fingers then sat down again.

— What about that map that Mimi saw. The one you found a copy of. Maybe that's what the driver was taking to the brother.

The implication hung in the air. He'd thought about it, of course he had, but like everything else it was all a big guessing game, and Marius wanted answers.

— Perhaps. But perhaps it's just a map that the school hands out to help people in Lagos.

— Then why is it from Kazuo's hotel? Lawrence Ashley hadn't even heard about it until I rang Kazuo that Sunday at your place.

— You're right. Sorry Takashi. I'm not thinking straight.

Takashi waved a hand and smiled.

— You're doing fine. Okay, tell me what else you found out. What about Lola's brother?

— Just that he's a pretty good hustler. No. I'm not being fair. Lola talked a bit about how Ibby took care of her after their parents died. Apparently the family planned to marry Lola to an old man – she was only thirteen – and Ibby got her away from them and managed to get a living, make a home, send her to school. For a while anyway.

— That must have been tough.

— Very tough. And who knows what layers of toughness he's built around himself.

Yao arrived with the mugs of Asahi and they waited while he set them out on the table. Marius took an exploratory sip through the foam but there was too much head and he put it down to let it settle. Mimi was feeling tired but it seemed too much of a struggle to get up and go to bed, so she settled back into the corner of the lounge.

— What about George Barnes? Weren't you playing chess with him?

That had only been a few days ago but there was something about today that had wiped all the other things from Marius' mind.

— I was. I did. Play chess with him that is. It's why I'm so sure Dave Gordon's up to something.

— So where does George Barnes sit on the scales: good or bad? Takashi asked.

— Good. Muddled but good. At least Ash was right about him. Well, right in that George isn't on the fiddle. But wrong to pretend that George hasn't got a problem.

— So...fill us in.

With an instinctive movement Marius edged forward on the lounge and leant towards Mimi and Takashi. No one was around to overhear – the customers had all left and only Yao was over at the bar – but it was a habit hard to break.

— It turns out that Ash had asked George to go behind Dave Gordon's back and get statements from the bank. Apparently Dave Gordon is the only one who handles all the banking for the capital investment account – that's an off shore account. George manages the day-to-day account for the current expenses, salaries and things like that. The off shore account was in the names of Dave Gordon and Lawrence Ashley until a few months ago. Then the account name changed to just one name....

— Dave Gordon, Takashi interrupted.

— You've got it. And around that time, some large amounts were going in and out of the account.

Takashi started to realise where this was heading.

— Something to do with the Russian. And convenient to have Lawrence Ashley out of the way. Do you think he said something to Dave Gordon about that phone call.

— It's possible. Probable even. My impression of Ash is that he desperately wanted to trust Dave Gordon. And George too.

Marius looked out at the dark garden. Thick clouds had covered the sky and he wondered if it was the long awaited storm that would break the dry season. For the first time he noticed the voodoo drums that must have been beating since he'd been here. It was time to make a move and he dragged himself away from the hypnotic sound and looked back at Takashi and Mimi.

— Sorry. I've got to get myself home. I think I'm beyond rational thought.

As he stood up Marius realised that all the drinking had had its effect. He could hear himself articulating too deliberately, though he felt clear-headed enough.

Takashi watched Marius from the doorway and noticed him stumble slightly as he walked up to the side of the road to flag down a taxi. What was Marius getting himself into this time?

19

Monday 4 April

Marius was relieved to see that the lights in the house were off when he got out of the taxi. No surprise there – it must be after midnight. He switched off the light at the front door and locked it behind him, then he felt his way up the stairs and looked in through the open door to Dzigi's room. The mosquito net had come loose at the bottom of the bed so Marius went over and tucked it in. Dzigi had thrown off the top sheet and was sprawled across the bed, deeply asleep. Marius tiptoed out though he knew it would take an earthquake to wake him.

In the taxi Marius had imagined himself in the shower, washing away a sour feeling that had settled around him. But when he closed his bedroom door and switched on the ceiling fan, all he could think about was sleep. It was a relief to take off the black T-shirt and the jeans that were too tight for his taste. As he pulled at them Marius felt damp patches of sweat and he took all the clothes into the bathroom and dumped them on the floor. Then he soaked a flannel in cold water and wiped himself with it as he shut the bathroom door and collapsed with relief on to the bed. He pulled the sheet up to his waist, spread the wet cloth over his forehead and closed his eyes.

But as he lay in the darkness waiting for sleep, the sound of drums took over from the night's silence. Tuneless but determined, they could go on like this for days. Voodoo drums, had to be. First out at Takashi's and now here; some sort of festival perhaps. Could be to help the rains come on time. Or then again, it might be for some private reason – love, fertility, revenge. Anything. There were people he knew who swore by the use of fetishes. That's probably what they'd say about George and his odd behaviour – someone had stuck a pin into his voodoo doll. Takashi had seemed certain that there was something odd – even suspicious about it.

A sudden shaft of panic shot through Marius like a punch in the stomach. He pulled the flannel off his head and sat up in bed. George. What was he thinking, telling George all that stuff? Who knew how many people he might have told by now? To calm himself he threw off the sheet and walked over to the window and looked out. Heavy clouds were low in the sky and a wind was blowing the dry leaves that had fallen on to the drive from the almond tree next door. The drums kept the same rhythm but Marius couldn't see any sign of life in the darkness.

He walked back to the bed and lay down again. And it wasn't only the forged signature on the bank account. It was those large amounts of money going in and out and the growing certainty that Dave Gordon was mixed up in something. To be honest with himself, he'd got too excited about finding those statements and George seemed so normal, so together, the way he'd gone through them in such detail. Maybe it was too late by then, but why didn't he just borrow them, bring them home to go through?

Looking back, he could see he'd allowed himself to think that George was just a bit forgetful, getting old. He should have listened to Takashi. Right from the start he'd been worried that there was something behind

George's behaviour, the way it had changed almost overnight.

Listening to the drums, his head suddenly clear, it seemed all too likely that George's behaviour might be manipulated somehow – drugs, juju, whatever. Gloria was the obvious suspect and of course he would end up telling her what they had found out! And what Marius hadn't told Takashi and Mimi was that Lola had as good as told him that she'd 'found' Gloria for George. Another connection that led back to Dave Gordon and linked up with Lola and Alabi.

One thing was for sure, he couldn't do anything about it right now. Marius pulled the sheet back up and rolled on to his side, then he took the pillow out from under his head and held it over his ear. The noise of the drums was muffled at least. He closed his eyes and forced himself to remember what he'd been reading this morning. Something about justice, but that was as far as he got.

20

Tuesday 5 April

Rain beating against the window woke him up a few hours later. Marius leaned over and picked up his watch from the bedside table. Nearly seven. Either the drums had stopped, or the sound of the rain was drowning them out. His night-time panic about George came flooding back and he thought back over it. Yes, he decided. Still a problem. Urgent, but he couldn't just rush off to see George now. He'd first have to make peace with Dzigi and Eva.

After a quick shower he was relieved to get back into his usual blue jeans and loose top and he joined the others downstairs. Dzigi and Seri were sitting at the table eating some left-over chicken and Eva was in the dining room using the mirror on the mantelpiece to put big silver hoops in her ears.

She looked smart in an orange and green outfit and Marius told her so. As he came and stood next to her she turned around, using both her hands to fasten the screw at the back of her earring.

— We were wondering where you were, she said.

Marius took the 'we' to mean Dzigi and glanced at him.

— Yes. Sorry. I've got something on at the moment that I want to talk to you about. How was Accra by the way?

The feigned indifference wasn't lost on Marius.

— Good. Seri had a lot of fun with her cousins.

— And you?

Eva turned back to the mirror and put the other earring in.

— A good break, she said, looking at Marius' reflection in the mirror. Then she turned back to him and smiled. Okay. I don't know why I ever try to keep anything from you Marius. I had a really good time. There's this guy that I met at Ifesia's wedding and we went up to Aburi on Saturday night. I haven't done anything like that for ages and it was fun. Good food. Good company. Just nice to have a real break.

It made Marius think about how long it had been since he'd done something like that. Definitely not since Selina had died. He smiled at Eva.

— Aburi. I love that place. Did you go to the gardens?

— Yes. But they were really dry. A bit depressing. Anyway, what do you want to ask me about?

Marius glanced into the kitchen. Seri was showing Dzigi a book she'd brought back from Ghana and there was still ten minutes before they'd have to leave for school.

— Do you know anything about the legal ins and outs of partnership agreements?

Eva took her mug of coffee off the mantelpiece and went over to the couch.

— Just the basics. It comes up sometimes when business partners buy and sell land. What do you want to know?

Marius sat opposite her on the ottoman and gave her a quick explanation of the little he knew about Ashley Lawrence and Dave Gordon's ownership of LICS.

— The thing is, the more I find out about Dave Gordon the less I trust him, and now I'm wondering if his claim to be the sole owner of the school has any legality. It would make things much easier if he hadn't.

— Is this to do with that mugging in Lagos?

— I don't believe it was a mugging. Killing more like it. And it's getting hard to escape the idea that the current head of the school might know something about it.

— God, that's terrible. I don't think the partnership law is going to help. I suppose you want to know what happens when one partner dies.

Marius nodded.

— That. And what would be the case if one partner does something by himself.

— Well that one is pretty clear. One of the partners can act on behalf of the firm and it's binding on both of them. If he's got the authority, of course.

— And what if a partner dies?

—Well, any debts pass on to the other partner. His share of the profits is part of his estate. Within six months the remaining partner has to either bring in a successor, buy out the interest of the deceased or commence to wind up the firm. But the reality is that partnerships can just be an oral agreement and unless somebody challenges it in court, it's pretty much between the two of them. Do you know if anyone is likely to challenge Dave Gordon? You know, next of kin, wife, kids.

Marius realised how little he knew about Lawrence Ashley. Something else he would ask George. He shook his head.

— Not really. There used to be a wife, I don't think there were kids. Dave Gordon must know, and he doesn't seem to be worried.

Eva checked her watch.

— Anyway, time to go. Will you be in tonight?

Marius had no idea, but he had some making up to do. Usually Eva didn't mind that he took advantage of their arrangement but the rule was to keep in touch. What had he been thinking last night?

— I'll make sure of it. And leave dinner to me – I'll sort something out.

He could see by Eva's look that she didn't trust him but she nodded.

— Okay.

Marius followed her into the kitchen and sat at the table next to Dzigi. He picked up the homework notebook that was lying on the table and checked through the things Dzigi needed for school today. Nothing special. He put it back on the table and Dzigi grabbed it and put it in with the other books in his satchel. Marius heard him say something like "what would you care" but it was muttered so quietly it wasn't clear. Was it just his conscience?

— Okay Dzigi, let me guess. Marius looked up as if he was searching, finger on chin. He had Dzigi's attention.

— Come on dad, don't be silly.

Marius ignored him.

— Wait. He lifted a melodramatic finger. I have it.

Dzigi pushed him, frustrated and friendly at the same time, and half laughed as he picked up his leather satchel and shrugged his shoulders into it. Marius helped.

— I should have rung you last night when I was late home?

Marius pulled the second strap so it sat flat and Dzigi turned round and looked up at him.

— Yes. Of course. That's the rule.

— Sorry Dzigi. What's the punishment?

— A hundred lines: I must ring Dzigi when I'm late.

Dzigi laughed and Marius was relieved. It wouldn't be much fun if Dzigi turned into a moody sort of kid.

From the kitchen window he watched them get into Eva's car and waved to them as she backed slowly through the big puddles the rain had left in the driveway.

As soon as they were gone he went upstairs and got his wallet, then he took the car keys off the hook at the front door and joined Jojo, who was washing the windows of the Toyota. It wasn't eight o'clock yet and there was a good chance that George would be still be at home. If he wasn't home he'd think of something. Better if Jojo drove, then at least there'd be two of them in case there was trouble.

Marius knew Jojo wouldn't go anywhere until all the car windows were clean and he waited impatiently for the last one to be rinsed down, the bucket to be emptied and put in its place. Then he threw Jojo the keys and opened the passenger door.

The rain had eased off, but low clouds still covered the sky and made a sandwich of the warm air trapped in it. All along the road cars had broken down because of the rain and even on the Boulevard the traffic was barely moving, except for the moto-taxis that crowded out the cars and slowed things down even more. When they finally turned off the Boulevard Circulaire, the street Jojo started to go down was so flooded that they decided to reverse and take a different one.

When they parked next to the wall in front of George's house it was after nine o'clock. Over one hour to come a few kilometres.

The gate opened, and Marius was happy to see that young Sam, the aspiring accountant, was on duty. But then he noticed Sam's face. Something was wrong.

21

Tuesday 5 April

The look Sam gave him was odd, as if Marius was the last person he wanted to see. He kept the green metal gate open just far enough to be able to talk to him, and had his left hand on the latch and half his body behind the gate, ready to close it at any second.

Marius took in the high plastered walls on either side of the gate. Properties on either side closed off George's house completely, so if Sam wouldn't let them in, there might not be any other way into the house. What on earth was going on? Why couldn't Sam look him in the eye?

It was in Marius' favour that Sam was young and well brought up. Before Sam could make his mind what to do, Marius moved closer to him and held out his hand.

— My friend, how's the study?

It wasn't what Sam was expecting and he couldn't refuse the hand. That gave Marius a chance to move even closer and into the gateway.

Sam looked at the ground as he spoke, and kept hold of the gate with his other hand, looking miserable and awkward.

— You can't go in.Mr Gordon's orders.

Marius snapped off the handshake.

— Mr Gordon? He's in there?

— No sir. But he was here last night. Mr Mensah's there now.

At least that was a relief. But Mr Gordon's orders? Where was George?

— Mr Barnes is expecting me. What's going on?

Sam shrugged his shoulders and pulled at the front of his kaki pants. He was definitely nervous. Why? Marius didn't have to be told there was something wrong with George. If he'd been worried before, he was doubly so now.

Well he wasn't going to find out by standing here. He leant against the gatepost so that his body was blocking the entrance and waved Jojo over from where he'd been leaning against the roof of the Toyota.

Sam pushed at the gate with his shoulder and Marius felt the wet metal digging into his calf.

— You have to leave now.

— Sorry Sam, I can't do that.

With some force, Marius thrust his leg through the gap in the gate and used his right arm to push Sam across the chest, forcing him to lose hold of the latch.

Sam lurched back, thrown off balance, stumbled against the chair and fell noisily on to the ground, the chair on top of him.

Marius flung the gate open and followed the paving stones down the side of the house, Jojo behind him. The earlier downpour had left pools of water on some of the uneven stones and sheets of water lay in the mix of mud and patches of lawn between, and on either side of the path. The storm had also left a gusting wind in its wake and the palm trees that lined the wall on the other side of the lawn were tossing around as if trying to break free.

Marius walked quite slowly, all his senses alert. Behind him he heard the gate slamming but he didn't turn around to see if it was Sam or the wind. The curtains in the front of the house were pulled back and he caught a glimpse of a face behind the open louvers. Not a surprise. Somebody must have heard the racket Sam made when he fell over the chair.

The path led up a couple of paved steps to a green and brown tiled veranda, sheltered to some extent by the overhang of the roof. There was a button to the right of a panelled door and just as Marius was about to push it, the door was opened by a big man with a large face and a self-important expression. He didn't look pleased to see them.

Mr Mensah, Marius guessed. A couple of the buttons on the tailored shirt of his beige coloured uniform were pulling against the buttonholes, straining to cover a paunch. He was a couple of inches taller than Marius and carried more weight. The uniform had LICS embroidered on the shirt pocket and suggested an official role of some sort. Manager, perhaps?

— Greetings, my good man. Marius moved his head in a vague gesture towards the gate. Your fellow didn't seem to want us to come in, but Mr Barnes is expecting me. We were held up in the traffic. All the rain, you know, so we're a bit late.

Marius spoke in French and it was clear the man didn't understand much. It was a fair guess he was an Ewe from Ghana.

Mr Mensah ignored Marius' greeting and kept the door open just wide enough to fit his body.

—You've no right to be here.

Sure enough, he spoke Ewe with a Volta accent. Marius pretended not to understand. He pulled out a rough sort of business card that he'd made in a hurry, and held it out towards Mensah.

— I'm Pierre Gautier. Mr Gordon might have mentioned me. Accountant.

Whatever trouble the man was expecting, he hadn't imagined it would take the form of a French speaking accountant who knew his boss. He hesitated, and that's all Marius needed. Surprise. He used his elbow and forearm and pushed past Mensah and into the entrance hall, Jojo following.

As he walked, fast now, Marius visualised the layout of the house. There was no sign of George in any of the living rooms, so he must be in the back of the house, a bedroom probably. Marius flung open a door that was the other side of the drinks cabinet in the lounge room and saw a long hallway with doors opening off it.

Mensah recovered his balance and hurried after Marius and Jojo, but he didn't seem to know what to do with them, and his voice was more of a whine than an order.

— You can't go in there. Mr Barnes isn't well. I've been told to make sure he's not disturbed. Mr Gordon said he needs to sleep.

Marius ignored him and kept walking. Only Mensah seemed to be here. Where were the others? It was obvious this was a bedroom wing and he walked up the hallway, pushing the doors open as he went.

Behind him there was a thudding sound then Marius felt a hand grip his shoulder, trying to spin him around and pin him against the wall. Marius grabbed the hand and used the onrushing weight of Mensah to throw him on the floor. He could see Jojo recovering from where he seemed to have been slammed against the wall, but there was no time to help him.

Mensah was struggling to stand up. Some men get their strength from hard training and intelligence. Mensah wasn't one of those. His power came from his position and only that. Now his first thought was to ring Dave Gordon. Still on his hands and knees he reached for the phone that he carried in a leather pouch on his belt.

Marius was quicker and bent down and snatched the phone out of his hand.

— I'll look after that for you. We're just here to see George. I have to say, it's not usually so difficult.

Marius kept walking to the end of the corridor and turned the handle of the last door on the right.

Mensah finally got to his feet and stood there rubbing his back. Marius opened the door of the bedroom and went in.

Embossed floral curtains under fringed pelmets covered the windows on two sides of the room but there was enough light for Marius to recognise the figure in the king-size bed. George. Marius went straight to the curtains nearest him on the eastern wall and pulled them back. Sunlight flooded into the room and he went over to the bed.

In the half darkness it had looked as if George was asleep but now.... If he wasn't dead he was close to it. There was no sign of movement and his face looked like wax. The air-conditioning was set so low that the room felt like a morgue, even with the long shafts of sun that spilled onto the tiled floor.

Jojo stationed himself at the foot of the bed, facing the door where Mensah was standing, unsure of what to do without his phone. Then he came further into the room, but made sure he was out of reach of Marius.

— Satisfied now? You can see he's not well. Now get out of here and let him sleep.

But Marius was bending over George, peering at his face, looking at the blue tinge that coloured George's lips. Then he bent further and put his left ear on George's chest. The heart was beating. Just. And now he could hear the shallow breath. He picked up George's right arm that was lying on top of the white sheet and looked over at Mensah.

— Come and see for yourself. Look at that blue under his fingernails.

Mensah muttered something that Marius couldn't make out and came close enough to get a look.

Marius put George's arm back on the bed and turned towards Mensah. The man looked panicked and undecided. It would be so much easier to work with him, rather than against him, and Marius tried direct appeal.

— Can't you see he's dying? Do you want that on your head? We've got to get him to a hospital.

Mensah held out his hand, more sure of himself and arrogant now, his bottom lip and chin thrust forward.

— Give me my phone. I'll ring Mr Gordon.

Marius shook his head. What a pathetic man.

— No. We don't need Mr Gordon. I don't want to move George, but I think we'll have to. I have a friend who runs a private hospital. It's not too far, we'll take him there.

Marius got his own phone out and called Alain's number.

Mensah took two angry steps towards Marius, his arm raised, intending to belt him on the side of his head, but Jojo grabbed both his arms and held them up behind his back.

— You're an interfering nobody, Mensah shouted. What would you know? Wait until Mr Gordon hears about this.

Alain's number was still ringing and Marius held the phone up to his ear and looked Mensah in the eye.

— I'd be very careful about taking orders from Mr Gordon if I were you.

Then Alain was on the line and Marius gave him a quick description.

Yes, they could move George. The thing to do was to keep him breathing, keep his circulation going. Could be an overdose of something, so have a look around. But get him to the hospital really fast.

Marius put his phone back in his pocket and looked at Mensah, strained forward under the pressure of Jojo's hold. What was he going to do with him?

He looked at the door of the bedroom. The lock was a traditional sort of style, with a big key in the door. There was a good chance the others would be the same.

Marius went over and stood next to Jojo.

— It's okay. You can let him go now.

As Jojo did so, Marius took Mensah's right arm and put him in a hammer lock. It was just loose enough to allow the man to walk and Marius steered him into the corridor and along to the next bedroom. It was all

Mensah could do to breathe and Marius talked to him as they went.

— This is probably better than you deserve, but I like to think the best of people. Maybe you don't want George to die, but just in case, we'll lock you in here for a while.

Like all the houses in the area, the windows were covered with heavy security bars. Should be safe for a while. Marius pushed Mensah into the room, took the key out of the door then closed the door and locked it from the outside and put the key in his pocket.

— Right Jojo. You bring the car in. I'll get George to the front door. He saw Jojo hesitate. I'm sure there's no one else here, he added. Don't worry about me.

Jojo raced off and Marius turned back to George. He remembered what Alain had said and did a quick search for signs of drugs. Working fast he turned over the pillows, threw back the bedclothes, then hurried into the bathroom and went through the cupboards and drawers. There was nothing that looked suspicious; no empty bottles or packets, no syringes or needles. Then he went back to George and tried a couple of holds that didn't work before he finally got a grip under his arms and pulled him off the bed.

— Sorry George, he said as he pulled his unconscious body along the corridor. It's not dignified but it's the best I can do.

Behind the locked door there was the sound of heavy banging and shouting. Marius barely heard it. As he dragged George through the dining room he noticed the chess board still set up on the table. Hard to believe that was only three days ago. He stopped for a second and changed his grip, then kept going past the giant television set and the velvet couches. Still no sign of Gloria. Not just that she wasn't here, but there was nothing of hers, as if she'd never been here.

From outside he heard the whine of the Toyota's engine as Jojo drove up and stopped right outside the front door. Together they bundled George into the back seat and Jojo astounded Marius by reversing at speed back out through the gates.

— Good man. By the way, how was Sam?

— Not very happy.

— What did you tell him?

—That Mr Barnes would die if we didn't get him to hospital. Then he seemed to understand.

— Nothing about Mensah?

— I told him that Mr Mensah said to make sure no one else went in.

Marius laughed.

— Well done.

22

The sun had come out while they were inside and the traffic was back to normal: congested, but moving. Twenty minutes later they pulled into the driveway of the Clinique d'Abovey. In earlier days it had been a residence for the French ambassador and it still looked more like a mansion than a hospital. But when they pulled up under the portico, the green neon sign said 'AMBULANCE' and the double doors opened immediately. Two orderlies in green uniforms wheeled a stretcher out and expertly transferred George onto it. They fixed a portable oxygen mask over his face and Marius left Jojo to park the car and followed them along a corridor and through a pair of swinging doors into what he recognised as an emergency room.

He was relieved to see Alain himself there, chatting to a short man in green scrubs. Marius went over to them and Alain introduced Dr da Silva. As soon as the stretcher was locked in place they both pulled down their surgical masks and went over to examine George.

Marius watched as they peered into his eyes, listened to his pulse, examined his arms then the rest of his body.

Alain lowered his mask and spoke to Marius.

— Do you know if he uses heroin?

It wasn't what Marius was expecting to hear.

— I'd say no, but then I hardly know him.

— Well, it looks to me like a classic heroin overdose, though I can't be sure until we run tests.

An image came into Marius' mind. Dave Gordon with his cold eyes and smooth looks. Why was he there last night? There had to be a connection. And why had Gloria moved out so suddenly? Come to think of it, what about the cook?

— Would it be possible for someone else to give him heroin. In food for example?

Alain took a few seconds to answer, then he nodded slowly.

— It's a bit hit and miss because you can't control the dose very well, but it's possible. I've had a case of it. It takes a lot longer to have an effect so you're not likely to get a regular user putting heroin in food because they wouldn't get a quick fix. But someone inexperienced might.

Alain stopped talking and turned to his colleague.

— Let's get some naloxone into this man right away. It's worth the chance. If it's heroin, it might save him. If not.... Look, we'll give him the naloxone, put him in intensive care and there's a good chance he'll pull through, even though he's nearly gone. An hour later and it would have been too late.

Already the other doctor was over at the glass fronted cabinet, taking a syringe out of its plastic wrapping as he reached for a bottle from the top shelf.

— Can I leave him with you? Alain asked da Silva.

The doctor turned around and gave him the thumbs up, but didn't stop what he was doing.

— Leave it with me.

Marius felt reassured.

Alain took off his mask and gloves and threw them in the disposal unit, then he removed the green scrub top and hung it on a hook. Brushing down the front of his tailored white shirt, he came over to Marius and touched him lightly on the shoulder.

— Let's go to my office and have a chat.

Marius followed him through the padded swinging doors. He glanced back just before they swung shut behind him and saw da Silva taking a syringe out of George's arm. He let himself relax for the first time that day. George was in good hands, at least he'd managed that.

It seemed a different world outside the emergency room. Alain stopped to have a word with a blue uniformed nurse who was pushing a heavily bandaged man in a wheelchair and Marius wandered over and looked at a framed black and white photograph that he hadn't noticed before. It showed a stately looking two storey building with big arched windows on the ground floor and matching square windows on the top. 1912, Gusthaus Abovey, the small neat writing said. The area around the building was bare and the portico was smaller than the one that was there now, but it hadn't changed much since that time. It was easy to see why the French ambassador might have taken up residence here.

Compared with the Tokoin Hospital, this was heaven. Marius looked up and down the hallway; the breadth and the high ceiling gave it an airy feeling, and it looked fresh and calm. In a way, the faint smell of disinfectant was reassuring. Alain had come a long way since the Moscow days. Back then Alain had been studying medicine and Marius was the one with the position and the connections. It hadn't been easy for Alain, and he always said that Marius had got him through that period in his life. Perhaps that accounted for the close friendship they'd had since then. These days Alain was busy running his hospital, but they never lost touch.

The nurse continued down the corridor and Alain opened the door to the left of the photograph and waved Marius in ahead of him.

In Moscow they'd spoken mostly in Ewe but these days it was usually French. Selina's mother tongue had been French, and almost by osmosis, Marius had become a French speaker too.

It wasn't the first time Marius had been in Alain's office, but it still took him by surprise. More like a library than an office, let alone a doctor's surgery, it had big arched windows that looked out onto a lawn with beds of red and orange flowers, and ended in a fringe of fan-palms.

Alain joined Marius where he was standing at one of the windows.

— Looks great, doesn't it? Come and sit down and tell me what's going on.

Some brown leather chairs were grouped in a semi circle facing the windows and Marius took the one nearest to him and sank into it.

— The thing is, Alain, I don't exactly know.

Where to start, Marius wondered. He knew he couldn't prove anything and it was going to sound improbable, but so was the idea of George Barnes using heroin. Encouraged by that thought he took Alain through the whole story, starting with Lagos, trying to keep things simple. Alain was a good listener and he let Marius talk, only asking an occasional question.

— Then this morning, Marius explained, I realised I'd made a huge mistake in trusting George to keep things to himself. I wasn't sure what I was going to do, but I wanted to find out if he'd told anyone, hoping it wasn't too late. As soon as I could get away, I got Jojo to drive to his house and found him in the state that you saw.

— Was he by himself?

Marius though of Mensah in the locked room and smiled. No time to go into that.

— You could say that.

— So you say that this George was…what? Forgetful? Confused? Aggressive?

— Not aggressive. The opposite in fact, but erratic. Sometimes he seemed uncoordinated. Definitely forgetful, but not about everything.

— You know all sorts of people take drugs. You might be surprised.

Marius accepted that idea and nodded slowly, staring out the window. What was it that made him so sure about George Barnes?

— They do. Who knows what the blood tests are going to show. But I'd put good money on the fact that someone else has been giving them to him. Last night it could have been Dave Gordon. Before that it could have been Gloria. Or the cook. I didn't say before, but I noticed this morning that Gloria has moved out completely. There's no trace of her in the house, not even in the bathroom cupboards. That has to make Dave Gordon's visit even more suspicious.

Alain took his glasses off, rubbed his eyes, then put them back on again.

— If it was anyone else I'd tell them to take a reality check, but you have a habit of being right about these things.

— Thanks Alain. How I'm going to prove anything is beyond me right now, but keeping George alive is going to help. He realised how that sounded and added quickly — but that's not what this is about. I'm convinced he's a decent chap and an innocent in all this.

— If you're right, the best way to keep him safe is to keep him here. Correct?

— It's a lot to ask, I know, but could you?

— Let's assume he recovers, there's a guest suite that's used by patients' relatives sometimes. No one's there at the moment.

Marius felt not just the lightness of relief, but a feeling of certainty that this was the turning point. He laughed and shook his head.

— Who would have thought in Moscow that you'd be getting me out of trouble!

Alain laughed with him.

— Who would have thought?

23

Tuesday 5 April

Alain took Marius back up the hall way and through the reception area. Before Marius opened the door he glanced up at the clock. Still only 11.00 o'clock, yet it felt as if a whole day had passed. He opened the door then turned back to Alain.

— So you'll let me know about the results? Any idea how long they'll be?

Alain shrugged.

— One day. One week. It's hard to say. It's best to give them time to get it right – I've asked them to check for a whole range of things.

— Fine. And thanks again.

— It's no trouble. Good luck with your sleuthing. And don't worry about the visiting hours.

Marius let the door go and heard the pneumatic hiss as it slowly closed behind him with a well-oiled click. Now to find Jojo. He looked over the cars in the parking area in front of him. Not one of those. Then he crunched over the gravel and spotted the Toyota under the shade of a cassia tree down the far end. As he got closer to the car he heard the radio through the open doors. Jojo had reclined the seat and was asleep but jumped awake as Marius climbed in and closed the passenger door.

Marius explained the situation and Jojo looked surprised and relieved in turn. He turned the key in the ignition.

— Where now?

— Home. No. I tell you what. You drop me at the local spot and then go on home. I need to think.

What was happening back at George's house. Was Mensah still in that room, or had someone let him out by now? Marius had not a single kind feeling for Mensah, but he regretted that he'd had to knock Sam over. Only a couple of days ago he had Sam marked as a good source of information about what was going on at George's place, but that wasn't going to happen now. Even if Sam was willing to talk, there was no way Marius could go back there. Not unless he wanted to put his own head on the chopping block, that is.

For that matter, what sort of a trail had he left for Dave Gordon? How easy would it be for him to trace George? Surely it would only be a matter of time before he found out about the Clinique d'Abovey. The expats mightn't know about it, but the clinic wasn't some back street place either.

And it wasn't only George that Dave Gordon might be looking for.

Had it been wise to use his own car? At least he'd given a false name to Mensah – along with that fake card – so that could send him off on a false trail. But then he'd given his real name to Sam on Saturday night.

The car stopped and Marius was surprised to see they were at the spot already. He opened the door and then leant back into the car, holding the top of the door in one hand.

— Okay. I'll see you back home. And thanks Jojo. Not bad.

Jojo's expression didn't change, but he waved his left hand in a way that said it was nothing. Marius closed the door and watched Jojo until he turned into the muddy driveway of the house.

Some men he knew were drinking at the front table of the spot and Marius greeted them before he stepped into the green glow of the annexe. When he walked through to the bar, Plaisance was stacking bottles into the top-loading freezer, and he waited until she had finished emptying the crate.

She stood up, pushing her hands into either side of the back of her waist, and Marius thought she looked tired.

— How's your mother? he remembered to ask.

Was that a smile?

— Much better thank you. The usual?

Marius nodded.

— Extra cold if you have one.

Plaisance bent back down into the freezer and pulled a bottle out from the bottom.

— Afua tells me that you were helping Bibi with her homework.

Marius hadn't thought much about Afua – too many other things had happened – but now that Plaisance mentioned her name he was conscious of an interest that he didn't bother to analyse. He hoped it didn't show on his face.

— Truth is, Afua was a lot more help than me.

— That's not what she said, but thanks anyway.

Marius took his change and picked up the bottle and glass from the bar.

— You know I'm always happy to help. That's if Bibi needs it. I'm sure you know how smart she is.

Plaisance nodded and watched Marius take his beer out to the table. She wasn't sure if he was good enough for Afua but at least he seemed reliable. Not like her husband. And that's what he still was, never mind that he'd been gone for all these years.

Marius sat down at the table under the ceiling fan. What to do next? After this morning he had no doubts left about Dave Gordon. As for what he might do next, there was no point worrying about that – he'd just have to try to stay a step ahead.

Marius took a few sips of his beer then leant back in his chair and looked up at the corrugated green plastic, the slowly turning blades of the fan.

What about the Russian contact? Could it be his old friend Sergei Krushnekov? And if it was, what did it mean? Marius wished he'd brought a notebook and pen because he couldn't seem to gather his thoughts. He went inside and found Plaisance still working behind the bar. When he asked, she pulled off a couple of sheets from the notepad that she used for her accounts and found a blunt, stunted pencil in the drawer.

Feeling more organised Marius refreshed his brain with some beer and wrote 'Sergei'. Then he added a question mark. The photo that Jojo had taken should be developed by now. He'd collect it and see if it was of any use. He wasn't hopeful, but it would be a start.

Under 'photo' he drew two arrows. Against one he wrote 'no'. Then 'who?' Against the other he wrote 'yes' and 'contact'. Then he put the pencil down and refilled his glass from the rest of the bottle.

What was he trying to do? As he drank his beer he took the other bit of paper and jotted down some answers.

i) do what Ash had asked him: find out about the school's finances

ii) find out more about Dave Gordon —contacts, possible drug use/dealing, where the extra money was coming from, plans for the school

iii) find out how Ash was killed – more details. Justice?

As for number i), he could almost cross that out. George had found confirmation of the change of name in the joint account and they'd seen in the statements that extra money was going through the account.

As Marius sipped on his beer he put the pencil down and thought some more. It made sense now, Ash asking him to go to Lagos and telling him about that phone call. If Ash had been alive, and still an active partner, then there would have been ways Marius could have helped him to take back control, to keep going with this education thing.

But Ash was dead, and it wasn't just the money. Marius had found out more than he'd bargained for, and he could feel himself being drawn into the school as if it were alive and in danger. Is that what people meant when they spoke of 'the school body'. Trouble was, now that Dave Gordon owned the school outright, what could be done?

Marius drank the last few mouthfuls of beer, took the empty bottle inside and put it on the counter of the black padded bar. He couldn't see Plaisance, but he could hear her cooking in the courtyard that was off the kitchen behind the bar area. And he could smell it. Something grilling on charcoal – fish perhaps? Suddenly he felt very hungry.

— Aunty Plaisance, he called.

Plaisance came through the kitchen door, wiping her hands on the orange and blue *pagne* that was tied around her hips.

— Another one?

— Thanks. And tell me, that's not tilapia you're cooking by any chance?

Plaisance confirmed that it was and Marius put in an order and sat back at the table with his beer.

So. What could be done? What should be done? Marius jotted down 'Do nothing' and looked at it for a while.

There would still be a school, though not the program – was it IB? – that Ash had been planning. The parents who wanted a sixth form course would have to find another school to send their kids to. Dave Gordon would keep playing his nasty games with the boys. Some would get over it, some wouldn't. Mibou and Mimi would lose their jobs.

Dave Gordon might use the school to make himself rich and move on. Or close the school.

Meanwhile the school would be headed by a man who had almost certainly engineered at least one murder.

Marius thought of the book he'd picked out of what he liked to call his library the other day. Actually it was just after he'd met Dave Gordon at the memorial service. There were a few things that he'd noticed that made him to seek out his old book on psychopaths. Despite all the fine words at the service, and the tears, Gordon's good-looking face was oddly expressionless. And the way he'd sent that memo around about taking over the school on the same day as the memorial service made it clear he had no empathy at all for the people involved. Then there was what Simone had said about his behaviour with the boys – the way he would give one boy too much attention, then suddenly withdraw it and pick someone else as a favourite. Play with them, set them against each other.

He'd have to check the details again, but he remembered the point that Hare made about psychopaths being very careful planners, and how well organised and meticulous they are. How they make very successful criminals, especially since they were often charismatic, and careful to present themselves well, to keep people on side.

One of the things they didn't have to hide – weren't even aware of – was a complete lack of conscience.

Looked at like that, Marius had to face it: Doing nothing wasn't an option. He crossed out 'Do nothing' and replaced it with 'Do something', and under that he wrote:

What?

i) get DG charged with fraud

ii) get DG charged with money laundering

iii) get DG charged with murder

iv) get DG charged with attempted murder.

With Ash dead, trying to prove i) would be impossible. Dave Gordon would claim that Ash had signed the form voluntarily and that would be that. Marius crossed it out.

Then he looked at (ii). He could find out who Dave Gordon's airport contact was, and take it from there. Even if it was a racket being protected at high levels, it was worth pursuing, and if Marius could prove there were illegal exchanges of money taking place it would at least be a bargaining point.

Then he looked at iii). Ash's death. Marius' gut instinct told him that Dave Gordon knew more about it than he wanted people to know. He'd seen it in his eyes on Wednesday. Then there was the suspicious white car – could he find a connection with Dave Gordon? It wasn't much to go on. Maybe he should go back to Lagos and ask around. Not a first choice, but it was something to keep in mind.

That brought him to iv).

Talk about meticulous planning! If, as Alain suspected, George had been dying from a massive overdose of heroin, then where would be the proof? Who would ever believe Marius' word against his? And even if there were traces of it in the kitchen, fingerprints, all of that, no one was going to be looking for them, including himself. It was far too dangerous to go back to George's house now. And Marius felt sure it would be pointless as well.

Plaisance arrived with a tin plate almost covered by a whole grilled tilapia with fresh tomato and pepper spilling down the sides. A steaming mound of *fufu* was on a separate plate. Marius folded the list and put it in his pocket. He washed his hands in the bowl that Plaisance had left on the table and picked up a piece of *fufu*. Decision time could wait.

183

24

Tuesday 5 April

The shop where Marius had left the photos was upstairs in a dirty concrete shopping arcade that looked as if it had never been finished properly. He came here because Rosie, the Korean woman who ran the place, was one of the few people in town who could develop photos that didn't look as if they had been dragged through a pool of muddy water.

This one had been a challenge, and Rosie apologised for the quality of the photo, pulling it out to show how she'd done the best she could.

Marius took the photo from her and held it up so they could both see it. The figure was only half in the frame, and badly out of focus, but it was good enough for Marius to recognise the face.

Sergei Krushnekov.

He put the photo back with the strip of black negatives in the green and white envelope, and folded the flap over it.

— You've done wonders as usual. Thanks Rosie.

Marius held the rusty metal rail as he went down the stairs. Something must have happened when they were being constructed and they'd ended up at an odd sort of angle.

Now what? Marius hailed a moto-taxi without any clear idea as to where he was going. He climbed on to the seat and then his subconscious made a decision and he heard himself say to the driver: Hôtel du Paradis.

The moto driver weaved in and out of the two lanes of traffic and sometimes the pack of moto-taxis around them was so close that Marius brushed the knees of other passengers.

There were only a few places where Sergei was likely to stay in Lomé. If he wasn't at the Paradis, then there was the 2 Fèvrier. As to what he was going to do if he found him, that wasn't clear, but Marius realised that the business of Dave Gordon aside, he was hoping to reconnect with someone who'd been a good friend to him all those years ago in Moscow. That Sergei was an arms dealer was pause for thought, but Marius doubted he would have changed completely.

Sergei had always had an eye for commerce and getting into arms sales must have seemed a natural move at the end of the cold war. Of course there were arms dealers who worked within the international agreements, and then there men like Sergei who provided flights to anywhere and to anyone at a price, flouting danger and arms embargos if that's what it needed. Sometimes the flights took in aid workers, or even negotiators, but most of the time the cargo was arms of some sort. Merchants of death, Marius had heard some of these gun-runners called.

But there was another side to the story. Governments were at the back of much of the arms trade and they would, Marius was sure, use Sergei's services when it suited them, sometimes as a way around embargoes. Angola had been a particularly awful example, and here in West Africa it was an open secret that the French government was behind much of the arms trafficking, arms embargoes notwithstanding.

As an ethical question it was hard to get a fix on: too simple to believe that arms and not men were the problem; too hard to know sometimes which side, if any, had right on their side. As a way to make a living it had to be high risk, no matter what backing the arms dealer might have.

The moto driver made a sharp turn to the left, just missing the cars that were taking off from the traffic lights, and then they were in the circular drive of the Hôtel du Paradis. The driver pulled over next to a row of potted palms, and Marius asked him to wait. He brushed the dust from the road off his shirt then went up the imposing stairs and into the foyer. It was all dark wood and stone, and had the sort of trimmings you'd expect from the most expensive hotel in Lomé.

Marius went up to a neatly uniformed woman who was looking at the screen of a computer behind the check-in counter

— Good afternoon Leila, he said, reading her nameplate. I'm here to see a Mr Sergei Krushnekov. Could you be so kind as to give him a ring for me.

— He's staying at the hotel, is he?

— As far as I know.

— One moment please.

Leila went back to the computer and started tapping keys.

— Could you give me the name again?

— Krushnekov. With K. K R U S

She was at the computer for what seemed like ages, and Marius had decided to try the 2 Fèvrier, when Leila stood up and smiled at him.

— I'm sorry, we're having trouble with the computer. He's in room 1023. Do you want me to ring him for you?

— Thank you.

Marius leaned against the counter and watched her dial the number. He could hear the phone ringing and after a few rings it was obvious there was no one there.

— Tell you what, he told her, I might just have a look around. He could be in the bar or at the pool.

Should he keep the moto driver waiting? Marius decided against it. He had a strong hunch that Sergei was here, and he could easily pick up another taxi if he wasn't.

Marius paid the driver then came back in and stood in the foyer to get his bearings. Pool first, or bar? Marius decided on the bar at the pool, and he followed the signs that took him along a hallway, past a hair salon next to a gift shop selling African souvenirs, then out to a covered breezeway where cane chairs and glass-topped tables were part of an open air restaurant.

The restaurant looked out over a pool that had a landscaped waterfall, and Marius stood for a minute and watched as a group of children darted in and out through the curtain of falling water. A swimming lesson seemed to be going on at the other end, and a couple of rather pale-skinned women in bikinis were lying on inflated mattresses in the middle of the blue water. Most of the others were lying in banana chairs around the edge of the pool or sitting at clusters of tables and chairs under the shade of trees on the other side of the pool. Some were perched on stools around the palm-thatched bar that was past the pool and to Marius' right.

Marius felt awkward and overdressed in his jeans and, and for a minute he had doubts about what he was doing. What if Sergei was in the middle of business? Maybe he didn't have time for old friends now.

Well, he couldn't stand here any longer and he looked around for somewhere that was less conspicuous. The bar looked like the obvious choice, and Marius walked across to it and sat himself on a stool that gave a good view of most of the pool area. It was something that appealed to him about these five star hotels: once you were in, no one asked any questions. Gulder beer was on tap and he felt better once a pint of it was sitting on the counter in front of him. He took a couple of sips and looked around.

Most of the people were Europeans but none of them looked like Sergei. There were some overweight men in tiny swimming costumes tanning themselves on banana chairs, and Marius was sure none of them would be Sergei. Not his style at all. Most of the other people were sitting in groups at the tables. There was one family that seemed to be French, and the only other Africans were a couple of men who looked as if they'd made it big in Europe.

Then Marius saw Sergei.

He was sitting at the far end of the pool in a shady spot partially screened by latticework that was designed to shield the table and chairs from the pool, and to create a private space. Naked from the waist up, his shoulders and chest were muscular and there was not a hint of a paunch. A small white towel was draped around his neck and as Marius watched, he used one corner of it to wipe his face. It was the hottest part of the day and even in the shade the air was thick and humid.

In an odd way, Marius wasn't surprised that Sergei looked right at home in this setting. He still had no clear idea what he was going to say, but if he was going to make the move, now was as good a time as any to do it.

His glass was beaded with heavy drops of condensation and he wiped the bottom of it on some towelling on the bar as he picked it up and slid off the high stool.

When he got closer to Sergei he noticed the familiar black and gold pack of Sobranies. Next to it was an ashtray half filled with gold butts. At least that hadn't changed. There was an ice-bucket on a stand next to the table and Marius smiled to himself when he got close enough to see the red lid of a bottle of Smirnoff. Apart from a mobile phone and a bowl of nuts, there was nothing else on the table.

Sergei picked up the pack of cigarettes. He flipped open the lid then pulled one out, put it in his mouth, picked up the lighter and bent over the flame.

Marius slipped into the chair opposite and watched silently. There was a very slight pause as Sergei noticed him, but then he clicked the cap back over the flame and took a drag of the cigarette as he put the lighter back on the table, his eyes on Marius, even as he leaned his head back and exhaled a cloud of smoke.

Then he relaxed and spoke in Russian.

— Marius. Thank God. I thought you might be someone about to make trouble.

Marius laughed.

— I still might! It's good to see you Sergei. And it was. Still working out I see. Sorry about my Russian. I don't get much chance to use it these days.

Sergei pulled the bottle of vodka out of the ice-bucket and re-filled a small tumbler. He waved the bottle in the direction of Marius.

— Pass, Marius said. I'll stick to beer thanks. Then he raised his glass and Sergei raised his.

— *Na zdorovye*. How did you know I was here?

Sergei looked friendly enough, but Marius knew he was on the alert, ready to act if he needed to. It would be easy to lie, but Marius, usually so cautious, had no inclination to make up a story.

— I had a tail on a man here who's causing trouble. My chap took a photo of you at the spot out near the airport. The hotel was a lucky guess.

Marius took a handful of nuts from the bowl and nibbled them as he watched Sergei.

— You must be talking about Gordon. Not my best decision. To use him that is.

Now that was interesting, and not what he'd been expecting to hear. Marius started to get a germ of an idea. He wouldn't put it in terms of using Sergei, but might it not be possible that their interests could coincide?

— You're right. Dave Gordon. I gather you're doing business with him.

Sergei tossed back the tumbler of vodka, threw a few nuts into his mouth then poured himself another glass. He held the bottle towards Marius again.

— Sure you don't want some of this?

Marius laughed and held up his hands in a gesture of submission.

— My friend, you know me too well. I'll get another glass. Then he drained the last of his beer. And another one of these. He waved the glass. One for you?

Sergei smiled for the first time and it seemed genuine.

— Why not? For old time's sake.

As Marius walked back from the bar with the beers, he reminded himself to be careful with the vodka. He knew his limitations, and the kick that vodka kept in store for later.

He put the beers and the tumbler on the table and Sergei filled it with vodka.

— *Na zdorovye* they said again, and despite his resolution, Marius tossed the vodka down.

Sergei had put on a white T-shirt, and the towel was gone from his neck.

— Why were you tailing Gordon? he asked.

Direct as usual. Marius felt the warmth of the vodka relaxing him and Sergei had already poured him another one. In more detail than he'd intended, he told Sergei about Ash's death, the attack on George.

— So what I was doing, putting the tail on him, was trying to find out more about him. Why was he able to throw money around in Lagos, what did he want from the school he seems to despise? You can see I have no reason to like him. Why did you say he wasn't a good decision?

Sergei lit another cigarette and leaned back in his chair, watching the smoke. Then he made up his mind.

— This is just between you and me, Marius.

Marius nodded and Sergei continued.

— I'm guessing you've heard about my business ventures?

Marius nodded again.

— Arms sales. An air-fleet. A rather grand place in Moscow.

Sergei relaxed his serious expression for a moment.

— Yes. You really should come back for a visit and stay with the family.

— Family? That I hadn't heard.

— Surprised? Why not? My wife's very understanding. Two daughters. How about you? How's Selina?

— She died. I have a son.

— I'm sorry.

— Thanks.

Marius waved his hand to show he didn't want to talk about it, then changed the subject.

— Was that money you were giving to Dave Gordon?

Sergei took a couple of deep puffs on his cigarette then leaned through the smoke and stubbed the cigarette out. He rested his elbows on the table and spoke quietly.

— The French government have their own ideas about suitable rulers in West Africa. For example, they supported Eyadéma and now his son because it suits them. The stability is good for trade of course. But Togo is also a good distribution point, and it's useful to have a strong government that turns a blind eye to certain transactions.

— Like arms deals?

— Exactly. But sometimes embargoes are put in place and the government can't afford to be seen to supply arms. That's where I come in. There's a man who contacts me from Belgium on behalf of the French Government. I have a Togolese contact in the embassy in Brussels and one here as well. Of course it costs them. Everyone wants a kickback and I don't come cheap. The buyers give money to the French contact and the government. The French pay me well for running the embargo. My problem is then to clean the money. It was the Togolese contact who put me onto Dave Gordon. You know you can only put so much money through the banks until questions are asked.

— So a school seemed like a good way to hide it.

— Just some of it. Trouble is, Dave Gordon is greedy. And he's naïve at the same time. Thinks he can pressure me to give him a bigger cut. As if. The governments need me. They don't need him. There's always some other way around the money thing. Last time he took out more than we'd agreed. He lied about it, and he also started to talk blackmail. Not directly of course, and all bullshit. That's something he's very good at, I'll give him that.

Sergei poured vodka into both their glasses and waved to the waiter behind the bar. Two beers and more ice were ordered.

— I wouldn't underestimate Dave Gordon, Marius said. I hardly know him, but from what I've seen and heard, he's very good at manipulating people and making them believe he's the nice guy who just wants to help everyone. And from what I know he's done, he's completely without scruples or conscience. Ashley Lawrence believed he could trust him right up until he was killed. Not at all the sort of person you want in your line of business. I'm sure trust is pretty important.

The waiter arrived with the beers and a bowl of ice, and Sergei waited until he had left before replying.

— It's funny isn't it? You're right. Some of my deals are set up to deceive on a big scale. But amongst the players on the ground, it's trust and keeping your word that makes it all happen. I don't like what you've said about Dave Gordon. Sounds like he's worse than I thought. Could be time to cut him out of the operation.

Marius wondered what Sergei might have in mind.

— Cut him out?

Sergei gave him a half smile.

— Don't worry, I'm not a thug. I sell the arms, but I don't go around shooting people. I think that might be one of your ironies you used to try to teach me about.

Marius smiled.

— You were always a good student Sergei.

— And you were never any good at making money, Marius. You should have come in with me in that cigarette racket.

They both laughed. It was an argument they'd had more than once, but Marius knew Sergei liked him for his principles and Marius respected Sergei's openness about his ambitions.

— So you're trying to get some evidence against this Gordon. Is that it?

— Yes. I want something that I can use to get him out of the school. And I really want to know the truth about what happened to Lawrence Ashley. Maybe I want to prove to myself that there was nothing I could have done to prevent it. Justice? I'm not very hopeful about that. But it would be something for the man to be forced to say "I did those things, I'm responsible, and it's wrong".

Despite his resolution, Marius tossed down the rest of the vodka then took a few mouthfuls of beer.

— I'm not sure I can help you, Sergei said. I'm trying to think of ways of setting him up but whatever I do could implicate other people. My guess is that he's going to be pretty upset when I pull the plug on his easy money. That I'm going to do. He's the weakest link in the chain and with the stuff you've told me about, who knows what's going to happen to him. I just wish I'd followed my instincts and not listened to this Togolese guy who persuaded me what a safe bet he was.

— You're right. Dave Gordon won't like losing his money.

— I wasn't too happy about handing over that suitcase on Sunday but it's in my interest to give him another chance. I've got a trip to Côte d'Ivoire in a few days, then I'll be back with more. Not interested in starting something up for me I suppose?

Marius smiled and shook his head slowly.

— Not really my line of business.

Sergei gave a hint of a smile.

— I thought not. But if you change your mind…

— Thanks Sergei. When I want to get myself on the wrong side of the law I'll keep you in mind.

Sergei raised an eyebrow.

— First irony and now sarcasm! You're really giving it to me.

— They both laughed and Marius pulled the bottle of vodka out of the ice bucket and looked at it.

— One more?

— Thanks.

Marius knew the vodka would make its usual delayed attack, but he didn't care. Forget about Dave Gordon – it was just good to talk to Sergei. Those years in Moscow hardly seemed real now and since Selina died, there'd been no one here he could talk to about them; no one, that is, who'd been through it with him.

Sergei glanced at his watch and gathered up the almost empty packet of Sobranies.

— Business calls. If I think of something I can do to help you, I'll let you know. This chap I'm meeting with is the one who put me in touch with Dave Gordon. I think he needs to be put straight at least.

— Yeah. He's probably in for a surprise. It's been good catching up with you Sergei.

— Maybe we can do it again. I'm in and out of here a fair bit.

They exchanged phone numbers and Sergei threw the towel over his shoulder, slipped into a pair of loafers and looked at the half empty bottle of vodka.

— Shall I leave this for you?

Marius laughed and shook his head.

— I don't want them to find me here in the morning!

Sergei put the bottle and his cigarettes, lighter and phone into a leather computer bag that Marius hadn't noticed before and he realised Sergei had probably been planning to work. Sergei saw Marius looking at it.

— Nothing I can't do later, he said, and picked up the bag.

Marius watched him walk around the pool and through the entrance to the hotel. The bag over one shoulder, towel over the other, he walked with a light, confident tread, straight, but not army style. His high forehead and close cut hair, the straight, rather severe looking mouth in a face that seemed devoid of laugh lines, was inclined to make people take a second look at him. Marius was sure he'd be a wanted man in some countries, but he seemed quite at home here.

25

Tuesday 5 April

The afternoon sun had found its way through a gap in the branches of the mango tree and Marius moved to a chair on the opposite side of the table where the palm thatch of the shelter was giving shade. From here he could see the edge of the pool and he watched the father of the French family teaching his son to dive. Marius could see the father losing his patience as each time the boy tried to dive, he belly-flopped onto the water. Then the father would show him how it was done. He would slice the water cleanly, in an elegant dive, and swim fast and gracefully across the pool and back. Then he would stand behind the boy, tuck his head in and launch him into the water. Another belly flop. Marius found it frustrating to watch. He wanted to tell the father to relax. If his son couldn't dive and swim like him, let him find out for himself what he was good at. Humiliating him didn't help anyone.

For that matter, Marius wondered, what would Dzigi end up being good at? He was much more like Selina than himself: even-tempered, intelligent, balanced. So far he showed no signs of the contradictions that Marius recognised in himself: sentimental and cynical; a sharp eye for justice, but not always worried about rules and conventions. Marius looked at his watch and it took a few seconds to work out that it was nearly 4.00. His sensible voice told him the vodka was kicking in with the delayed reaction he had chosen to ignore when he was drinking it. Better to stay here for a while and wait for his head to clear than to go rushing off somewhere else. But this time he remembered to call Jojo and ask him to tell Dzigi he'd be late.

His conscience clear, he called the waiter over and asked for a large bottle of water, then he set about sobering up as methodically as he'd got drunk.

Meeting up with Sergei – not to mention the vodka – had put Marius in nostalgic mode and he found himself going over the night that Sergei had invited him and Selina around to his government apartment for dinner. There were some others there too, but Marius could only remember his friend Ivan. The chess sets had come out after the meal and they'd drunk vodka and played knock out rounds of speed chess. Selina wouldn't touch the vodka but she joined in the chess and amazed them all by wining the most games. She was the only woman there and he could still feel that special excitement they both had walking home, as if they'd taken on the world and won. What would Selina think of his life now?

Suddenly another image popped into his head and Marius found himself thinking about the woman he'd met at the spot the other day. Afua – she said she was interested in Russian literature. That was the day that the Moscow connection had first started creeping back into his life. Should he give her a call? She'd given him her number so it was reasonable to think she'd expect him to ring. He clicked through the names in his contact list. She might be free. He didn't feel like going home and trying to be normal. What was there to lose?

He pressed the number and after a few rings Afua's voice was on the other end.

— Afua? Marius here. We met at Plaisance's place the other day.

She laughed and her voice sounded friendly and natural.

— Yes. How are you?

— To be honest, a bit the worse for wear. I'm at the Paradis – been drinking vodka with an old friend. Not a good idea – the vodka, that is, not the friend. I've got some free time now and wondered if you felt like catching up. I could do with some company.

— Give me an hour or so to tie some loose ends up here. I'll really be ready for a drink by then. Maybe a bite to eat too.

They settled on 6.00 pm at Greenfields Pizzeria. It was an easy walk for both of them, and the pizzas were well known around Lomé. Marius hit the off button and sat gazing at the phone for a minute. He was glad he'd gone ahead and made the call. He couldn't remember the last time he'd done something impulsive like this. Maybe Eva was right; he should get out more. Well today seemed to be the day for it.

And thinking of Eva, he'd better give her a call. It was only as he was waiting for her to answer that he remembered he'd said he'd sort out dinner tonight. Too late now. She sounded resigned and maybe a bit smug. No, she hadn't taken his word about dinner tonight and had picked up something on the way home.

Marius looked at his watch again. It would only take fifteen minutes to walk to Greenfields so he still had a bit over an hour to wait. There wasn't much to do so he went back over to the bar and ordered some yam fries and more water. Now the cocktail happy hour was starting, and along from him a freshly scrubbed young couple perched themselves at the bar for a pre-dinner drink. Marius watched the barman as he made rainbow-coloured drinks with what looked like half a fruit salad on top of them. In one way they looked tempting – maybe it was the ice tinkling – but he decided to stick to water.

The shadow of the building had fallen over the far side of the pool and only the boy and his father were left. It got Marius thinking about Socrates and one of his more interesting questions: can virtue be taught? Would it be harder, he wondered, than teaching someone to dive? What if one was to break it down into virtues? Now that was different. You could have virtues but not be virtuous. How many virtues would it take to be virtuous? Look at Sergei. He definitely had a few virtues – loyalty, honesty – but he could hardly be called virtuous.

What about Dave Gordon? Did he have any virtues? Would hard work count? Funny how that was seen as a virtue, yet a person could be working hard to do the worst possible things. Dave Gordon had definitely put a lot of hard work into organising Ashley Lawrence's death, but even a sophist would be hard put to find any virtue in that. Marius finished the last yam chip and brushed his hands together to get rid of the salt. No. Anyone who fell under the spell of Dave Gordon's charisma and believed him virtuous would sooner or later be disillusioned. Marius felt sure of that.

26

Tuesday 5 April

When Marius walked down the granite stairs of the Paradis the sun was a hazy orange ball hanging over a fringe of tall palms behind the buildings on the Ghana border.

Fifteen minutes later when he turned into the entrance to Greenfields Pizzeria, it had dropped below the rooflines and replaced by lobster coloured clouds.

The pizzeria covered a sizeable area that was defined by Spanish style arched colonnades. Directly opposite him was a well lit bar with art deco stools, and in front of that a large paved area was filled with wooden tables and chairs. The lanterns hanging from scattered poles had been lit, anticipating the sudden darkness that would come soon. To his right there was a smaller, covered space with leather chairs and polished teak tables. It looked welcoming and there was no sign of Afua, so Marius chose a seat that faced the entrance and kept an eye out for her.

He went over in his mind what he knew about her. She was interested in Russian literature, drank Star beer, lived down town somewhere, wasn't a teacher. That was about it. Not much really. But he guessed that Plaisance might have talked to her about him. Not that Plaisance knew much to tell. As far as she was concerned, Marius was someone with a lot of time to spend at her bar.

Ten minutes later when Afua came through the gate, he didn't recognise her immediately. She really had come straight from work, and the slim fitting dress and chunky high heels made her look older than she'd seemed in her shorts and T shirt. Thankfully, she stood just inside the entrance and looked around for him. That was all the time he needed, and he stood up and waved his arm, making the low hissing noise that was an essential communication tool around here. She heard it and came over.

As she pulled out the chair opposite Marius she apologised for being late then sat down and looked around.

— Good choice. I like the lights. Where's the waiter?

She spotted him leaning against the bar and waved him over.

— I'll have a *pression*. Small. And a menu please.

— Same for me, Marius said. Then as the waiter walked away he turned back to Afua. You're looking very businesslike.

— Could that be because I've just come from work?

They both laughed and Marius felt comfortable.

— Do you mind me asking what your business is?

— Ask away. Interior decorating. Well, it's more than that. I advise people then organise the purchases, get things made up. Sometimes import things from America. It's fun. Everyone in the States told me it would never work, but it has so far.

So he was right; she'd been living abroad. He wasn't surprised about her business success. It was a common belief that African women made great entrepreneurs, and there was a lot of truth in it.

The waiter arrived with two glass mugs of beer on a tray. He wiped the table then carefully positioned them. There was only one menu and Marius and Afua swivelled it round so they could both read it. In the end Marius let Afua decide, and it took her no time at all to choose a Supreme for them to share. The waiter picked up the menu and left. Marius raised his glass.

— *Sante*.

Afua leaned forward and touched his glass lightly with her own.

— *Sante*.

Marius took a sip then put his mug down.

— What took you to America?

Afua sipped on her beer and took her time replying, as if she had to think about it.

— I usually say my husband, but that's not the real story. Now I think I married him because he was going to the States. She laughed. Not really a good reason to marry someone. No wonder it didn't last.

— Children?

Afua smiled and shook her head.

— That wasn't part of my plan. Still isn't. For that I may as well have stayed in Togo!

Marius got the picture, unusual though it was. One thing there was no shortage of in Africa was children.

— So you studied?

— Studied. Worked. Made contacts, got experience. Lucky for me my husband was working in New York. That might have been another reason for marrying him. Had he been heading to Louisiana, for example, it wouldn't have seemed such a good proposition. Hey.

You must think I'm a calculating sort of person, but you know, at the time I didn't realise all that. Sorry, I don't usually talk about myself so much. It's a relief to meet someone who I know isn't going to lecture me about … she searched for the right word… about my choices.

—You're right. I get a bit of that myself.

— Plaisance told me a bit about you. Your wife. Sorry. And a son?

Marius nodded.

— Dzigi. That's probably all she knows about me.

— According to her, you're not good enough for me!

— She's probably right. All she ever sees me doing is drinking beer and eating kelewele.

They were laughing when two things happened.

The waiter put a steaming pizza in the middle of the table. The cheese was still bubbling and mounds of minced ham and salami just managed to keep afloat.

At the same time a group of four or five people came past their table. They were laughing and excited in a way that spoke of an afternoon drinking. The men were European and the two women were Lola and Dora.

They passed by, and Marius pretended not to see them, but then he saw Afua looking behind him. He felt an over friendly hand on his shoulder and looked up at Lola.

— If it's not Sam the music man, she said.

Marius had always thought that wanting the earth to swallow you was an exaggeration. Now he knew it was a cliché for a reason.

— Lola, was all he managed to say.

— Don't worry. I know when I'm not wanted. Lola laughed and gave Marius' shoulder a squeeze. See you round Sam.

Afua watched her saunter over to the others. Her dress was an interesting mix of purples and pinks, and the flounce around the skirt needed a figure like Lola's to carry it off. She turned back to Marius, who looked so uncomfortable that it made her laugh.

— Sam! Music man! What's that about?

Marius looked behind him. Lola and her friends were sitting at the table directly behind them and he couldn't say anything that wouldn't be overheard. He'd had a bad feeling about the way he'd got information from Lola and he'd been right. Nothing felt good about the situation. What would Afua think of him if he told her the whole story? But what would she think if he didn't explain? He could make up something. Or just say nothing. But he didn't want to start things off like that.

— It's a bit complicated, he said finally, and flinched at the cynical look on Afua's face. I can't talk about it with them sitting so close. How about we eat this pizza and then go to a place where I can talk.

He watched Afua's face as she thought about it. She wasn't laughing now and she was looking at him as if she was trying to see into his mind. Then she shook her head.

— It's not what you think, he said, and realised how pathetic it sounded.

Afua tried to sound light and breezy.

— Why would it bother me who you go out with? Or what they call you?

But even to her own ears it sounded unconvincing.

— Look, Marius said. Do you like jazz? I have a friend who owns a jazz bar not too far from here.

Suddenly Afua just wanted to be back in her own place. But she loved jazz. In New York there had been plenty of it, and she'd been searching for the local jazz scene since she'd been back. On the other hand, all she had wanted was some good company and a drink after a day's work, and now it was getting complicated. She weighed up the effort of going to another place and getting more involved, against the prospect of listening to some music at home. The jazz bar won out.

— Okay. I'll give it a go. But let's eat this pizza while it's hot. I'm starving.

Marius didn't even try to hide his relief.

— Thanks, he said, and picked up a slice of pizza. The cheese stretched like elastic and wrapped itself around his chin.

The night had taken on the velvet softness of the tropics and the air was a perfect blood temperature. Afua was the one who suggested they walk, and that was perfect for Marius. He knew his way around the back streets pretty well in this area, and there was an occasional streetlight that helped, not like some other parts of Lomé where the streets were so dark you could hardly see your hand in front of you.

Once Marius found a way to start, it was easy enough to tell Afua why he'd taken on the persona of Sam.

It took over half and hour, and by the time they got to Le Jazz Spot Afua was trying to understand how Marius had got so caught up in what seemed like an improbable but very sinister situation.

Tuesday was a quiet night. There were probably no more than a dozen or so people drinking at the tables in the friendly darkness of the garden, and a couple more were sitting at the well lit bar. One of them was Mibou.

As Marius led Afua along the path lit by soft ground lights, he could see Akosua say something to Mibou, who turned round and gave them his trademark smile. A flute piece that Marius didn't recognise was playing over the loudspeaker and Marius could feel the tension leaving him.

— Nice music. Who's the artist? I don't recognise it. By the way Mibou, meet Afua.

Mibou greeted her and held her hand for a few seconds while he explained.

— It's Hervey. He sent me his new CD. Not bad hey?

— Who's Hervey? Afua asked.

— He's a French guy, a friend of Mibou, Marius explained. He comes here on holidays and plays with Mibou and the others. You'll have to come and hear him next time he's in town.

— Try and keep me away! This is exactly the sort of place I dreamed about in New York. I could remember places like this, but the ones I went to in the old days have all closed down.

Mibou gave an excited shout.

— New York! You've been living in Charlie Parker land?

He sat them down at the table in front of the bar and ordered beers all round. Then he quizzed Afua about the jazz she'd listened to in New York, exclaiming at all the familiar names — Michael Brecker, Roy Hargroves,

Wynton Marsalis – as excited as if he was going there himself.

Hervey's album ended and Afua turned to Mibou.

— Marius tells me you're quite a musician. How about playing something.

Nothing could have pleased Mibou more. Playing was like breathing.

— Why not? What would you like? Sax? Guitar?

— You choose.

Mibou drained the last of his beer and went across to the storeroom behind the palava hut where he kept his instruments. As he walked back to the table he draped a lanyard around his neck and attached his old Selmer to it. Then he sat back down, licked the reed and started playing.

At first Afua couldn't make out the tune. There were riffs and chords and references to bits of tunes she recognised, then suddenly the melody resolved into New York, New York and she laughed.

— Perfect.

Marius relaxed into the night and the music. Afua was looking at Mibou, totally absorbed in the music, her eyes shining, and Marius hoped it was just the music. Mibou himself was barely conscious of it, but lots of women seemed to fall for him. What they didn't know was that Mibou's only two loves were music and Francoise, and Marius, like Mibou, still hoped that she'd come back to live here.

But there was no point thinking about all that, and Marius sipped happily on his beer and lost himself in the music.

27

Tuesday 5 April

Dave Gordon scraped the gravy and mashed potatoes onto his fork and put it in his mouth. Then he rested the cutlery on his plate while he chewed this last mouthful. Once finished, he re-arranged the knife and fork so they lay together, the tines of the fork facing up, the blade of the knife just touching the fork, so the plate was dissected exactly in two.

Only then did he allow himself to pick up his phone from the table and check for messages. Odd that Alabi hadn't got back to him. Flat battery? Out of range? No point worrying about it. But the boy had better watch himself. He pushed the phone away from him in disgust and leant back in his chair, his hands behind his head. Alabi was starting to get boring; maybe it was time to move on. He was useful though – no doubt about that. Or was that in the past tense now that Ash was out of the way?

Dave smiled to himself. It felt good, having the school to himself. Maybe he should do something to celebrate. A pool party for the teachers? Why not? Even those language teachers would be eating out of his hand. Invite a few parents as well, get Lola to do her thing.

Lola. What was she up to? He unclasped his hands and folded his arms, staring at the framed hunting scene on the wall opposite, but not seeing it. She was freaking him out. All she had to do was to act like his girlfriend – or partner, as people wanted to call her. Turn up at a few school things looking good, not act like a slut. Jesus. How hard could it be? You'd think she'd be grateful.

But now she'd started asking for more money. Not so much that it was a big thing, but it seemed like a bit more each time. And she was always out somewhere. She said she was discreet, but why should he believe her? The creepy thing was the way she was acting, as if she had something over him. Not that she said anything directly, but he could tell, he could see it in her eyes, as if she was daring him to say "no" to the money. Then what? Blackmail? Is that what it was all about?

Well she'd find out the hard way if she thought he was easily frightened. Neither of them seemed to realise — not Alabi and not Lola — that his word would always count more than theirs. No. It was Lola who should be worried, and if it got too bad, he'd think of something to do with her. There were plenty of choices. No one at the school would take much notice if she just disappeared one day — they'd believe whatever he said. Poor Lola, her sister died and she had to go back to Nigeria and look after her children. So sad! Despite himself he half laughed at the thought of it.

He pushed back his chair and stood up, then clapped his hands.

— Franck!

The door on his left opened almost immediately and Franck stepped through as if he'd been waiting on the other side.

— Take this away. And bring me the bottle of Glenfiddich, some ice and a tumbler. Not the tall one, you understand. The short one. I'll be out by the pool.

He walked through the living room and up to the far end of the swimming pool, then settled back into one of the white cane armchairs.

The sliding door from the house opened and Dave turned and watched Franck carry a laden tray across the lawn, so upright he almost seemed to be leaning back. He put it on the glass table and stood there waiting while Dave checked it; a half full bottle of Glenfiddich, a square crystal tumbler, an ice bucket, and a pair of silver tongs. For once it was what he'd asked for. Franck looked on, expressionless, and only started back inside when Dave gave him the nod.

He poured half a glass of whisky, added three ice cubes, then sat back in the chair and took a satisfied sip. With the extra money coming in maybe he could get some work done around the pool. A bit of landscaping – rocks, ferns, a waterfall – something to give it a more tropical look.

Thinking of the money, he probably should be getting it into the bank soon. Put the whole lot in, or keep a bit more aside? If there was an easy answer to that, it would be in the bank already. No point asking Sergei for a bigger cut – that hadn't gone down too well. But skimming a bit of cash…. Last time it worked and that was no surprise. With all that money coming in, was Sergei really going to keep track of it down to the last dollar? A bit risky though. Maybe best to keep his nose clean for now. If the fighting in the Ivory Coast kept going – and who was going to stop it? – Sergei would be running plenty more arms. More arms, more money. The kickback he gave to that bank clerk was nothing much, and in a couple of years he could be a millionaire. Dave smiled to himself, took a sip of the whisky, and stretched out his legs.

A millionaire. He'd never doubted he'd get rich somehow, it was just a matter of taking opportunities when they came up. Not everyone could have done what he did; all that planning, the sucking up to people, the acting. He should be on the stage! A few more years working things here and he could be on the Mediterranean somewhere, big mansion, garden going down to the water, and a private beachfront. Some Greek boys. Or maybe Spanish….

But first there was more organising to be done. Better give that bank clerk a call and line up an appointment. What was his name? K something. Kobi? Kofi? He took his phone out of his top pocket and went through the contact list. Kojo. That was it. He selected the number and listened. All he got was a woman's voice talking in French – god knew what she was saying. What was the use having these mobiles if no one answered them! He couldn't just turn up at the bank with all that money.

While he had the phone out he checked for messages and then tried Alabi's number again. Still no answer. He reminded himself of all the things that went wrong with the phones here and thought about next weekend. He was going to Lagos no matter what. If it hadn't been for Sergei insisting on the Sunday meet up, he could have gone over last Friday. Had some fun with Alabi, done a few lines, got away from this boring place.

Dave picked up his glass and shook it gently so the ice cubes clinked together and mixed with the whisky. He liked that, the tinkle of the ice; it was the sound of the old empire. It might be long gone now, but you only had to look around at people like himself still making good money out of this place. All he had to do was to take things slowly, plan carefully and think of the long term. He held the glass up so the late afternoon light turned the whisky a deep amber. Almost the colour of that local brandy George kept raving about.

George Barnes! A pulse started on the side of his head and the mood was gone. Why was there always something else to do? Someone else causing problems? And that fool Mensah. Dave put his glass down and rubbed his temples slowly with a circular movement until he felt calmer. How could Mensah have let those men into the house?

It was odd. No doubt about that. Now he had time to think about it, maybe it was too odd. Freaky. Could Mensah be lying? It was true he'd been locked in the bedroom; Dave had seen that for himself. Mensah claimed that armed men forced him in there, but Dave only had his word for that. Was he was working with them? They could have locked him in to make it look as if he'd tried to stop them.

213

But why would he do that? Dave couldn't think of a reason. He'd promoted Mensah because he knew they had something in common. Mensah only cared about two things: his position and the power and money he got from it. Those two things depended on doing whatever Dave asked him to, no questions asked. That made him if not trustworthy, at least predictable.

There were definitely two men at George's house, that was a fact. That useless security guard had described them and their car. But who were they? That was what he had to find out now.

Yes, he'd find out. But there was no point worrying about it. In fact, there was nothing to worry about, just things to do. He'd made sure he cleaned everything up before he left George's place, and what could possibly be suspicious about taking some palm nut soup to a sick friend? No, it was a damn good plan, though if he did it again, there were one or two things he might change.

George was alive so he must have been treated for an overdose. Simple as that. The kindest thing to do was to ship him back to the UK, courtesy of Bupa, and no questions asked. George could talk as much as he liked – and so could anyone else for that matter – but no one was going to believe him. Not after his odd behaviour in the past few months.

And at least he knew where George was now. Some local place with a stuck up name. No point even thinking about trying to get to him there – he'd stick out like a dead fish….

But then it didn't have to be him. What about the super efficient Adele? She'd love it. Always wanting to help someone. Tomorrow first thing he'd get her on to it.

Dave smiled to himself. One less thing to worry about. But as for those men – no way he was going to let them get away with it. No way at all.

It almost looked like they'd gone to help George, as if they knew what had happened, but it hardly seemed possible. How could they know? There'd been no ransom demands or anything like that. No question that George had been unconscious when he'd left the house last night. With the amount of heroin in that soup there was no way he should have come round. Not without assistance, that is.

It didn't make sense. And what was this African connection? As far as he knew, Gloria was George's only black 'friend'. But Dave had seen her pack up and leave the house before he did. It was almost obscene the way she was so happy to take the money and get out of Lomé with that cook.

The colour was suddenly sucked out of the sky and garden lights lit the dusk. Dave got up and went into the storeroom and took a packet of mosquito coils and some matches off the shelf. Then he went back to his chair, pulled out the metal frame, inserted a coil, lit it and put it on the ground next to the table. The smell was disgusting but in all these years he'd never had malaria. He sat back in the cane chair and took a sip from the almost empty glass.

There was that man who'd been there on Saturday night. Playing chess seemed harmless enough. But it was after that when Gloria said how upset George had been, and that he kept talking about how he could have saved his friend Ash.

There had to be a connection. George was doing well just to push a chess piece around the board, so someone must have put those ideas into his head. Gloria had told him the name - something weird as usual. God. Why couldn't they have ordinary names?

Who could it be? Think. Who were George's friends? Someone from school? The only locals close to George were those men that worked in the office, but it was a stretch to imagine any of them playing chess. It must be someone else, someone who was snooping around George's place, giving him ideas. What if he was a friend of Ash's? Maybe that was it.

Dave felt he was getting closer and he pushed at his head with the fingers of both hands until it hurt.

Then it came to him. That black guy at the memorial service – the one who said he'd been in Lagos with Ash. The way he'd looked at him was creepy, as if he knew more than he was saying. What if that man was the same as the one who'd been at George's place on Saturday night, the one who was stirring up trouble? Maybe George had got in touch with him somehow. The thing was to find out.

And then to sort him out.

The fellow had said something about Ash giving him a lift to Lagos. Yes. And Ash hadn't even told him, was being all secretive. It was only when Jerro got back from Lagos that he'd found out. Of course, that's who would know. Forget about Mensah; Jerro was the one to ask. He was a lot more than a driver; he seemed to know everything that went on around the place. For a native he was pretty smart – always had the latest gossip. He'd know for sure.

Dave turned his back on the pool and walked back to the table. He felt the adrenaline surging the way it always did when he was working on what he liked to think of as his 'projects'. Identify the obstacles and find a way to remove them, that was the Dave method. Now that he had a plan he felt more alive, excited. He half whistled 'My Way' to himself and poured himself another whisky. Well done you, he thought. Then he sat down, picked up his phone, and called Jerro.

28

Wednesday 6 April

Marius woke up buzzing with energy. It felt early and when he picked up his watch from the bedside table and checked the time, sure enough, it wasn't even 6 o'clock yet. He dropped the watch on the table and lay on his back, his hands behind his head. What to do? No point trying to get back to sleep.

He felt fired up for the day – nothing to do with an early night. By the time he'd dropped Afua off it must have been after 01.00 am when he got back home. Interesting. When he thought back over the evening at Le Jazz Spot, apart from the music, it seemed as if all they did was laugh. Now he couldn't remember anything they'd been laughing at, but that wasn't the point.

What Marius did remember was what Afua had said as she gave his hand a squeeze then climbed out of the taxi. "You'll think of something, Marius. Follow your instincts. And look after yourself." He hoped she was right about his instincts – if only he had as much confidence in his sixth sense as everyone else seemed to have. Well if he didn't think of something soon, it would be too late.

Yesterday seemed more like a week than a day. First the drama with George, then meeting up with Sergei, and then Afua. Marius laughed at the thought of Lola appearing out of nowhere at the pizzeria. Not that it had been funny at the time; it was like something out of a Nigerian drama. Classic farce. Thank god it hadn't ended badly. The truth was it had been fun and he suddenly realised what the buzzy feeling was. He felt happy.

Meeting up with Sergei like that was part of it. When Selina was alive Marius hadn't missed the edginess of his time in Moscow. Not too much, anyway. But since she'd died he had to admit his life had become – well – dull. It made him realise just how much he missed her, but he pushed that out of his mind.

Now that he'd shared his theories about Dave Gordon with Sergei and then with Afua, he felt less obsessive. More determined. Not like Monday night when he'd felt as if his head was filled with concrete.

He unclasped his hands and sat on the edge of the bed for a minute, looking around. Then he found what he was looking for and picked up a pair of boxer shorts that were on the end of the bed. He stood up, pulled them on, and walked over to the window.

A thick bank of clouds was streaked with orange and it looked like a good morning to be out. Still early enough to have a run before it got too hot. He pinched some flesh around his waist and was surprised to be able to take a good handful. A run was definitely what he needed. Curious, he went over and opened the wardrobe door with the mirror on it then looked at himself critically. He pulled his stomach in. That looked better, but the slight paunch was still there. Then he ran his hand over his almost shaven scalp. It felt good. Maybe Takashi was right, he decided, he looked younger with his hair like this. Sergei was the same age as him and he was all muscle. Seeming older than his age had appealed to him since his twenties, but now he wondered why. He went closer to the mirror and turned his head so the light caught it better; the grey was still there but much less obvious.

By the time he found his running gear and went downstairs, Eva was in the kitchen making coffee.

She looked up as he grabbed a glass out of the cabinet.

— Do you want a coffee?

— No thanks. I'll just have water.

He filled the glass with water and drank half of it. Eva took a sip of her coffee and looked at him, then raised an eyebrow and smiled.

— You're looking pleased with yourself. Good day yesterday?

Marius thought of the drama with George, the meeting with Sergei, dinner with Afua. He'd be here all morning if he tried to tell half of it.

— An interesting day, he said.

Eva put the coffee on the table and started laying out the lunch boxes.

— Tell me about it sometime. Enjoy your run.

Marius started off without much thought about what roads to take, and followed his nose along the streets that looked inviting. He didn't notice the time. Running was thinking time and his mind was going over yesterday. As he sifted through the events he started to plan his day. Alain might have some more tests back on George. And for that matter, how was George doing? Recovering? How long would it be before he was normal again? The school would need him to handle the money once Dave Gordon was gone. Eva could help with the legal stuff. Marius hadn't a clear idea how he was going to get Dave Gordon out of the school, but it was something that had to be done one way or another.

When Mimi had told him about the business card in Dave's wallet, Marius admitted to himself he'd thought the worst about Sergei. It wasn't so much the thought of arms dealing per se, but the corruption, the government contacts that made it all possible. What he realised now was that friendship was in a place outside all of that and Sergei had been a good friend. There were some values they had in common, despite their differences. Hard to put your finger on, but both of them hated bullies and, for want of a better word, injustice. Marius believed Sergei when he said he delivered the things people wanted faster and in riskier situations than anyone else. Mostly it was arms bought by governments and rebels alike, in defiance of embargoes. They'd get them from somewhere if not from Sergei.

Part of Marius acknowledged the rationalisation that went into that thought, but right now he didn't feel like scrutinizing it any closer. Sometimes the way he had to analyse everything was annoying, even to himself. The thing was that he liked having Sergei in town and the timing couldn't be better. Takashi and the others were great but there was the constant problem of putting them in danger. No need to worry about that with Sergei – if anyone could handle himself, he could. He had training, experience, toughness.

Marius crossed a half empty four lane road then noticed that he'd already come as far as the Caisse. In this residential enclave the streets were laid out in a grid and lined with plane trees. Behind those were whitewashed walls and neatly maintained grounds and houses. He looked at his watch. 6.45. He'd been running for thirty minutes. By the time he got back home, the others would be leaving. Undecided, he stopped for a minute and was glad of the break. What to do? If he turned back now he might just make it home in time to say goodbye to Dzigi. What would be the point in that? He was here now. He may as well do a circuit then head back a different way. Dzigi would forget about it once he was at school.

Marius got back into his stride again and thought about Dzigi. What if people were right when they said that Dzigi needed a mother? What was wrong with an aunty? Eva didn't seem to mind; Dzigi was almost as much a son as a nephew. But of course it was never meant to be permanent. The first couple of years had been a blur and he'd just kept going like a robot, he realised now. It was hard to believe that it was now more than four years since Selina had died and when he thought about it, he and Eva had never really talked much about their arrangement. But if he was reading the signs right, Eva seemed to getting serious with this chap in Ghana, and good for her. Where did that leave him?

When he was a couple of blocks away from home his right ankle was feeling tight and he decided to walk the last stretch. He wiped the sweat off his face with the bottom of his T-shirt and crossed to the other side of the street and walked in the hard dirt under the shade of the trees. This end of the road was quiet as usual and the overgrown gardens in front of run-down old houses gave it a peaceful feel, as if time had stopped.

As he got closer to his own place, the roots of the trees were exposed and he moved back on to the bitumen. As he did, he noticed a car parked on the road opposite his driveway. It wasn't one he recognised. What was it doing there? Everyone who knew him parked their cars in the driveway, or even on the lawn sometimes.

Marius stopped to have a good look. The car was dark green and he could see what he always thought of as a peace sign on the back of it. A Mercedes then. And one that looked familiar.

Suddenly Marius felt exposed and he moved behind the trunk of the nearest tree.

There was no mistaking it. Of course, it was the Mercedes that he'd travelled to and from Lagos in. He recognised Jerro at the wheel and in the front passenger seat was a white man. The man's face was in profile because he was leaning forward and looking across the road towards the house. The headrest obscured the back part of his head but it was enough for Marius to recognise Dave Gordon.

29

Wednesday 6 April

Just as Marius spotted them, the Mercedes pulled back on to the road and in seconds it had turned left at the end of the street and was out of sight.

Marius watched it go then walked the short distance back to the house. He took his shoes off and shook the dirt off them, then let himself in through the laundry door. There was nothing that seemed out of place downstairs at least, but he felt different about the house, as if it had been compromised, and it wasn't until he'd checked out all the rooms upstairs that he relaxed a bit. He tossed down a glass of water and then decided it wasn't too early for a beer. The shower could wait.

With a bottle of Star and a glass in one hand, he used the other hand to lift open the glass doors to the patio, then sank into the old cane chair. He put the glass and bottle on the weathered glass topped table, filled the glass, drank most of it, filled it up again then settled back in the chair, ready for some hard thinking.

So Dave Gordon must have put two and two together, otherwise what would he be doing outside his house? No point wondering how he found out – the fact that Jerro had brought him here told its own story. Judging by the way they were so focused on the house, Marius felt pretty sure they hadn't seen him and at least that was something to be grateful for. On the downside,

Dave Gordon hadn't come here just to look at real estate.

What exactly might he have in mind? And who would he get to do it?

What about that friend of Philippe's? The antique dealer Marius had met a few times, bought one or two things from. Only last week a group of armed men had forced their way into the house and killed the dealer and his wife. Just like that. There was no investigation, it wasn't in the news. Philippe only heard about it when he called in to the shop.

But Dave Gordon wouldn't have those sort of contacts.

What he might have were contacts with the government. There were plenty of stories about the cozy relationship between the school and the president, and that could be disastrous. All Dave would have to do was to tip off the right person – probably with something obvious, like Marius dealing drugs to students – and he'd end up in jail like Mibou had. It was a common way of getting rid of enemies here – and in Ghana, for that matter. All you needed was a friend in the right place.

Getting spooked about things wasn't going to help, but two things were really clear. One was that no one should stay in the house until what he thought of as 'this thing' was sorted out. And the other part to it was that he was the one who had to sort it out.

The man had to be confronted, and soon. As soon as tonight! Having made the decision, Marius felt better. All he needed was a plan.

Marius took a few sips of his beer, but it was already warm and flat and he threw the rest of it onto the grass.

Okay, so inspiration wasn't going to come out of a bottle. He got up and walked across the patchy grass to the tall wooden totem, half-hidden now by low-hanging branches . The wood had gone silvery grey from age and weathering, but the blind eyes on the carved face were still just as compelling as when he'd first spotted it in Porto-Novo.

Marius joked about using the totem as his medium, but he thought it wouldn't do any harm to look there for some inspiration, and he was doing just that when he thought he heard someone moving in the trees that grew along the fence.

There was nothing to see from inside the garden, so he walked slowly over to the driveway, and down towards the road.

He was level with the garden wall when a man seemed to appear from nowhere.

Marius took a step back and was working out what to do when he realised who it was: the security guard from George's place.

— Sam?

The young man had dark skin and was wearing brown jeans and a green polo T-shirt. He had both hands on the zipper of his jeans, and he quickly finished pulling it up then glanced down nervously.

— Mr Marius. Sorry. I was waiting under the tree, then I needed to… then you came. Sorry.

Marius laughed and gave him a friendly slap on the shoulder.

— I hope you come in peace.

Sam nodded and Marius led the way back down the drive and through the front door. By the time they sat down in the living room – Sam with a glass of water, Marius with a beer – Marius had established that Sam was a cousin of Ato, the man with the wife who takes in ironing.

— What I don't understand, Marius said, is why you want to see me. If I remember, the last time we met I was in a bit of a hurry. Sorry. Nothing personal.

Marius let the worn old cushions on the couch take his full weight and sipped his beer, watching Sam, who was perched on the edge of the cane chair opposite him, the glass of water held with both hands resting on his knees. Marius hoped it wasn't the prelude to a request of some sort. Money? Work?

Finally, Sam found his tongue and he leaned forward even further, very young and earnest.

— Is Mr Barnes dead?

The blunt question surprised Marius.

— No. We got him to the hospital in time. He's still there, but they think he should recover.

Sam looked relieved. He drank some of the water and put the glass on the small wooden table that Marius had put next to his chair.

— What made you think he was dead?

Sam still looked nervous and awkward, so Marius encouraged him.

— It's okay. It might seem odd, seeing what I did, but you can trust me. I'm sure Ato must have told you that. Think about Mr Barnes' place. Maybe you noticed something?

Of course he noticed something, Marius thought. A house like George's would have a cook, house help, a security guard and at least one gardener. They would talk amongst themselves so they'd know everything that went on in the house. There would probably be a network of similar workers from other houses in the area, especially the ones in houses occupied by people who worked at the school. That's why at one point Marius had thought it would be worth having a chat with Sam. And now here he was. The thing was to get him talking. Marius tried a different tack.

— Was Mr Barnes a good boss, Sam?

Sam nodded.

— He's a nice man, Mr Barnes. Too kind. He was helping me with my accountancy course.

So George had been the one to get young Sam started on his accountancy. Good for him. Marius wasn't the only one who noticed how sharp Sam was.

— With study? Money?

— Both. Sometimes I asked him questions. He gave me what he called a study bonus to pay the fees. He didn't mind at all if I studied while I was working – he thought he didn't need a security guard. He used to say he felt safer here in Lomé than he did in England. But he didn't know about the bad things.

— And you couldn't tell him?

Sam looked unhappy and nodded again.

— Now I think I should have.

Marius fought against his impatience. Why was Sam so reluctant to talk when he'd obviously come here for more than an idle chat. Embarrassed, ashamed? Maybe a bit of both. Marius leaned forward and smiled at Sam.

— Look here Sam. I'm going to get you a nice cold beer. You can drink it or not, but I'll feel a lot better if there's one there ready if you want it. Don't get up – I'll be back in a second.

He laughed and thought Sam looked relieved as he passed him on the way into the kitchen.

Marius put the bottle of Star and a glass on the table next to Sam's water, and sat back down. He waited until Sam had poured some beer, then held up his own glass.

— Good luck to us both.

Sam raised his glass and smiled. He took a few mouthfuls of the beer and put his glass back on the table. For the first time since he'd arrived, he started to look less like a nervous school boy, and he leaned back in the chair.

— Where's a good place to start, do you think? Marius asked. How about with Gloria?

The beer had broken the ice and now Sam started to talk.

Yes. Trouble had started when Gloria moved into the house. Mr Barnes was different. Then there was Serge, the cook, who had seemed okay, a sort of friend. He changed too, and he and Gloria were 'doing things' when Mr Barnes was asleep. Every night! Serge told him that Gloria was putting stuff in Mr Barnes' food – drugs brought over from Lagos – and sometimes they tried them themselves. Serge said they were to make Mr Barnes crazy, and that he and Gloria added some stuff to make him sleep. Sometimes Mr Barnes remembered the bonus for the study. Sometimes he didn't.

Sam had started his shift at 10 o'clock on Monday night and things were weird. Mr Gordon had been there, and he gave Gloria and Serge money and told them to leave, right then and there, but not to tell Mr Barnes.

While Gloria and Serge were waiting for the car to pick them up they told Sam they were going to go to Accra to set up a restaurant there. When the car came he recognised Jerro and the green Mercedes. Nobody said exactly what, but everyone knew Jerro did things for Mr Gordon.

It was Serge who told Sam that Mr Barnes wasn't well. He'd seen Mr Gordon helping Mr Barnes up the hallway to his bedroom. Serge thought Mr Barnes looked drunk and he knew they'd had a lot to drink. Or Serge could remember that George had. He wasn't sure about Mr Gordon.

Sam had a bad feeling after Serge and Gloria left and some time in the early morning – maybe 4 or 5 – he let himself into the house. Just to look around, make sure things were okay. Sam could see Gloria and Serge had taken everything. Because of all the drugs they'd been giving Mr Barnes he thought something might have happened to him, so he went into his bedroom, but Mr Barnes was snoring and Sam thought he was just asleep.

Half choking from the heroin overdose more likely, Marius thought, but there was no point in telling Sam and making him feel worse.

It was creepy in the house with no one else around and Sam started to think that someone might be hiding. He lifted up the valance around the bed George was in and noticed something.

Sam picked up the grey canvas satchel he carried his books in and pulled out a dirty looking handsewn pouch, made of some old hessian bag. He brought it over to Marius, and sat on the couch next to him.

Sam prised open the pouch and pulled something so it was half out of the bag.

There was something altogether repellant about it and Marius had to force himself to lean close enough to make out what it was.

At first glance the skin the mamba had shed looked like a live snake. There were hollows where the eyes had been on either side of the flat head, and the mouth was gaping open, as if it were about to strike. The thing Marius thought was the tongue turned out to be a large nail. That explained why the pouch was heavier than he'd expected. Sam pulled the snakeskin out a bit more and Marius could see that the scaly, dry skin was stuffed with smaller nails.

Marius watched Sam poke the snake head back into the pouch. He was impressed. There weren't many people around here who would touch that thing; they'd be much too worried that the bad juju would transfer to them.

— Well done Sam. You say you found this under George's bed?

Sam got up off the couch, went back to his chair and picked up his beer. He seemed to have shed the last bit of awkwardness the way the snake had shed its skin.

— At first I thought it was a dead rat and I should get rid of it, so I got a broom and dustpan and pulled it out. When I realised what it was I almost left it there, but then I thought what if….

Sam's voice trailed off and Marius helped him.

— What if Mr Barnes died?

Sam nodded.

—Something like that. I don't really believe in that stuff… but you hear stories.

Marius had heard plenty himself.

— I would have done the same – no point taking chances. So what do we do now? Any ideas?

There was a lurking feeling of menace about the thing, and despite what his logic told him, Marius definitely didn't want it in his house, especially not now.

Sam glanced down at the canvas bag and he looked just as keen as Marius to get rid of it.

— Well, one of my cousins is at Akodessewa.

— The fetish market? Do you think he could help?

Sam nodded.

— He's training to be a *féticheur*. To help people – not the other thing.

— Then he's our man for the job. My only question then is how soon can you see him?

30

Wednesday 6 April

Marius gave Sam some money for a taxi and watched him walking down the drive. Looking at the grey canvas bag slung over Sam's shoulder you'd never guess what was inside. It was probably nothing – just a dead snake and some nails – but Marius knew he'd feel a lot better when Sam had handed it over to his cousin.

If only Jojo had been here he could have sent Sam out to Akodessewa with him, but today of all days, Jojo had gone back up to Kpalimé for a couple of days – something to do with sorting things out after his uncle's death. And to see his family of course. Not the best time for Jojo to have time off, but at least he'd be safe up there. One less person to worry about.

Next thing on his list was to call in and see how George was getting on.

It was already past 11.00 am by the time Marius turned into the entrance to the Clinique d'Abovey and followed the signs to the visitor's car park. The Toyota shook and made a dying noise as he switched the engine off and pulled on the handbrake. His was the only car in the car park but Alain had said not to bother about visiting hours.

The harmless looking clouds of the early morning had gathered into a thick, dark mass. As he closed the door of the car it was as if those clouds had been holding back a damn, and water seemed to fall from the sky, smashing on to the roof of the car and throwing up little piles of gravel. Marius ran around the building and into the shelter of the ambulance drop off point. His silk top was clinging to him and he pulled it off his skin and shook it out, then pushed the water off his head and face.

At the reception desk he was put through to Alain, who asked him to wait for a few minutes. The row of chairs looked comfortable enough, but Marius chose to walk around, flapping his shirt, and by the time Alain arrived it was almost dry.

He was wearing green scrubs and explained to Marius as he clicked off from the handshake:

— I've just been checking on some patients. I like to wear this. He pointed to the loose green cotton top and matching pants. If I turn up in a suit they go all formal on me and clam up. You might remember my mantra: keep the patient talking.

Marius did remember. They'd discussed it a lot in Moscow and many times since then.

— How could I forget? Interesting that a green pyjama top does the trick.

Alain laughed.

— You could write a sociology thesis on that! Anyway, come and see the patient. Your timing is perfect – I just had some results delivered a few minutes ago. I haven't had a chance to look at them yet, so let's go past my office and I'll take them up to the room.

— How's George?

Alain paused with one hand on the door of his office and Marius didn't know what to make of the look on his face.

— Well, it was definitely a heroin overdose, that much we know, and he's recovered pretty well from that. But there's something that's still not right with him and I can't make out what it is. Hang on a minute.

Alain went over to his desk, picked up a manila envelope, then came back out and closed the door behind him.

— Lift or stairs?

— Stairs.

Marius followed Alain along the corridor and up a polished timber staircase. He spoke to Alain's back as they climbed the stairs.

— What's the recovery like from a heroin overdose?

Alain looked back at him.

— Well, you saw Dr da Silva giving him an injection of naloxone. Apparently your friend didn't come round after the first shot, so he kept him breathing, gave him a couple more grams and ten minutes later he was breathing by himself.

— How long before he's back to normal?

— Normally he should recover in a few days. It was a near thing though. Another minute or two and he would have died. By the time you got him here his breathing had stopped and his heart was pumping at a crazy rate to try to keep the oxygen going. You saved his life.

— You seem to be saying that things aren't normal.

— Yes and no. You'll see for yourself.

The hallway branched off in two directions and Alain turned to the right. Marius followed him to the end of a wide corridor and they went down a couple of stairs to a small reception area with a grey marble floor and two healthy looking palms in timber palm stands.

Alain gestured towards them.

— Not bad, hey? They were here when I bought the place. I'm told they belonged to the original owner. The stands, that is.

Alain knocked on the door between the two palms.

— It's Dr Amevor and Marius.

There was the rattle of a safety chain being slipped across and George opened the door. He was wearing blue striped cotton pyjamas and a loose brown robe tied around the waist that did nothing to allay fears about his health.

Alain and Marius went into the room and George locked the door behind them, pulled the chain across, then came up to Marius and shook his hand.

— Dr. Amevor tells me you saved my life. Can't thank you enough.

Marius waved his free hand.

— I was just lucky to get there in time. How are you feeling?

George shook his head as if he didn't want to talk about it and led them over to a small lounge area.

The room was airy, with high ceilings and two long windows looking onto the side garden. The queen-size bed only took up half the space. There was a closed door on the far side of the room that Marius guessed was the ensuite, and a kitchenette in an alcove to the right of that.

George sat in one of the padded leather chairs and Marius took the chair opposite him.

George was holding himself straight in the military way he had, but as Marius watched him sit down in the chair opposite, he could see what an effort it was. His face had lost its usual healthy tan and the pallid skin and sagging cheeks made him look ten years older. Marius wasn't sure if he was succumbing to the power of suggestion, but he found himself thinking that there was something haunted about his eyes.

— I say, it's all a bit cloak and dagger isn't it? George said suddenly.

— Yes. It must seem like that to you. What can you remember, George?

Alain had slit open the manila envelope with a knife from the drawer in the kitchenette and now he came and sat down in the chair next to Marius. He'd been glancing through the laboratory reports and he put them on the round wooden coffee table that filled the space between the chairs.

Before George could answer Marius' question, Alain leaned back in his chair and said almost as if he was talking to himself:

— Interesting.

— What do they show? Marius asked.

Alain looked at George, seemed undecided as to what to say, then he leaned forward and picked up the reports again.

— According to these lab reports, as well as heroin, your samples show significant amounts of a type of cannabis, something that goes by the name of yellow honey.

Marius and George both looked blank so Alain explained:

— It's a type of ganja, but much stronger than your regular marijuana. Most of it comes from Lagos —

homemade stuff. I've seen it cause a complete brain meltdown on one unfortunate soul.

Alain took the top sheet off and looked more carefully at the next page.

— The amount of heroin still in your system is more than I'd expect from a single dose, even one that was meant to kill you. Sometimes they cut the ganja with heroin – it could be that.

George shook his head and seemed to be struggling to take it in.

— I don't understand.

Alain looked at the next sheet.

—There's alcohol showing up as well. That was a strong mix.

Marius wasn't sure if Alain was deliberately provoking George, trying to get at the truth perhaps, but his next question, although he asked it gently enough, took him by surprise.

— When did this drug thing start, George?

George didn't seem to have the energy to do more than shake his head in disbelief so Marius helped him.

— Can you think about how they got into your system, George? Could someone have put things in your food, for example?

Alain picked up the sheets of paper, folded them and put them back in the manila envelope, then stood up.

— I'm sorry, but I've got a lot to do. Keep up the vitamins and rest.

He walked over and opened the door and Marius followed him and stepped outside so he could talk without George overhearing. He went straight to the point, talking in a low murmur.

— Before you go, Alain. It's probably nothing, but just before I came here the security guard from George's place showed me a nasty looking bit of juju junk. He found it under George's bed.

Alain sighed.

— I was wondering about that dead sort of look that George has. His eyes. I've seen it before. There's only so much we can do to help that side of things. It's up to George to pull himself out of it. See if you can get him talking. Right now he looks as if just wants to give up.

Marius went back inside and locked the door. George had sunk back in his chair with his eyes closed and Marius sat down quietly opposite him. He could see what Alain was talking about. There was something defeated in George's manner.

Keep him talking, Alain had said, but the only thing Marius could think to say was to ask him about Monday night. Should he do that? Or would it make things worse. Marius looked around the room for inspiration and saw the electric kettle in the kitchenette.

— I'll tell you what, he said, I'll make us a cup of tea.

Marius went across to the kitchenette and looked for some tea bags while the kettle boiled. He was taking down a bowl of sugar when he saw that George had come over and was leaning against the wall, watching him. There were a few questions that Marius wanted to ask and now was as good time as any.

— Who was it George? Who gave you that heroin? Can you remember anything?

Making the effort to talk seemed almost too much for George and he sighed deeply before he answered.

— Dave Gordon was there on Monday night. He came round with some of Lola's palm nut soup.

— Did you eat it or keep it for later?

— We ate it. You know, after a few drinks. I remember I opened a couple of bottles of red.

— Out of the same bowl? Did you all eat out of the same bowl?

George thought for a minute then shook his head.

— No. Separate bowls. I thought how nice it was for Lola to do that.

Marius dipped the tea bags in the boiling water in the cups, dropped one of them into the water, then burnt his hands pulling it out. He dumped the sodden tea bags into the plastic flip-top bin, stirred a couple of teaspoons of sugar into each cup and carried them back to the lounge area. George followed him and collapsed back into the chair.

— I remember the soup. It tasted really good, you know. And you think he.... Was that where the heroin came from?

George looked at Marius, who was shaking his head, and added:

— He was being so nice.

What was there to say to that? Of course he was being nice. Dave Gordon was good at being nice... when it suited him.

— Can you remember anything else George? Like what you talked about?

George put his mug of tea back on the table and slumped further down in the armchair so his head rested against the leather back. He closed his eyes and Marius worried that he might be going into some sort of stupor, but then suddenly he sat up again.

— Gloria. She was laughing and laughing. Does Gloria know where I am?

Marius leaned forward, his elbows on the armrests. There wasn't any easy way to break the news.

— George, Gloria has gone. When Jojo and I took you out of the house it was as if she'd never been there. Everything was gone. The cook was gone too. You were alone in the house. There was just a rather nasty man called Mensah who seemed to have been told to keep people out.

For the first time that morning George started to look more alive. He picked up his tea and took a few sips then looked at Marius as he put the cup down.

— Gone? You're sure.

— Completely.

— With Serge?

— If that's the name of your cook, then yes.

George nodded to himself then looked at Marius as if he was about to say something, then stopped.

It wasn't hard for Marius to read between the lines.

— You knew about them?

George leaned back again, and turned his head away as if he'd rather not think about it.

— It was hard not to notice.

But then quite suddenly he pulled himself up straight and Marius noticed a difference as if George had made up his mind about something. Whether it was willpower, or some physical improvement wasn't clear, but a change it was.

— You know Marius, George went on, I don't know how to explain it, but just then I had this feeling as if something of my old self was coming back. I'm sure now I'm going to get better. You can't imagine what a relief that is – that it's drugs and not some horrible mental thing.

— And, speaking of drugs, how do you think they got into your system? Let's say they were in your food, when could that have happened?

George took a sip of his tea as if to fortify himself.

— Well, let's see. Breakfast. I make that myself. Lunch. I always used to have that in the dining hall at the school, but since Gloria moved in, she insists that she makes lunch for me.

George realised what he'd said and dropped his head on his hands and shook it from side to side. Marius could just hear something like "what an idiot".

—Did you notice a pattern? For example, did you always eat the same sort of food? Or would you – I don't know – have a sandwich sometimes?

— It was always something hot and spicy. Let me see: light goat soup, ground nut soup, that sort of thing. She said she was educating me about African cooking.

— So the sort of food that you wouldn't notice if something was added.

— There was always plenty of chili. I used to joke about getting addicted to it and she said…

George didn't finish the sentence and gave a rueful smile.

Marius finished the sentence for him.

— She said chili was addictive, and in a way it is, but it was the ganja, probably with a bit of heroin and who knows what else that you were getting addicted to.

George looked at him and nodded.

— I couldn't work out what was happening and most of the time I didn't care. But then I'd get these anxiety attacks and I was sure I had a brain tumour or something. It was as if my personality had been taken over. Of course I couldn't say anything to Gloria and just kept going somehow.

— And that's when Dave Gordon started to tell Ash and others that you had dementia and were making mistakes with the orders. I don't know if you're ready for this George, but I think you should know. It was Dave's so-called girlfriend, Lola, who 'found' Gloria for you. He masterminded the whole thing.

George had been about to take a sip of the last of his tea, but he put the cup back down, pushed himself out of the chair and walked over to the window that looked out over the garden. There was a pinging noise and Marius pulled his phone out and checked the messages. Sam. 'Package taken care of'. So that side show was finished at least. He was putting his phone away when George came and sat back down and started talking again.

— I did think it was odd when she – well, she sort of picked me up. It was at the Club Tropicana, so I guess I thought that made it okay. And it was fun, you know. At first, anyway.

Marius was relieved to see some of the colour back in George's face, but he felt that he'd done as much talking as was good for one day.

— I've got to go now George. There's some unfinished business with Dave Gordon that I have to attend to.

He remembered to take the cups back to the sink and gave them a quick rinse. George got up as well and waited for him.

— But what about Dave? I mean, if he really tried to…. Shouldn't we tell someone? The police?

Marius wished it were so easy.

— There's nothing at the house George. Not a single thing. No dirty bowls, no signs of Gloria being there. Nothing. It would be Dave Gordon's word against ours.

George unlocked the door and held it open for Marius.

— I see what you mean, but you know I don't really feel safe. What's going to happen when I leave here? And what about you?

Marius stepped through the doorway into the corridor and turned to face George.

— I have some ideas about how I can get Dave Gordon out of the school and away from Lomé. It's not enough, but it's better than nothing.

— Well, if there's anything I can do….

— Thanks George. Right now, the main thing is to get you better and keep you safe.

George shook Marius' hand then held it in a strong grip while he talked.

— Thanks again Marius. And perhaps it's my turn to say look after yourself.

Marius opened the door and stepped out into the hallway.

— I'll do my best. And lock that door behind you.

31

Wednesday 6 April

As Marius was arriving at the Clinique d'Abovey, Mimi was watching students file out the door of her classroom. None of them wanted the extra help she'd offered, (that was a relief), so she cleaned the blackboard, picked up a pile of books to mark, and headed back to the staff room.

She crossed the foyer, and stopped to chat to the art teacher who was pinning up some new paintings on the display boards. They looked at them together and Mike pointed out different things, explaining what the students had been trying to do. Mimi was absorbed in what he was saying and she jumped when she heard a voice behind her.

— Can I interrupt?

She turned around and hoped the panic she felt when she saw Dave Gordon didn't show on her face.

— No. I mean yes. Mike was just telling me about these paintings. They're good, aren't they?

Dave Gordon looked at the paintings without really seeing them but he nodded.

—Very nice. Well done Mike. And to Mimi. When you've finished, could you come and see me in my office? Maybe sensing the panicky feeling she was trying to cover up, he added. Don't worry, you're not in trouble. Then he smiled, the nice, affable, Dave smile.

Mimi gave what passed as a laugh.

— That's a relief. I can come now. See you later Mike.

As she followed Dave across to his office, it reminded her of Monday morning, and his eyes looking down at her. She half expected him to take out his wallet and confront her. There was no way he could know she'd been looking in his desk, but the guilty feeling made her anxious. What it must be about, she told herself, was the letter she'd left there, and she was ready to talk about that.

The solid teak desk looked exactly as it had on Monday; the few items on it squared and tidy. Dave sat in the adjustable leather chair behind the desk and he waved a hand at the two straight-backed chairs in front of him.

— Take a seat.

Mimi felt as if the chair was designed to make whoever sat in it feel uncomfortable. With the hard seat and straight back, the only way to sit comfortably was an awkward 'sitting up straight' posture that made her feel even more on edge. She watched as he opened the top drawer on the right. She knew what was in there; all those books of empty order forms and the map. But he produced a manila envelope and flourished it like a conjuror, then put it on the desk in front of Mimi.

— Your reference, he said. No need to open it now.

Mimi put it on top of the books she was holding on her lap and wondered if it would be of any use, given what little he knew about her.

— Thank you.

She tried to seem natural, but now that she knew things about Dave Gordon she felt as if he must be able to notice the difference. Not that she'd ever been relaxed with Dave. He was so different from Ash, who seemed to enjoy chatting to her about her classes. She took a firmer grip of the awkward pile of books on her lap and began to stand up.

Dave Gordon gave what Mimi took to be an official smile. There was no friendliness, no warmth in his eyes.

— You're welcome. Tell me, have you had any thoughts about what you'll do when you leave here?

Mimi sat back down again and rearranged the books.

— Not really.

It was the truth. The bit she didn't tell him was that she was pinning her hopes on Marius finding a way to get Dave Gordon himself out of the school.

— Terrible about the money business. Mr Lawrence was a great educator, but sadly, not a good economist. Maybe you have some friends who could help you find some work. What about that fellow you introduced me to at the memorial service? Marius I think it was.

All of Mimi's senses went on to red alert.

She was the only one at the school who knew what Marius had done yesterday morning, and the only one who knew where George Barnes was. Is that what Dave was going to ask her? Could that be the reason for Dave Gordon's sudden interest in Marius? Well, there was no point in denying that she knew him.

— Yes. That was Marius. He's a friend of my father's.

God. Now she was involving Takashi!

Dave Gordon rested his elbows on the desk and leaned forward. His unusual green eyes were staring at her intently as if he'd caught her out in a lie. Mimi felt her face flush and she was sure he must have noticed it.

— And a friend of Mr Lawrence too, I suppose. I think he said something about going on that ill-fated trip to Lagos with him.

I have to do better than this, Mimi thought. I've got to stop looking awkward and guilty. The books were half falling out of the pile on her lap, so she picked them up and put them on the desk in front of where she was sitting.

— Mind if I dump these here for a minute? Then she leaned back, smoothed the creases in her skirt, and crossed her legs, feeling more at ease. But to answer your question, I imagine that Mr Lawrence knew Marius through jazz. My dad's a big jazz fan too. She looked at Dave and saw his lack of interest. I guess that's not your thing.

Dave fell short of the smile he was aiming for.

— No, not my thing. Poor Mr Lawrence. If only we knew more about who killed him. You know I've been thinking that your friend – Marius is it? – might be able to tell me more about it. He said something about being there just after it happened. You wouldn't have his phone number by any chance would you?

So this was what Dave had been aiming for. Instinct told her not to give him Marius' number. Dave sounded well meaning, really concerned even, but now she knew better than to take that at face value. On the other hand, she was hopeless at telling lies.

To give herself some time, she took her phone out of the little bag that was looped over her shoulder and switched it on, then started scrolling through the numbers.

— I don't think it's here, she said. But let me check.

Dave Gordon leaned back in his chair, his elbows on the arm-rests. He lifted one hand and waggled his fingers.

— Thanks.

Mimi scrolled all the way through her address book then switched the phone off and put it in her bag and snapped the clip shut.

— Sorry. I don't have it.

Dave looked as if he didn't believe her, and for a second Mimi thought he was going to ask if he could check for himself.

— I guess your father would have it.

Mimi had to agree. She smiled as if she hadn't thought of it.

— Yes, of course. I'll ask him.

She looked at her watch and then stood up and picked up her books off the desk.

— Sorry, I'll have to run. I have a class in five minutes.

Dave stood up and walked around the desk as Mimi pushed the pile of books under one arm and walked towards the door. Her back was to him and she had the crazy thought that he was going to snatch her phone out of her bag. Almost as bad, he asked another question she wasn't expecting.

— I suppose you know what happened to George?

Mimi could feel her heart beating faster, and it seemed, louder. She clutched the books more tightly and turned around to face Dave making her face as cute and innocent as she knew how.

— George? She managed to say. I haven't seen him around for a while. Is something wrong with him?

Dave shook his head and really did look concerned and sympathetic.

— Poor chap is much worse.

This was getting too confusing.

— I'm sorry to hear that, she mumbled, then turned her back on him again and hurried across the foyer to the staff room. She really did have a class in five minutes. That was true.

32

Lagos: Wednesday 6 April

Omowale sits in his car with the door open and listens to the radio. His parents' house is the other side of the road but he's parked here because there's some shade from the concrete skeleton of an unfinished house.

When his mother gets back from the bank he'll accept the beer she's sure to offer him and tell her more about the block of land she's helping him to buy. He knows she'll be happy that he's moving over to this side of town, and if she has time they can drive over and have a look at the block. It won't be until much later that his father will get home from his job with Eco Bank on Lagos Island. He's relieved his mother has been able to get the money for him without having to involve his father.

Thinking about the house he's going to build he looks over at his parents' place. There's a paved driveway that's plenty wide enough for two cars and he can see the carving on the front door they paid so much money for. Apart from that it's respectable, but too plain for his tastes.

On the radio Efi Abeni is doing her crime watch segment and he turns the volume up so he can hear better. Today she's talking to a woman who's been mugged by some men in a white Mazda. He's heard the same sort of thing before. The woman is telling Efi that she was driving back to her friend's place after getting some money out of the bank. She was planning to travel the next day so she had more money than usual. When she stopped on the road opposite her friend's house there was no one around. Then as she got out of the car and closed the door there was a white car that seemed to come from nowhere and almost ran over her feet. The next thing she knew they were driving off with her bag. In the bag were her passport, her ticket and her money. She sounds as if she's almost crying as she tells Efi what happened and he feels sorry for her and wonders if she's going to travel after all.

Efi asks her if she remembers anything about the car like the make or a number plate. The woman says she didn't notice the make of the car but she thought she saw part of the numberplate. It looked like CRY. She said it stuck in her mind. Efi says that's interesting, because the numberplate of the white Mazda wanted in connection with the murder of the British man in Ikoyi was LX704CRY.

Omowale opens the glove compartment and finds an old receipt and a pen that works, and writes the number down.

When he looks up his mother is back and she's pulling on to the right hand side of the driveway where she always parks, so there's room for his father's car. Omowale reaches back across the passenger seat and puts the paper and pencil back in the glove compartment. Then he switches the radio off and gets out of the car. When he looks across and waves to his mother she's standing next to her car with her big brown bag on her shoulder.

He waits to cross because a white car comes along the road and he thinks it must be one of the neighbours. The next thing he sees is the car turning into the driveway and he thinks they're going too close to his mother, that they're going to run over her. It's all so sudden he's frozen to the spot but then he starts to run across the road thinking he'll do something but having no idea what he might do. A man leans out from the back seat and grabs hold of his mother's bag then the car reverses out of the driveway and Omowale has to jump to one side so they don't hit him.

His mother is trying to scream but her throat sounds all blocked. She's saying 'Your money. They've taken your money.'

He knows that what he's just heard Efi talking about is happening right here, and this time it's the money for his land they've taken.

Without thinking it through, he's back in his car and chasing after the white Mazda. They're driving fast, but the roads around here are in a grid and they can't get a clear run. If he does catch up with them what can he do? Without some help he'll never get his money back. He's seen other people doing it, so he starts blowing the car horn, hoping someone might stop them.

The only way out of this estate is the road past the market that's the only thing around here until the new shops are built. People are crowded around the stalls and the traffic is bumper to bumper on both sides of the road. He keeps his hand on the horn and yells out thief and points ahead to the Mazda.

Some people stare at him but they don't do anything. Then a lorry pulls out in front of the white car and it looks to him as if the driver's going to force them to stop, but the Mazda turns on to the footpath and keeps going around the truck and back on to the road. A woman has been knocked into the gutter and a group of people are helping her up.

The lorry pulls off the road and Omowale keeps going, trying to catch up to the Mazda that has pulled ahead.

He knows the roads this side of the market because that's where his block of land is. The further they get away from the market the fewer the houses. It seems to him that they're headed for the link road that would meet up with Admiral Way and take them back into Ikoyi. Then he would be sure to lose them because there'd be too much traffic. Before they get to that road they have to go along the beach road for a few miles and maybe there will be a chance then. He hasn't thought about what he plans to do, he's just desperate to get his mother's money — his money — back.

He can see in his rear-view mirror a string of cars behind him. They're all blowing their horns and for the first time he starts to *wonder what it is that he's started. But it's too late to change his mind, and as the Mazda makes a sudden turn to the left on to a dirt road filled with potholes – a shortcut to the link road – he breaks sharply and follows them. He seems to be catching up while they go through the housing area, but the Mazda has an advantage after turning off and they're starting to pull ahead again.*

They're driving through an area marked out for development. The land is rough dirt and sand with some clumps of bushes scattered across it. Building has already started on some of the land but so far all that's there is clumsy piles of grey concrete blocks.

Suddenly he's got his foot flat on the brakes and he's waving his arm out the window to warn the cars behind him to stop. A truck piled high with some of those concrete blocks is backing right across the road, planning to dump the blocks on the heap that's already there.

The Mazda has pulled off the road to get around the back of the truck but there's a ditch on that side of the road and now the car has ploughed into the ditch then rolled over and is on its roof. The wheels are spinning in the air like the legs of a helpless beetle.

Now everyone is piling out of their cars and he realises that even if he had a plan, it would be no use because the people all rush towards the helpless car in the ditch. There's a big man out the front of the crowd and he's shouting "thief, thief" and urging everyone to follow him.

Omowale stays in his car and watches as one of the car doors is pushed open from inside. A man crawls out through the half opened door. He's not bleeding and doesn't seem to be hurt but he looks dazed and he stands up and holds his head in his hands and shakes it from side to side. Then he sees the mob rushing at him and tries to run, but the big man who seems to be the energy of the mob is holding a metal bar and he swings it hard and hits the man on the head. The thief falls to the ground and the man beats him again. A few others surround the thief and are kicking him. Other men are milling around. Some of them look as if they don't know what to do and there's a lot of shouting. Omowale can hear arguments. Then he sees a group of four men picking up a huge cement block, one of the blocks that the construction workers have unloaded from the truck that was blocking the road. He's not sure what they're doing that for, but then he sees them pushing through the men who are still beating and kicking the man on the ground.

The circle of men opens to let the four carrying the cement block through, and they drop it on to the man on the ground. Omowale feels sick at what he sees and yet one part of him is working out when it's going to be safe enough to get his money out of the car.

Another man crawls out of the passenger door on the other side of the car. Omowale watches as he keeps low, running in the opposite direction from where the mob has just killed his friend. By now Omowale hopes that the man will get away. If this is jungle justice then he hasn't got the stomach for it.

The men have finished with the first victim and they chase after the other man. It doesn't take them long to catch up with him and they drag him over to the pile of concrete blocks and beat him to the ground, then they drop one on him too.

Some of the men have turned their backs on the lynch mob and they're in their cars and driving off. Omowale feels like doing the same but he has to get his money first.

Then he sees three or four men coming from the other side of the road where they've been unloading more of the concrete blocks. They're holding short planks of wood and at first it looks as if they're going to join in the lynch mob, but when the men see them coming they seem to realise what they've just done and they run down the road and drive off in their cars.

The construction workers see Omowale sitting in his car and they come over to him. He gets out of the car and his legs feel like jelly and at first he can hardly speak. When he clears his throat and finds his voice he tells them about the men grabbing the money from his mother and they all go over to the car. The part of the roof over the driver has crumpled and he is trapped behind the steering wheel. While the construction workers free him from the car, Omowale leans into the back seat because it was the man behind the driver who snatched the bag. Sure enough, there's the big brown bag, lying on the roof that is now the bottom of the car. He pulls it out and isn't sure what to do next. The other men have pulled the man out from behind the wheel and he's lying unconscious on the ground on the side of the ditch. They want to look at the bag and Omowale is scared they're going to take it, but they look inside and give it back to him because they believe that it really does belong to his mother because of the photo of him in her purse.

Then they all go round to the back of the car where the boot has popped open with the impact of the crash. Maybe they're hoping that there's more money here, but they hear a car stopping on the road just behind them and it's the police. Omowale thinks that he should have called them but he didn't. It's a relief that someone else has.

He's not sure if the police will believe him and he feels guilty about having started the chase. But the construction workers explain about his mother and the police just nod. They're looking all over the car as if they know something is there. Omowale remembers what Efi said about the Englishman who was killed and he gets the paper that he wrote the registration number on out of the glove box and tells the police about it. Now they're really interested and they look all around the back of the car and in the boot.

One of the officers goes over to the police car and comes back with some clear plastic bags. Omowale watches him put a screwdriver and some other tools in one of the bags, and an old T-shirt with brown marks all over it in another one.

He asks them if these men really did kill the Englishman, and they say it's too early to say for sure, but it looks like it. The officer *who had put the things in the bags holds up the one with the T-shirt in it and pushes the plastic so they can all see the brown stains on the stretch cotton.*

— It's definitely blood, one policeman says, I'd stake my life on it.

He holds up the bag with the screwdriver.

— And the Englishman was killed with a screwdriver.

Then they tell Omowale he can go, and as he's getting back into his car he sees them put handcuffs on the man lying unconscious on the ground.

After driving for a while he feels calmer, but he can't get the image out of his mind of those giant concrete blocks dropping on the thieves, squashing them like oranges.

How did the men in those cars behind him turn into a lynch mob? He thinks about how frightening they were and how he was too scared to get out of the car. Everyone talks about jungle justice as if it's nothing, but he thinks that justice is the wrong word because justice makes things right and what the mob did wasn't right.

He admits to himself that he's happy he got his mother's bag back, and he looks across to make sure it's still there on the front seat.

33

Wednesday 6 April

The downpour had flooded some of the roads and it was a slow drive from the clinic to the house. The driveway was one huge puddle, and Marius pulled the car onto the grass to avoid the water.

As he was walking up to the front door his phone rang.

— Marius, a voice said, and there was no mistaking the accent.

— Sergei. What's up?

— I'd rather not tell you over the phone. Can we meet up?

— Now?

— If you can. Not the Paradis. Somewhere private.

Marius looked at his watch then wasn't sure why he bothered. The time didn't matter. Eva was going to pick up Dzigi and the only thing he had to do was to work out a plan for tonight.

— Sure. I'll pick you up. Give me half an hour.

Marius was at the Paradis with five minutes to spare. He was parking the car next to the palms in the circular driveway when Sergei came through the glass doors and down the stairs, so he drove forward a few feet and Sergei let himself into the front seat.

On the way to the hotel Marius couldn't think of any place in town that could be called secure; there was always the chance that he'd run into someone he knew. Someone like Lola! Chez Miki was twenty minutes away, but at least they'd be private there.

Sergei liked the idea of a drive along the coast.

— It gets very dull, waiting between deliveries, he said. But I have to be in Lomé to make sure things go to plan.

When Marius knew Sergei in Moscow, he'd just finished a stint with the Russian air force in Afghanistan. Sergei didn't talk about what made him make the change to the KGB, but he liked to talk about flying.

— Still flying?

— Of course. On Friday I'll fly over to Côte d'Ivoire. Do you know those Swiss planes? The PC-6? Sergei took in Marius' blank look so he explained. I can't resist them. You wouldn't believe what they can carry with only a few hundred metres of runway. Straight up and straight down. Apart from the fun, it keeps everyone on their toes as well – knowing the pilot might be me.

— Do you fly out of Lomé?

— No. Not possible. We use a bush runway a bit north from here. You should come with me some time.

— Maybe. Anyway, Sergei, what's up?

Sergei turned and looked closely at Marius.

— Dave Gordon came to see me in the hotel this morning.

Nothing too surprising there. Not considering he was working for Sergei.

— So? What did he want?

Sergei gazed at the oncoming traffic and took a few seconds to reply. Marius had the impression he was thinking about what to say next. When it came, he wasn't ready for it.

— Well, I'm almost certain it was about you. He used some round about way of saying it, but in the end I realised he was asking if I knew someone who would…in English you might say 'bump you off'.

The quaint idiom did nothing to make it seem real, especially in a thick Russian accent, and Marius would have laughed if Sergei wasn't so serious.

— Are you sure it was me he was talking about?

— Well he mentioned the name Marius. The story he went on about was that some local guy was pushing drugs at the school. I strung him along for a while, to see where he was going with it and he said the man had tried to kill one of his men. I thought it could be some other Marius but it's not a common name. Then I asked him to describe this man. When he did, it sounded just like you, even down to what you wear. And of course I know the problems you've been having with him. Then I asked how I'd find this person. Easy, he said, I can show you his house. I was there this morning.

Marius had to give it to Dave Gordon – he was quite the organiser. He must have gone straight from his place down to the Paradis.

— That bit he wasn't lying about. He knows where I live for sure. When I came back from a run this morning he was sitting in his car right outside my house. He didn't see me, but that's not much comfort.

Sergei punched Marius on the shoulder and gave one of his rare laughs.

— I thought it must be you. Pretty funny hey? That he comes to me to knock you off.

And Marius had to admit that there was something darkly humorous about it. He managed a smile despite himself.

— Yeah. Pretty funny.

— But not really. I see that. I think it's time we did something about him. Any thoughts?

— Confront him. Scare him off. But I'm not really sure how yet.

— It's not the sort of thing you should do by yourself. Look, I know you won't ask, so I'm offering. I'll go with you.

— You don't have to do that.

— I do. There's something in it for me. He still hasn't banked the last lot of money yet and I'm not at all impressed. The more I find out about him, the less I trust him.

The adobe walls and soaring thatched roof of Chez Miki were just ahead of them and Marius let the conversation drop while he pulled off the road and parked to the left of the entrance.

— Let's talk some more over a drink.

Sergei nodded and climbed out of the car. He took in the giant clay water bottles and the granite stepping-stones winding through the neat bamboo.

— Nice, he said, and followed Marius along the path to the entrance.

As they parted the *noren* and slid open the slatted wooden door, they could hear drumming.

Marius greeted Yao, who was washing glasses behind the bar, and walked across the room to where the timber floor gave way to terracotta tiles and then into the garden. He pointed to the row of drummers seated in a semi-circle inside an outdoor stage.

— That's Takashi, the one in the middle. Looks like he's giving a workshop. Come on. Let's get a drink and something to eat.

They settled on a shared plate of fresh seafood and sat at a table that fronted on to the garden, front rows to a concert. This wasn't the repetitive voodoo drumming that disturbed Marius; this was Takashi's mix of Japanese and African drumming with some jazz thrown in.

Yao put a bottle of vodka, two tumblers and two tall glasses of Asahi beer on the table. Sergei poured himself a glass of vodka and held the bottle towards Marius.

Marius shook his head and put the empty tumbler to one side.

— No thanks. I need to keep my wits about me.

But Marius didn't have time to pick up the beer before he felt his phone vibrating then heard it ring. He pulled it out of his back pocket and looked at the name. Mimi.

— Sorry. I'd better take this, he said to Sergei. Then to Mimi. You won't guess where I am.

— No. Where?

— At your place.

— Good.

— Why? What's up? Where are you?

Marius could barely hear Mimi's voice over a background noise of traffic.

— I'm walking along the esplanade – waiting to cross to the beach. Hang on.

For a minute Mimi stopped talking and all Marius could hear was traffic. Then the noise disappeared and Mimi came back on.

— There. That's better. I had to get away from the school to tell you this. I think you should watch out for Dave Gordon.

Marius listened while she told him about her meeting. He could picture Mimi walking under the tall date palms that separated the esplanade from the wide sandy beach.

— What about you?

— Stop worrying about me Marius. This place is fine in the daytime – I often walk down here in the lunch hour to get a smell of the sea.

— Okay, okay. And thanks Mimi. I'll tell you about it later.

But Marius realised he was talking to himself. When he rang back it went straight to voice mail. Just a case of bad reception? It was always hit and miss along the beach front, but still….If something happened to Mimi….He fought against panic. There were always so many people on that part of the beach. It must surely be the reception.

Sergei had pushed his chair back so he was facing directly over the garden, legs stretched out in front of him, sipping on his beer and smoking a cigarette.

— Looks like your friend's finished his class.

Sure enough, the drumming had stopped and now the group had split up and people were wandering back to their cabins. A couple had stayed to talk to Takashi.

— That was Takashi's daughter. She works at the school. Apparently Dave Gordon was after my phone number.

— Why? I can't see what use it would be to him. Unless he's planning to threaten you. He surely can't imagine he could trick you into some sort of meeting?

— I don't know. Maybe Mimi only thinks it was the phone number he was after. It could have been an excuse to find out something else.

Sergei pulled his chair back into the table and faced Marius. He ground the stub of the cigarette under his foot and poured another tumbler of vodka.

— Or it could be a way to feel more in control. Everything Dave Gordon does makes him look like a textbook psycopath.

— I'll go along with that. And now he's got plans for me ...

— But that might be in our favour, Sergei interrupted. Look at the way he came straight to me for help this morning. He's too confident and that means he'll make a mistake. In fact he has already. I know what he's thinking, not putting that money in the bank. He's wondering how much he can get away with. And the answer to that is nothing!

They stopped talking while Yao put a plate of tempura fish and prawns in the middle of the table, along with French fries and some plates and cutlery. At the same time Takashi came up to the table, pulling off his headband and smoothing back his hair.

He greeted Marius and held his hand out to Sergei.

— Sergei, a friend from the Moscow days, Marius explained. Still busy, or can you join us?

Takashi pulled out a chair and sat down next to Sergei.

— I'm finished for the day and I'm hungry. And curious.

It didn't take long to bring Takashi up-to-date and when Marius told him about seeing Dave Gordon outside his place Takashi broke in with a sharp intake of breath and shook his head.

— That's too close. What do you think he's going to do?

Sergei explained about how Dave Gordon was looking for someone to 'take care of' Marius, and Takashi sipped his beer and looked over at Marius.

— What about Eva and the kids?

— They're not going back there. Eva's arranged for them all to stay at her sister's place until it gets sorted.

— I guess she's not very happy.

Marius shook his head.

— Not happy at all.

— So what do you think you can do? Takashi asked.

— Confront him. Tonight.

— Confront him with what?

Sergei looked at Marius and lifted an eyebrow and Marius could feel the two pairs of eyes boring into him. Trouble was, Marius had nothing definite in mind.

— Well…I've got a pretty good idea how he organised for Ash to be killed, and I know for sure about the attempt to kill George. No hard evidence of course….

Sergei looked impatient and broke in.

— But there is for the money laundering. That's where we have him. He thinks he's got protection and that's where he's wrong.

Sergei was right, Marius could see that. The money was the only thing they could nail him on. But would that be enough?

— Unless something turns up in Lagos, we're never going to get proof. But I want to look him in the eyes and force him to recognise what he's done. Get him out of the school, out of Lomé.

Even to his own ears it sounded lame. Takashi's expression didn't change, but the way he put his beer down and leaned back in his chair spoke volumes.

— So he can do the same things somewhere else?

Marius could see his point but what else could he do? Sometimes Takashi's logic was hard to take, and he shrugged his shoulders.

— We're not vigilantes.

— But we can be very intimidating, Sergei added.

Takashi decided that Sergei could probably be very intimidating indeed when it suited him. He was still thinking about that when he heard a text message come through on his phone. From Kazuo. 'Urgent', it said.

Takashi explained and went in to his office to log onto the internet. Sergei helped himself to the prawns left on the plate then lit a cigarette and poured another vodka.

— Your friend's right Marius. We need to have a better plan.

Marius agreed and they started going over their options. Yao brought over two more beers and he was taking away the empty plates when Takashi came back.

He'd brought his own beer, and he sat back down next to Sergei and put it on the table. Then he said in a voice so quiet that the others could barely hear him.

— I think you'd better listen to what happened in Lagos this morning.

34

Wednesday 6 April

— *Come.*

Dave Gordon watches as Jerro sits down on the other side of the desk.

— *Well?*

Jerro smiles and pulls a mobile phone out of his pocket. He puts it on the desk.

— *Any problems?*

Jerro shakes his head.

— *My friends know what they're doing.*

— *Thanks Jerro. I won't forget this.*

A man with contacts was Jerro. The sort of man who gets things done.

Jerro knows not to outstay his welcome and stands up.

— *Sir.*

— *Close the door could you.*

Dave picks up the Nokia and plays with it, feeling its potential. He finds the call log: Marius at 1317. The call she was making when the phone was snatched. And all that carry on in his office!

Mimi. So fake. And poking her nose into his business, like the other day. What was all that about? Why was she snooping around his office. All that stuff about the letter, as if he couldn't see through it.

Of course he can do what he wants to Marius without the phone. That isn't the point. The point is Mimi can't mind her own business and this morning she sat there and lied to him. What he has to do now is make her see what a bad idea that is.

First she has to know he's got her phone.

Dave pulls out his own phone and enters Marius' number in his contact list. Then he smiles to himself and puts the phone in the top drawer. He picks up the phone on his desk and rings Adele.

She copies down a message for Miss Kasahara and puts it in the 'out' tray with the staff mail. Then she picks up the office phone and dials the number for the Clinique d'Abovey

Dave puts the phone down and thinks back over his plan. So easy. If she comes for her phone, all he has to say is that one of his chaps found it on the beach, and watch her squirm. If she doesn't come for the phone it will be even better. He laughs when he thinks how that will make her feel every time she sees him.

But that won't be for too long because there's step two. Dave thinks about the drumming place her father runs. It shouldn't be too hard for one of his government contacts to find something wrong with the paperwork. Or better still, an old place like that could easily go up in flames. Whatever. Then they can both piss off back to where they came from. Nice. Very nice.

But first there's this Marius business to sort out. If Sergei had been more obliging it would all be done and dusted. What was it with him? Not as if he deals in used clothes. And what was with that "Not my thing", as if he's never used one of those guns he sells?

Well there's more than one way to skin a cat.

Dave takes out a piece of paper and starts jotting down some ideas. He's irritated when his phone starts vibrating, and glances at it to see if it's worth wasting time on. It's a message from Alabi and Dave picks up the phone and reads it.

problem come now yr place

What's Alabi playing at? Dave looks at the message again and feels like throwing the phone at the wall. That's not a good idea so he switches it off, drops it into the top drawer and slams it shut.

Alabi can wait. Whatever trouble he's in, Lomé is not the place to bring it to.

Dave reaches down and grabs his wallet out of the bottom drawer. He pulls the photo of Alabi out and looks at it, then he tears it into half and quarters and eighths and keeps tearing until it's only tiny flecks of paper.

35

Wednesday 6 April

A few minutes after seven Marius parked the Toyota on the road in front of Dave Gordon's house. He waited for Sergei to get out then reached over and locked the passenger door before following him along the street.

Vendors had turned the area into a mini-market, with stalls on both sides of the road. There were no streetlights, but the darkness was punctuated with the smoky orange glow from dozens of kerosene lamps.

A few people were sitting in the dark, eating and drinking. Others were buying cigarettes, peeled oranges, little pastries, things in packets and cans, shoes. All the usual things. Marius caught the smell of yams frying in coconut oil but now wasn't the time to stop for a snack, and he followed Sergei past the market stalls and over to the green metal gate in front of Dave Gordon's house.

The staff knew Sergei from when he'd been here to set up the deal with Dave. It rankled with Sergei that he'd been taken in, not least by Lola who had played her role so well that he was convinced Dave was a safe bet.

Sergei knocked on the gate and the security guard came over from where he'd been chatting to a man cooking kebabs on a charcoal brazier. He recognised Sergei and didn't seem surprised to see him.

— Good evening sir.

Sergei didn't think much of a security guard who hung about eating kebabs, but he turned and acknowledged the man.

— They're in?

The guard pushed in front of Sergei and made a show of opening the gate for them.

— Yes sir. Go on in.

Sergei gave the guard a nod and walked past him through the gate. Marius followed him along the paved pathway and up the concrete stairs to the covered porch. The lights were on in the room to the right of the door but there was no sign of movement so Sergei gave Marius a 'here goes' look and knocked loudly on the door.

There was something odd about the silence. No footsteps, no voices, no music. If they were at home like the guard had said, what were they doing?

— Try again, Marius suggested.

This time Sergei pounded the door with his fist and called out.

— Dave? It's Sergei.

Still no sound and Marius went across to the other side of the porch and tried to peer into the room. The slit in the curtain was too narrow and all he could see was a strip of painted wall. Something didn't feel right. He heard some sort of low rumble but couldn't place it.

Marius held up one finger to signal to Sergei not to knock again, and they stood quietly, listening. Suddenly the silence was broken by the sound of a car starting and Marius realised the noise was coming from inside the garage that was attached to the side of the house. Before they had time to react there was a throaty roar of a car accelerating and the screech of tyres.

— Shit, Sergei said.

Then they were both racing back down the path. Sergei was in front and he pulled the gate open. It crashed against the wall and sprung back. Marius pulled it open again and stopped on the side of the road, his back against the wall of the house. On his right Sergei was running towards the green Mercedes, pulling a gun out from under his jacket as he ran.

The car had reversed out of the garage and it was slewed at an angle across the street with the acrid smell of burnt rubber drifting around it.

As Sergei drew abreast of the car there was another roar from the engine and the high-pitched squeal of rubber slipping on tarmac.

But instead of accelerating away the Mercedes started to fishtail along the road.

Headlights suddenly floodlit the street and as the car careered towards him Marius jumped further back along the wall.

People eating at the kebab stand on the corner ran under the trees and seconds later the back of the car sent some wooden benches sliding across the road. The tail of the car swung back up the other way and made a crunching noise as it hit the wall, then it jerked out of control back across the street.

Now that he wasn't blinded by the headlights Marius could make out the figure of the passenger, and he found himself looking straight into the frightened eyes of Lola.

It was harder to make out the driver but he saw enough to know that it wasn't Dave Gordon. The face was dark, the same as Lola's. In fact so much the same it had to be her brother. Alabi. Ibby.

Whoever it was had no idea how to control the jackknifing car, and it swung back and forth as if it had a mind of its own.

Dodging around the car, Sergei ran ahead of it, both hands on his pistol. There was an explosion of sound as he fired at the headlights, then kept firing through the engine.

The Mercedes spun round and faced back the way it had been coming, then the back of it ploughed into the trunk of the almond tree on the corner, and the engine cut out.

There was a moment of absolute quiet, then people started to emerge from the darkness and converge on the car. The driver's door was flung open and a man jumped out, pulling with him a large Adidas sports bag. He tried to push through the group of men who had gathered around him, striking out with his free hand, but they were angry now, and kept hold of him. One man in particular was yelling, pointing at the broken benches lying across the road,

Lomé wasn't Lagos, but Marius was relieved to see Sergei waving the crowd out of the way with his gun, shouting something in Russian that seemed to calm them down. They retreated to a safe distance and watched Sergei wrench the bag off the man and pull his arms behind his back.

Marius went over to the passenger side of the Mercedes and peered in the closed window. Lola was running her hands over her head as if she'd only just found it. Knocked out, perhaps, Marius thought. Might have hit the windscreen.

He didn't feel it was his proudest moment, but there was nothing for it. He half helped, half pulled her out of the car, then put her in a hammer lock.

The security guard seemed to have vanished into the night and there was no one to stop Marius as he pushed Lola ahead of him through the gate. It wasn't where Lola wanted to go and she tried to lash out with her free arm. Then she found out the hard way how painful that was and she stopped. Instead she looked over her shoulder at Marius and sounding desperate pleaded with him.

— Who are you Sam? Let me go. You have to let me go. You know who I am.

But there was something heavy, menacing and unspoken, that hung in the air, and Marius took no notice and pushed her ahead of him up the path and on to the porch. He could hear Sergei behind him.

The lights in the house were still blazing, just as before, and the front door was unlocked.

Marius pushed his way through the door and stood in the entrance, not sure where to go next. There wasn't a script for this but he followed his instincts and kept going to a door on the left of the hallway. It was the kitchen, and kitchens had all sorts of useful things. He looked around at Sergei, who was keeping a tight hold of Alabi.

— What do you think? In here?

Sergei nodded.

— I don't know what these two are up to, but it can't be good. Let's get them tied up and have a look around.

The kitchen had a scrubbed wooden table and chairs at one end, with a granite topped bench between that and a sink and stove up the other end.

Sergei dropped the Adidas bag on the table, and he and Marius flung open the drawers, looking for anything they could find. Marius had tried to think ahead, be ready for anything, but this? Definitely not this. It was a relief when they had Alabi and Lola strapped to chairs and gagged with electrical tape. A sort of calm settled on the room.

Marius gestured towards the chairs and spoke to Sergei.

— On the left, Adelola, on the right her brother Alabi.

— The boyfriend, Sergei said, and Marius nodded.

Alabi's face was half covered by the black tape but above it the whites of his eyes looked huge with anger. Then he let them close as if he was bored with it all.

Sergei turned his back on him and went over to the table. He opened the zipper on the Adidas bag and pulled out wads of US banknotes. They were fastened with rubber bands in parcels of $5000 and he waved some in the air to show Marius.

— I wonder how he managed to get these off his boyfriend. Let's find out.

If a house reflected the personality of its owner, then Dave Gordon had kept himself well hidden. As Marius and Sergei went across the hallway and through the dining room into the living area, everything was correct and neat, but soulless, more like a display home than a place to live in.

And where was Dave Gordon? Marius wanted answers to his questions and right now he didn't care how he got them.

To their right heavy shantung curtains were pulled over the French doors that Marius had tried to peer through when they first arrived. On their left an open door by the cabinet led into a hallway with two rooms opening off.

Pulling his gun out, Sergei grabbed the handle of the door closest to him.

— I'll take this one, he said.

Marius opened the other door.

The smell was enough: elusive, expensive and feminine. Even without the untidy piles of clothes on the chair and the bed, and the array of bottles and jewelry reflected in the mirror of the dressing table, this had to be Lola's room. Through an open door on the inside wall Marius could see part of a toilet, black and white tiles: an ensuite.

Then he heard Sergei call out.

— In here.

There was no sign of Sergei as Marius went through the door into the bedroom opposite. Everything was neat and in order; a silky looking deep blue bedspread matched the striped curtains.

Marius skirted around the end of the bed and now he could hear Sergei talking on his mobile.

On the far side of the bedroom a sliding wooden door led into a long narrow room with clothes hanging on the right and open shelves on the left. In the middle of the shelves was a large, heavy safe, the door hanging open. Another door led from the dressing room to the bathroom, and Sergei was standing just the other side of the door, his back to Marius.

Sergei put his phone away and turned towards Marius as he came alongside. He didn't' have to say anything – it was only too obvious.

In front of them was a bathroom floor of small blue Italian tiles. Then a white freestanding bath. In the bath was Dave Gordon. He was on his back, his head over the plughole. His feet, still in brown loafers, were halfway up the other end of the bath and the brown handle of a large knife was sticking out of his chest.

The blood he was lying in was mixed with water. It looked fresh and bright. His T-shirt and chinos were soaked in blood and water, but the trousers below the knee and his shoes were dry.

Marius wanted him to be alive, but he looked very dead.

To make sure, Marius leant over the bath and made the usual checks, then he looked back at Sergei and shook his head.

Sergei joined him on the side of the bath.

— No prizes for guessing who did this.

Of course he was right, or Marius hoped half right.

— Alabi, yes. But Lola?

Sergei bent over closer to Dave Gordon's face and then stood back up and pointed to the wet clothes.

— Looks like he was stabbed then finished off in the water.

— Or the other way around. Held under the water then stabbed.

— I think you could be right Marius. It looks as if they've been giving him the water treatment. Trying to get him to talk.

Sergei walked into the dressing room and went up to the safe. He felt inside to make sure nothing was left in there, then closed the door. In the centre of the door there was a solid looking combination lock, black numbers against a silver background. Sergei pointed to it.

— And that must be what they were after. The combination.

Sergei stood back from the safe and looked around the shelves, then he reached up and pulled at a handle that was just visible on the top shelf. A soft brown leather suitcase appeared over the edge and Sergei flicked it off the shelf, caught it and put it on the floor.

Marius pointed to the suitcase. It was exactly as Jojo had said: identical to his own.

— That's when I first thought it might be you. When the guy tailing you described the suitcase. Remember that Estonian work we did?

Sergei gave a half smile and raised an eyebrow.

— More like a holiday. The only thing I remember about it is that tall blonde.

Marius laughed.

— That's because she wouldn't sleep with you.

Marius walked into the bedroom and sat on the end of the bed and Sergei dropped the suitcase on the bed then went over to the door.

— Back in a minute.

Marius wondered how Sergei was planning to get them out of this mess. They hadn't locked the door and if anyone were to come in the first thing they'd see would be two people gagged and bound, a body in the bath, and a suitcase full of money. This was way beyond what he could ask any of his own contacts to help with so there was nothing for it but to trust Sergei. Who was it he'd phoned? No doubt whoever it was would get the job done. It was how they'd do it that worried Marius.

Sergei came back into the bedroom, carrying the Adidas bag.

— All quiet in the kitchen, he said as he opened the suitcase and dumped the money from the bag into it. He counted the bundles of notes and when he was satisfied that it was all there his face relaxed a little.

Marius watched him and wondered what sort of help Sergei would have given him if it wasn't for the money.

Sergei zipped up the suitcase, pulled the strap through the handle and fastened the clasp.

— Now what?

— You know me, Sergei. I'm not happy until I find out the truth. Let's see if we can get Alabi to talk.

The look Sergei gave Marius was ironic.

— Leave it to me. You know it's what we Russians are good at!

36

Wednesday 6 April

The neon light in the kitchen was unsparing, and seemed to drill into Lola and Alabi, leaving them exposed and pathetic. Unlike the rest of the house, there was no air-conditioning here, and as Marius pushed open the door and walked in, the hot air wrapped around him, and with it the smell of sweat and fear.

Sergei walked over to within a few paces of the pair and stood still, looking down at them, his mouth in a tight line and the shadows from the light picking out the angular lines of his face. When he spoke, his English was heavy with a Russian accent and sounded full of menace.

— Here's the deal. There are things we want to know. If we get the answers we want, you're free to go. If not... Sergei pulled out his Glock, snapped off the safety catch, and aimed it at Lola's face. I have this and I'm not shy about using it. You can hear from my accent I'm not from around here. I can disappear like that.

There was a loud snap as Sergei clicked his fingers. Even Marius jumped. Sergei put the safety catch on and tucked the pistol back into its holster.

— So, he said, when we take off the tape, you know what we expect.

Tears came into Lola's eyes as Sergei ripped off the electrical tape. Alabi had steeled himself and his only reaction was to mutter something in Yoruba.

Sergei flicked his head back with a slap under the chin.

— Not a good start. You said?

— How do we know we can trust you?

— You don't. But what choice do you have?

Lola looked resigned, defeated, and she glanced across at Alabi.

— For god's sake, Ibby. Just tell them what they want to know.

Sergei moved away and sat on the wooden table and Marius positioned himself in front of Alabi. He leant back against the kitchen bench, his elbows resting on the granite surface. In contrast to Sergei he spoke quietly, his tone conversational.

— They tell me you're not safe in Lagos now, Alabi. Not after what happened yesterday. Your friends in the white Mazda... they weren't very popular. And the one who survived, he's told the police all about you.

Alabi just looked at him, and Marius went on.

— So what I want to know, Alabi, in your own words, is what happened to Lawrence Ashley, Dave Gordon's business partner, the quiet Englishman. How did he come to be murdered? A nice safe neighbourhood, everyone says, and yet there he was, bleeding to death on the side of the road. I was there.

Alabi's face had relaxed into the insolent look that Marius recognised from the photograph, but his eyes showed surprise.

— No, I thought you mightn't know that. Yes, I was there and Lawrence Ashley wasn't dead. Not quite. He managed to give me your name, so I know you were there too.

Marius folded his arms and shifted his weight.

— Look Alabi, I know that Dave Gordon was probably behind it. Maybe he made you do it.

That was too much. Alabi pulled his head back and spat hard on the floor. Suddenly the insolence was gone. Rage seemed to flick a switch inside him and it wasn't hard to imagine him stabbing somebody to death.

— If you think Dave Gordon could make me do anything, then think again. Who do you think came up with the idea? He was always complaining about Ashley Lawrence but without me he'd never have had the balls to do anything. I had the contacts, Gordon had the money. Then when this shit happens in Lagos suddenly he doesn't want to know me. Do you know how much he tried to buy me off for? Five hundred dollars. That's all I was worth. So what if I got caught? "No one is going to take your word over mine", that's what he said. Arrogant cunt. As if I was his boy. Anyway, he found out the hard way not to piss on me.

— And Lola had told you about the money in the bag, so you forced him to give you the code to the safe and then killed him.

Alabi had regained his cool and he looked at Marius knowingly.

— I've done you a service so you can let me go now.

Marius shook his head.

— What I want to know first is how you set it up. The Lagos thing. It was all very clever, wasn't it? Everyone just blamed the Area Boys and forgot about it.

— Without that bitch on the radio.

Marius ignored him and kept going.

—How did you know when Lawrence Ashley would be walking along that road?

Alabi gave a dry laugh.

— Dave's map, courtesy of Jerro. He couldn't do enough to keep in good with me. Thought he was living the high life. Couldn't resist the sweet stuff.

— And then?

— And then we drove to the place and waited. Put the bonnet up, like we had a problem with the car. Works every time. But then it looked like Lawrence was going to walk straight past. I was in the back seat and he couldn't see me so I put on this posh voice and said "excuse me".

It was a chilling imitation of a polite English accent. No wonder Ash was fooled.

— But he knew it was you?

— Not until he got right up to the window. Big surprise-o. *Na mugu*.

The lapse into pigeon gave the statement an extra twist, as if it was all a game.

Lola looked as if she'd heard it all before.

— Okay Sam, or whoever you are. He's told you all about it. Now you can let us go.

— What about George Barnes, Lola?

— That old guy at the school? Dave said he wanted some girl so I got him one – he should thank me.

Marius turned back to Alabi.

— What about you Alabi? Know anything about George Barnes. What about drugs, for example. Has that been part of the deal with Dave Gordon?

Alabi sniffed and threw his head back.

— Coke. Yellow honey, heroin. Mixed, straight. Whatever.

— There's one more thing. He spoke to Alabi as if Lola wasn't in the room.

— What about Lola, Alabi? Do you think you've done a good job looking after your sister? Would your parents have been proud of you? Is that what they would have wanted?

Alabi couldn't hold Marius' gaze and he turned his head aside and said something Marius didn't catch.

— What was that?

Alabi turned back and shouted at Marius.

— She didn't know!

Lola cut in, her voice thick, her eyes even bigger and darker than usual.

— You didn't have to kill him. What's happened to you?

Sergei had been sitting at the kitchen table, smoking and sending an occasional text message on his mobile. Now he stubbed out his cigarette under his foot, stood up and spoke to Marius.

— Got what you wanted?

Marius felt he'd reached the limit of what he could listen to and he nodded.

— That's enough.

With quick slashes of the knife that he'd used before, Sergei cut Lola and Alabi free.

As she stood up, Lola smoothed the skirt of her dress and adjusted the shoulder straps. She held herself straight as usual and seemed defiant, but anyone could see it was an act, and Marius had a strong urge to help her, to get her out of the mess she'd landed in. Instead he watched her follow Alabi down the hall and out the front door.

Sergei waited until the gate had closed behind them, then he and Marius went back into the kitchen and sat at the table opposite each other.

— How far do you think they'll get? Marius asked.

— Not far at all. I told the colonel to follow them for a bit so they were well away from this house.

— Do you think you got it?

Sergei pulled a mini-recorder out of his pocket and held it in front of him, looking at it as if it might have been a pet he was especially fond of.

— Never failed me yet. I need this little gadget in my line of business.

Then he put it on the table, pressed the rewind button, then play.

It was Alabi's voice: "...then we drove to the place..."

Sergei pushed the 'off' button and let it rewind. He looked up at Marius then pulled out another cigarette and lit it.

— Even the corrupt ones like to have some proof, he said. Especially them. We know all about that in Russia.

Then Sergei leant towards Marius, his elbows on the table.

— Hey. You're not soft on that chick are you? She seems alright. I told them to leave her alone.

No, Marius wasn't soft on her, but he felt for her. Sergei wouldn't understand. Russia had its problems; Africa had its own. He shook his head.

— No. But I'm glad she's a scammer, not a murderer.

Sergei gave his tight-lipped smile.

— A scammer like us. Come on Marius. Let's get out of here. We need a drink.

37

Saturday 9 April

— Here, hold this.

Marius was sitting propped up against the wooden bedhead and he took the tray that Afua was holding out for him.

— Smells good.

On the tray was an espresso coffee maker, two glasses with black silicon grips and some milk and sugar in angular green and red porcelain. Next to them a plate was piled with tiny sugar coated doughnut balls, and the freshly fried smell mixed with the coffee aroma. Marius held the tray while Afua propped herself against the pillows, then put it down between them.

It reminded Marius of some mornings when Dzigi brought him lemongrass tea, and he felt familiar stirrings of guilt, but that was something he could deal with later. For now, Eva and the kids were safe at her sister's place and as far as he knew, Dzigi was happy there.

The stylishness of Afua's apartment was a world away from his old rambling house, but Marius felt – well, not exactly at home, but as if he was in the right place. He took the glass of coffee and thanked her.

— How do you do it? he asked.

— Do what?

— Make me feel so relaxed.

Afua laughed and settled back on the cushions then took a sip of her coffee.

— I thought it was you.

It was ten o'clock on Saturday morning and Marius was hungry. He picked up one of the doughnut balls and held it out towards Afua.

— My favourites. How did you get your hands on them?

He put it in his mouth then picked up a couple more.

— The woman who sells them comes past here every morning. She makes them fresh.

Afua picked up a doughnut and looked at it before she put it in her mouth.

— Another one of the things I missed in New York. Anyway, you were saying...

— Well, that's pretty much it. By the time we let those two go, the colonel and some of the elite guard were waiting outside. They followed them for a while, but then Alabi started to hotwire a car and it was easy to pick him up for that. Sergei and I met up with the colonel yesterday – gave him the tape. Apparently Alabi's getting a military escort back to Lagos. Well, to the border anyway. Then the Nigerian police will take over.

— What about Lola?

— They let her go, but put her down on the Ghana side of the border.

Afua took a sip of coffee and looked thoughtful.

— I wouldn't want to be in her shoes.

Marius nodded.

— I know what you mean. Part of me feels sorry for her. But she's – how shall I say – resourceful. Probably has some guy looking after her already.

There was something in the way Afua was looking at him that Marius recognised in himself. It was questioning, maybe puzzled, as if there should be deeper answers to her questions.

— I don't know how to think about all the things you've been telling me. Or maybe it's more how to feel about it. It's horrible – that lynching in Lagos. Imagine, crushing them with those blocks! Then the way Dave Gordon was killed. But it's not getting through, it's all on the surface.

Afua had put in words what Marius himself had been feeling and it was a relief to be able to talk to about it.

— I know what you mean. I barely knew Lawrence Ashley, but in some way I almost felt responsible for his death.

Afua gave him a surprised look and Marius tried to explain.

— Well, not his death exactly. But I should have listened to him, paid more attention. Then when he died I wanted to find answers at all cost. Now I can see it was never going to work, but I was so sure I could force Dave Gordon out of the school – out of Lomé. It seems naïve, but I really wanted to make him own up to what he'd done. Don't laugh!!

With her free hand, Afua pretended to wipe the smile from her face, and she nudged him with her elbow.

— As if he had a conscience like you.

— Exactly. Of course what I really wanted was to see justice done, as they say, and that seemed impossible.

But look at the way it's turned out! If I believed in god, I'd say it was divine retribution.

Afua gave him a teasing look.

— Now don't go all religious on me. But it fits. The gods always overreact. Then she rested her hand lightly on his. Come on Marius, you've done enough. It's time to admit that you can't find the answers to everything.

A K (Kate) Jenkins is an Australian who is currently living in Hobart, Tasmania. As an international educator, Kate lived and worked for many years in West Africa, including several years in Lomé.

Lomé is the capital of Togo, a very small country sandwiched between Ghana on the west and Benin (and then Nigeria) on the east. Located on the Gulf of Guinea, Lomé has a coastal feel, and a wide sandy beach stretches the length of the city. In the 1980s it was a popular tourist destination until the political situation worsened in the 1990's and investment and embassies were withdrawn. *Twice No One Dies* is set in 2004, when Africa's longest serving ruler, President Eyadéma, was in his 38th year. *A Certain Kind of Justice* is set the year after, when there were major political upheavals following Eyadéma's death in 2005.

Twice No One Dies

West Africa, 2004. In Togo, Africa's longest serving dictator is determined to hang on to power. Marius, amateur philosopher and jazz enthusiast, has almost forgotten his former life as intelligence officer. He would much prefer to stay out of politics and drink a few beers at Le Jazz Spot, especially when his friend Louis plays trumpet.

But late one night Louis is found hacked to death on a lonely beach near Lomé. Could it be a drug deal gone wrong as the gendarmerie claim?

Marius and his friends know that can't be true. Against his better judgment, Marius determines to find the real killer and clear Louis' name. With the help of friends he gradually pieces together Louis' last hours and it's then Marius realizes that someone is trying to stop them at all costs. Someone who wields power in the tangled politics of Togo.

Finding Louis' killer becomes a race against time as Marius has to draw on all his cunning and experience to stay one step ahead.